I0678976

Gathering of the Chosen

Tournament of the Gods Book #1

by Timothy L. Cerepaka

An Annulus Publishing Book

Annulus Publishing, Cherokee, Texas, 2016

Published by Annulus Publishing

Formatting by Timothy L. Cerepaka

Contact: timothy@timothylcerepaka.com

Cover design by Elaina Lee of For the Muse Design

ISBN-13: 978-0692627808

ISBN-10: 0692627804

Acknowledgements

I would like to thank my uncle, James Wilhite, for helping me get this manuscript into publishable shape. I'd also like to thank the rest of my family for supporting me while I wrote this novel. You guys rock.

Chapter One

BRAIM KOTOGS—A tall, green-eyed, red-haired mage who had been told that he was a necromancer—was pretty sure that he had been resurrected wrong.

It was a feeling that had plagued him for the past couple of months or so, ever since he had returned to life in the graveyard of the Arcanium, the main campus of North Academy, the most prestigious magical school in the world, which was located in the Great Berg, well to the north of the Northern Isles. He had at first tried to ignore it, thinking it might just be a normal part of the resurrection process (although, being the first human to come to life, he had no idea what was 'normal' about coming back to life). But it seemed to follow him wherever he went and whatever he did, like his own shadow.

Yet Braim had said nothing of it to any his friends. He had not mentioned it to Darek Takren, a fellow mage who specialized in pagomancy, or ice magic, nor had he mentioned it to Aorja Kitano, yet another fellow mage, although that was probably because she had vanished a couple of months ago and no one knew where she was. He was glad that she wasn't around anymore, however, because the others had told him that Aorja was an escapee from the most secure prison in the world and very violent.

And he still said nothing of it as he walked through the pure white streets of the island city known as World's End, or the Throne of the Gods, along with his friends. Darek Takren was in the lead, wearing the pure white robes that all Xocionian Monks —that is, mages who served the god Xocion, God of Ice—did, in conversation with Jenur Takren, the current Magical Superior of North Academy and Darek's mother (or adopted mother, according to Darek).

Jenur was a middle-aged woman, though her dark, curly hair made her look a bit younger to Braim. According to Darek, Braim had once known Jenur prior to his first death thirty years ago, when the two of them had been younger. Or, rather, when *Jenur* had been younger, because Braim's body was still the exact same age as it had been when he had died years ago.

Although Braim had had his old body back for a few months now, he still looked down at it every now and then to make sure it looked normal. He was wearing the black-and-red robes that all North Academy students wore, not because he himself was a student of that school, but because it was the only clothes that they had on hand for him when he returned from the dead. When he had been a ghost, Braim had worked entirely without clothes, but Darek had reminded him that nudity was generally not tolerated among the living, so Braim had agreed to wear the robes in public.

Even so, Braim found them stifling. While the robes kept him quite warm up in the freezing north, World's End was located in the warm southern seas, and the sun was out today. He tugged at the collar of his robes, trying to let his neck breathe, but that did little to cool him off. It didn't help that the huge skyscrapers that towered around them reflected the sun's rays and increased the intensity of the heat, but neither Darek nor Jenur seemed to notice or care.

As for walking, it was a task that Braim had learned quickly, but still he found it harder to walk with a solid, flesh-and-blood body than with a ghostly one. As a ghost, he had been very light, able to jump great distances with ease. As a human, however, he was largely restricted by physics and his own weight. Magic wasn't of much use to him, as he no longer remembered what specific branch of magic would allow him to jump like how he did as a ghost.

As a result, Braim was highly aware of how awkwardly he walked. He was made even more aware of it by noticing how naturally Darek and Jenur walked. The two of them certainly did not give much thought as to how they walked, which made Braim slightly jealous, despite the knowledge that he would learn how to walk more naturally with time.

Another thing that Braim found hard to deal with were the intense sensations that assaulted him from every direction. As they walked through the streets of World's End, Braim heard the odd clicking sounds that the native katabans—minor spirits who served the gods and who called World's End their home—made as they walked among themselves, smelled his own somewhat sweaty body and the delicious scents wafting from what appeared to be a katabans bakery as they passed it, and was aware of how tightly his shoes clung to his feet. He supposed he had gotten used to these strange sensations prior to his first death, but even after two months of living, Braim was sometimes still overwhelmed by the information that his body's senses fed his brain at all times.

3

Stop thinking about yourself so much, Braim thought. *You're a living being now, not a ghost. Every other living being on the planet doesn't think about walking or any of this other stuff. Go with the flow. Take it easy.*

Of course, whenever Braim did that, he became aware of all of the dozens of katabans watching him and his two friends as they made their way through the city's streets. The katabans *looked* human enough, except for their wild and crazy hair colors and styles that no human had. One katabans in particular had hair that looked like the remains of a hair explosion, sticking up in every direction and looking like a mess.

But even if the katabans had normal hair and hair colors, Braim could have told that they weren't human right off the bat. The way they stood, the way they watched him, Darek, and Jenur walk … it wasn't the typical way some humans might view foreigners in their midst. No, these were the eyes of completely alien creatures watching intruders on their domain, intruders who they could do nothing about.

What a silly thought, Braim thought. *Us, intruders. Don't these katabans know that we were invited to World's End by the gods themselves?*

That was the truth. Only a week ago, a messenger from the gods—some horrific titanic creature, its head covered in smoke and its body constantly oozing the worst smelling slime that Braim had ever had the displeasure of smelling in his life—arrived at North Academy with an invitation to World's End for Darek Takren, Jenur Takren, and Braim Kotogs. Braim recalled it because he had been standing in the sports field, watching the students practice makhaimancy (a magical discipline that combined magic with swordplay), when the titanic messenger appeared out of nowhere and invited Braim, Jenur, and Darek to World's End.

At the time, Braim hadn't understood why the titan had come to him with the message first. Jenur was the Magical Superior. Surely she should have been the first to receive the invitation, shouldn't she have?

But now, since he and the others arrived on World's End about a day ago, Braim finally understood why. The three of them had been met by a katabans named Hashan, a chubby little man with long, purple hair that looked like snakes. Hashan had told them that he was going to be their guide, as none of them knew their way around World's End very well, which seemed like a good thing at the time.

Until Hashan began grilling Braim on questions about the afterlife. The questions had been rude and invasive. In fact, they had been so annoying that Braim had pulled out his wand and attacked the katabans with a fire spell. Braim barely remembered it, mostly because his memory as a mortal was poor, especially whenever he was under any kind of stress.

All he remembered was Jenur stopping him before he could kill Hashan, and Hashan himself running away for his life. After that, the three humans received yet another message from the gods informing them that they would not be receiving another guide and that they could simply go straight to the Temple of the Gods the next day.

But Braim had read between the lines of that message. He knew that the gods were interested in him, even more so than they were in Jenur or Darek. And the reason why was as plain as the sun: Braim was the first ever human to return from the dead. He wasn't just a reanimated corpse, but a true blue, flesh-and-blood living human being. His heart beat, his lungs needed air, and he could tell when his shoes were too tight on his feet. It was the only thing about Braim that was special or unique, and the only thing that would make him stand out to the gods in general.

As for why Darek and Jenur had been invited, that was easy. Darek had helped save the whole world from the villainous Uron, an evil spirit that had used Braim's own body for a while to commit great evil, so the gods respected Darek a great deal, even considered him a hero to an extent. And Jenur was the Magical Superior of North Academy, a position which gave her a unique link to the gods and which was respected by the gods in general.

Despite that, however, none of them knew what the 'momentous event' mentioned in the original invite was supposed to be. Darek had spent the last week or so running down a list of possible events, ranging from a simple thank you ceremony from the gods for what they did to save the world from Uron all the way to an ascension ceremony in which one of them would rise to godhood as a reward for their efforts.

The Powers know that we could use new gods, though, Braim thought grimly as he followed Darek and Jenur around a corner. *Or at least I think they do, anyway.*

During the conflict with Uron, five gods had been killed by that monster, including Skimif, the God of Martir himself. Aside from Skimif, none of the other gods had been particularly prominent or important. The Northern and Southern Pantheons of Martir, however, had existed in a very fragile balance for a long time. With both the death of Skimif and the deaths of members of both Pantheons, Braim was surprised that another Godly War had not started yet.

Not that I'm complaining, of course, Braim thought. *Uron already did a number on the world. We don't need a divine conflict among the gods to make things even worse than they already are.*

Braim found his thoughts becoming too depressing for his tastes, so he said aloud, "Hey, Darek, how much longer 'til we get to the Temple? My feet are killing me."

"Not much longer now, I think," said Darek as they went up a small slope. He held a map of the city before him, which he had received yesterday from Hashan before the katabans ran off. "According to this map, we should be arriving at the center of the city, where the Temple is, any minute now."

"Good," said Braim. "Say, have either of you two ever been to the Temple of the Gods before? I've heard about it, but have never actually visited it."

"I have," said Jenur, glancing over her shoulder at Braim, although he noticed that it wasn't with a smile on her face. "Years ago, before I even met you. I went on a voyage to the southern seas with King Malock, King of Carnag, on a trip to this very island, though that was before he became King."

"You did?" said Braim. "What happened when you got here?"

Braim knew that he had asked the wrong question the moment those words left his mouth, because the stony silence from Jenur radiated from her like the heat from the sun above. What made Jenur's silence worse was that Braim had no idea what the matter was, as it seemed like an entirely innocuous question to him. And based on how puzzled Darek looked, Braim could not rely on him

7

for help in this matter, either.

Finally, Jenur said, "Let's not talk about it. That was a lifetime ago, literally in your case. Let's instead focus on the reason why the gods invited us here. We have all had enough tragedy in the last several months. You don't need to be burdened with the tragedies of the past, too."

Braim was none too sure about that, but he remembered enough about basic social etiquette not to push the point. Besides, he decided that it wasn't really relevant to their current situation.

"But I must say," said Jenur, frowning as the slope evened out, "World's End seems very different from how I remember it. Of course, I am getting older and my memory isn't what it used to be, but I don't remember having to go up a slope before."

"Well, World's End was attacked by Uron when he was here," said Darek. "Remember? He led an entire army of half-gods to destroy the place. No doubt they've had to make a lot of repairs on it, which is probably why it looks so different."

"That is true," said Jenur. "But they must have had access to the original blueprints, because despite the differences, the city still seems familiar to me. It is both familiar and foreign, I guess, is how you'd put it."

"Familiar and foreign," Braim repeated. "Same here. Except it's just foreign to me, like everything else I've seen since coming back to life."

"I wonder if we'll get to stay here any longer after the big announcement," said Darek, excitement in his voice. He looked around at the large skyscrapers like they contained the deepest secrets of magic behind them. "I mean, think about it. This is the Throne of the Gods itself. We could learn so much about magic and the gods here and bring back so much knowledge with us to improve our teachings. We could advance our magical knowledge by a century at least."

Braim rolled his eyes. While he liked Darek well enough, he thought that the guy was a bit of a dork sometimes, always going on about the minutiae of magic and the gods anytime anyone gave him a chance. Braim didn't have a lot of interest in that stuff, despite being a mage, but then, he had found that he had interest in very few things, ever since returning from the dead. Most of his days felt quite aimless, because he barely remembered anything about his past life and his past interests, not helped by the fact that North Academy had little records about him and his original life in general.

"I just want to go home as soon as it's finished," said Braim. He leaned in closer to Darek and Jenur as they walked and whispered, "I don't think the katabans like me very much."

"Katabans don't like humans in general," said Jenur. "I wouldn't take it personally. In my younger years, I knew a katabans who I did not get along very well with, due to the fact that she tried to feed me to her goddess once."

"You don't think that's what the gods have summoned *us* for, do you?" said Braim with a gulp. "Because I just got back from the dead and I really don't want to go back to the Spirit Lands any time soon."

"I doubt it," said Jenur. "After all, only the southern gods eat humans. If they tried to eat us, the northern gods would probably put a stop to them."

"Yeah, but aren't we beyond the Dividing Line?" asked Braim. "Doesn't that mean the southern gods can eat us, if they want?"

"Don't worry about it," said Jenur, patting him on the shoulder. "The southern gods are not very subtle, so it is unlikely that this is an elaborate trap set to kill us. It's not worth worrying about."

"If you say so," said Braim.

The party of three rounded one final street corner and ended up in a wide-open plaza that took Braim by surprise for a moment. It was probably the abrupt change from the narrow streets to the wide-open plaza that had taken him by surprise, especially when he saw the huge building in the center of the plaza.

It was a massive temple. Not as massive as the skyscrapers of ruby and emerald that towered around them, perhaps, but so large that it made the Arcanium of North Academy look like a rundown shack in comparison. A shallow moat, full of water so clear that it looked like shiny air reflecting the rays of the sun, surrounded it, with more water pouring from the channels along the sides of the building. A tiny bridge of gold crossed over the shallow moat to the marble and pearl gates, reflecting the rays of the sun from above.

Not only that, but the building had dozens of turrets arranged along the top, such as one that resembled a lightning bolt and another that resembled a raging fire. A massive glass dome rose from the midst of the turrets and towers, while the building itself radiated the energy of all of the gods of Martir. It was almost too much for Braim to handle.

"Wow," said Darek. "It looks even more amazing than I thought it would. Does it look like how you remember it, Mom?"

Jenur nodded, her eyes fixed firmly on the beautiful Temple standing before them. "Yes. It looks almost exactly the same as I remember it."

But Jenur didn't sound happy when she said that. There was an unmistakable tinge of sadness in her voice and she looked at the Temple the same way that a person might look at the grave of a deceased one. She even looked older, as if the mere presence of the Temple was enough to age her considerably.

"Well, what are we waiting for?" said Braim, causing Darek and Jenur to look at him in surprise. "That's where the gods said the big announcement is supposed to take place, right? Let's head on in, then. Don't want to be late."

They crossed the plaza and the tiny bridge over to the massive gates of the Temple itself. Braim was at first confused about how they were supposed to open the large gates before the gates opened inwards on their own without warning, allowing the three of them to pass through without delay.

The lobby of the Temple was immense, almost as wide-open as the plaza was. Huge marble columns supported the ceiling, while thousands of stone statues of the gods—similar to the ones in the Magical Superior's study on World's End—stood on pedestals everywhere, although there was a clear red-carpeted path from the front door to the end of the lobby.

But as Braim, Darek, and Jenur entered, Braim immediately noticed that they were not alone. Standing about halfway between the front door and the doors at the end of the room were five people who were probably not katabans or gods, standing together in a group chatting among themselves idly.

Two of the five people he recognized immediately: Archmage

Yorak, an aquarian mage with a whale-like head, who was also the headmistress of the Undersea Institute, the best magical school in the Undersea, and her pupil and student, Auratus, another aquarian mage whose head resembled a goldfish's head. He had met the two shortly after his revival, as they had been helping defend North Academy from Uron at the time, but he hadn't gotten to speak with either of them long, as they had left for the Undersea Institute shortly afterward.

As for the other three, Braim did not recognize them at all. One was an old, almost elderly, dark-skinned man with piercing gold eyes, leaning on a fancy black cane with the head of a golden hammer for its tip. Braim pegged the man's race as Carnagian based on his dark skin and light hair. Not just Carnagian, but Carnagian royalty, because he wore fancy red robes with the symbol of Grinf, the God of Justice, Fire, and Metal, on them, and a golden crown topped his head. His face was horribly disfigured, as if it had been badly burned at some point. Nonetheless, Braim imagined that the man had probably been extremely handsome in his youth and would probably still look good today if not for his face.

Standing next to the man, wearing bright yellow robes like the butter flowers Braim had seen a botamancy student summon once, was a much younger woman, probably in her early thirties at the oldest. Though her blonde hair was hardly alarming, Braim sensed that she was a katabans. He found it odd how she held the Carnagian man's hand, as if she was his wife.

And finally, standing next to the female katabans was a young girl, probably no older than eighteen, who looked like the old man and the young katabans put together. She had darker skin, like the old man, but also strikingly blonde hair like the female katabans. She wore dark red robes, just like the man, but she held herself more like the female katabans, with an air of haughtiness that made her seem unfriendly at first glance.

As a result of not recognizing those three, Braim held back, while Darek waved at Auratus and Yorak, saying, "Hi, guys! What are you doing here?"

Auratus noticed Darek and waved at him with a large smile on her own face, while Yorak cut off her conversation with the elderly Carnagian man and turned to face them. The man, the katabans, and the young girl looked at them as they approached as well, the man with a large smile on his face.

"Jenur Takren? Is that you?" said the man. Despite his age, his voice was strong and firm, but also friendly, which sounded odd coming out of his disfigured mouth. "How are you doing?"

Braim looked at Jenur, who was staring at the old man in surprise.

"Malock?" said Jenur, the disbelief etched in her voice as she, Darek, and Braim came to a stop before the other people. "What are *you* doing here? I didn't know you'd be here."

"I was invited by Lord Grinf himself," said the old man, who was apparently named Malock. "But I didn't expect to see you here, either. Were you also invited by the gods?"

"I was," said Jenur, nodding. "They sent me an invitation, but they did not say that they had invited anyone else."

Then Malock's eyes darted toward Braim and Darek. "And who are these two young men? I don't believe I have had the pleasure of meeting either of them before."

"Oh, excuse me," said Jenur. She rested one hand on Braim's

shoulder and another on Darek's. "This is Darek, my adopted son, who you met years ago during the Katabans War when he was much younger, if you don't remember. And this is Braim Kotogs, the man who just recently came back to life. Darek, Braim, I would like you two to meet King Tojas Malock, the King of Carnag."

Darek, as friendly as ever, held out a hand and said, "Pleased to see you again, Your Majes—"

"Hold on a moment," said King Malock, his eyes fixed on Braim as if he was the only thing that existed in the room at the moment. "Did you say Braim Kotogs? You mean *the* Braim Kotogs, the only man to ever return from the dead?"

Braim normally liked to be the center of attention, but for some reason he found Malock's gaze unnerving, perhaps because it was coming from such an ugly, distorted face. It didn't help that the female katabans and the young girl were staring at him as well. Especially the young girl, who was watching him as carefully as if she was trying to figure out how to fit him into her own little plans, whatever those may have been.

"Yes, that's him, all right," said Darek. He still held out his hand. "Anyway, pleased to see you again, Your Majesty. It's been a long time since we last met, but I still remember you very well."

"I'm sure you do," said Malock, although Braim was under the impression that Malock was not paying much attention to Darek. "This is quite an honor, Braim. I did not expect to meet the man who came back from the dead. You are famous throughout the whole world, you know, from the highest king to the lowliest peasant, for having returned to life."

"I am?" said Braim, scratching the back of his head. "But I've

14

never even left North Academy until yesterday."

"Word travels quickly along the sea winds," said Malock. "Even into the ears of old men like me."

The female katabans coughed loudly, causing Malock to start and look at her.

"Oh, yes, how rude of me," said Malock. He gestured at the female katabans and the young girl. "Please meet my wife, Queen Hanarova, and my daughter, Raya Mana."

Queen Hanarova smiled at Braim and Darek, though it reminded Braim of that same patronizing look that the katabans in the city earlier had given him and the others on their way to the Temple. "Hello, you two. It is quite an honor to meet the man who came back."

Darek, as with Malock, held out a hand and said, "Pleased to meet you again, Queen Hanarova. I—"

"So you really *did* come back from the dead?" Hanarova asked, interrupting Darek as if he hadn't said a word. "Truly?"

"Yep," said Braim, nodding, not sure what else to say. "I did. You can ask Darek. He was there when it happened."

Darek puffed out his chest and said, "Yes, I was. I could tell you all about the Spirit Lands, if you'd like."

"I don't care," said Hanarova, without missing a beat. She then gestured for the young girl to approach. "Come and introduce yourself to the most famous man in the world now, Raya. Don't be rude or shy."

Much to Braim's surprise, Raya curtsied him and said, "Hello, Mr. Kotogs. I am very pleased to meet you. You are far more handsome in real life than the descriptions of you suggested."

"Really?" said Braim, perking up. "Well, no surprise there.

Words can't describe this." He gestured at his face as he said that.

"And quite humble, too," said Raya.

It took Braim a second to realize that she was mocking him, but before he could respond, Queen Hanarova looked at Jenur and smiled, although it was hardly a friendly smile. "Hello, Jenur. I almost didn't notice you. You've grown quite a bit quieter with age, haven't you?"

"Hello, Hana," said Jenur. She sounded polite, but she stood as straight as a board, like she was trying to keep herself from doing something she would regret. "As untactful as ever, I see."

"Tact is a human construct," said Hana. "If anything, I would suggest that *you* should show some tact to me, seeing as I am royalty."

"And I'm the Magical Superior," said Jenur, "which means I know all sorts of ways that I can make your day worse without even thinking about it."

"Cute threat," said Hana. She hugged Malock's arm. "If you tried anything, Tojas would simply order the Carnagian Army to tear your silly little school apart. Right, Tojas?"

Malock now looked rather uncomfortable with both Jenur and Hana looking at him. "Er, ladies, why don't we move the conversation to something a bit more … lighthearted? I mean, it has been many years since we have all been together like this. Why not enjoy it, rather than fill it with petty insults?"

"Mal has a point," Jenur said. "I really don't have any time to spend arguing with an old katabans, anyway."

"*Old*?" Hana said indignantly. "I am only one hundred and fifty years old. That's young in katabans years."

"Hold on," said Braim, causing Jenur and Hana to look at

him. "You really *are* a katabans?"

"Of course," said Hana, tossing her hair back. "What else would I be?"

"And you're married to a human king," said Braim, pointing at Malock.

"Indeed," said Hana. "I am just going to assume that your resurrection must have messed with your ability to notice the obvious, so I won't hold your denseness against you."

Braim didn't know what to say to that. So he pointed at Raya and said, "And this is your daughter? As in, your actual, blood daughter?"

"Yes," said Hana.

"So that makes her half-human and half-katabans, then," said Braim.

"Of course," said Hana. She looked at her daughter affectionately. "And she's the best daughter in the world, best child in the world in fact. You would have to be a fool not to see her greatness."

"I didn't even know it was possible for humans and katabans to, uh, mate like that," said Braim.

"It is very much possible," Malock assured him with a wink. "And no, Raya does not suffer from any deformities or terminal illnesses as a result of her upbringing. She used to be quite ill as a child, but I had only the best doctors and healers in the Northern Isles to take care of her, and she has been a healthy girl ever since."

Braim scratched his chin and looked at Raya. She seemed too quiet for his tastes, but he supposed that she might just be shy. In any case, she certainly didn't look like she was sickly or suffering from any physical deformities that one might expect from an inter-species hybrid, so maybe it was not worth pushing the subject further.

Darek, on the other hand, said, "So can Raya access the ethereal and stuff? Can she live as long as a human or does she have the typical lifespan of a katabans? Furthermore—"

"Do shut up," Hana said to Darek, glaring at him as if he was intentionally annoying her. "Our beautiful daughter is not some unusual specimen for you mages to study and dissect. If you want to talk to her later, you can do so, but right now your questions are obviously distressing her. See?"

Hana was right. Raya looked rather stressed, as if every one of Darek's questions had been as difficult as a complex mathematical formula. She had pulled her hood over her head, which seemed rather over the top to Braim, not to mention rude. He certainly didn't like how it hid her beautiful features, as Braim was of the opinion that a beautiful woman should never be afraid to show her beauty wherever she was.

Then again, she is a princess, Braim thought. *She can do pretty much whatever she wants, regardless of what we think.*

Darek looked a little annoyed at being told off by Hana, but he nodded and said, "All right," before turning to face Auratus and Yorak, neither of whom had said a thing during this entire exchange.

"I'm glad to see you two again," said Darek. "How's the Undersea Institute?"

"Wonderful," Yorak said. Unlike other aquarians Braim had met, her voice lacked the distinct gurgled accent that all aquarians who learned Divina as a second language spoke with. "We have just recently built a new dorm to house the large number of new students we've received over the last couple of months. We named it the Kuroshio Dorm."

Darek nodded solemnly, although Braim had no idea what that meant. He figured that Kuroshio was the name of someone important who must have died, but he decided to ask Darek that question later, after the announcement.

"We were just speaking with King Malock and his family while we were waiting to be let into the rest of the Temple," said Yorak, gesturing at the Carnagian Royal Family. "But we certainly did not expect to see you three here."

"Same here," said Darek. "We thought we were the only ones invited to the Temple."

"Clearly, you were wrong about that," said Hana, brushing her hair out of her eyes, "although I don't understand why they invited you five, aside from Braim, of course."

Darek—whose patience with Hana seemed to be running thinner and thinner—folded his arms across his chest and said, in a strained tone similar to Jenur's, "Well, it can't *possibly* be because I helped save the whole world and the gods themselves, now can it?"

Jenur put a hand on Darek's shoulder and shot him a warning look. Darek looked at her and said, "What?"

"Your mother is obviously trying to tell you not to speak that way to royalty," said Hana. "That honestly surprises me, though, because Jenur hasn't exactly had a sterling record when it comes to showing respect to royalty herself."

"Sorry, Hana, but you aren't exactly right about that," said Jenur. "The truth is, I was simply trying to let Darek know that he shouldn't be wasting his time responding to such obvious bait."

"Bait?" Hana repeated. She put one hand on her chest. "Me? I would never bait anyone. Baiting people is quite uncouth, especially for royalty such as myself. But if I *were* to 'bait' anyone, it would be you, Jenur, because you are so easy to bait that I don't even have to try."

Jenur shot Malock a look that clearly said, *What did you see in this woman?*

Malock shrugged sheepishly and said nothing. Braim decided that Carnag was probably a very good place to live, if Malock was wise enough not to get in between two fighting women. Perhaps he'd move there once he got fully acclimated to the physical world again. Braim had heard that Carnagian women were quite beautiful, after all, which seemed as good a reason to move there as any.

"Queen Hanarova, I do not approve of you speaking so unkindly to Jenur," said Yorak. "While I don't know the history between you two, I do know that Jenur is the Magical Superior and is thus my peer. As a fellow mage, I do not like to see her treated in this way by anyone, even by royalty such as yourself."

"Fine," said Hana. "I was getting tired of talking to her, anyway. Does anyone know when the gods will call us into their meeting chamber?"

"Good question, Hanarova," said a familiar deep voice above them, causing the entire group to look up toward the ceiling in response. "The answer to that question is, very soon."

At first, Braim saw nothing on the ceiling, but then a large figure slowly materialized into view. The figure lacked legs. Instead, he had a wispy, ghost-like tail. He was also heavily armored, with fingers like chains and a human-like face that lacked a nose. His green eyes and crooked teeth only added to his creepy appearance, especially as he floated down toward the front of the group, blocking off their path to the doors at the end of the hall.

Though Braim had not interacted with this particular god often, he still recognized him, although it was Darek who said, "Hello, Ghostly God. I didn't expect to see you today."

The Ghostly God, God of Ghosts and Mist, smiled. "And a good day to you, too, Darek. You seem as a rude and disrespectful as ever, which surprises me, seeing as you still owe me eight years of service."

Braim looked at Darek in surprise. "Eight years of service?"

"Long story," said Darek, without looking at Braim. He then put his hands on his hips, looking up at the deity floating before them. "What are you doing here, Ghostly God? I thought they were going to send a katabans to fetch us."

"This is the Temple of the Gods," the Ghostly God pointed out. "And seeing as I am a god, it should be obvious why I am here. It would be sort of like asking why the Magical Superior lives in North Academy."

"You still didn't answer my other question," Darek said.

"Yes, well, I decided to give you all a hero's welcome," said the Ghostly God, in the least convincing voice Braim had ever heard anyone use. "Everyone here today, perhaps with the exception of Princess Raya, has contributed to saving the world at some point or another. I believe that heroism should never go unrewarded. Therefore, I wanted to greet you all myself."

The Ghostly God was not nearly as good a liar as he thought

21

himself to be. He didn't make any eye contact with any of them the whole time he spoke, but that hardly surprised Braim. The gods—especially southern gods such as the Ghostly God—tended to think they were too smart for mortals to notice when they were lying. It was one of their annoying tendencies, though you usually didn't point it out unless you wanted to get punished for speaking disrespectfully of the gods.

Anyway, Braim suspected that the Ghostly God had really arrived to greet them because of his interest in Braim. When Braim had come back to life two months ago, the Ghostly God, who had been at North Academy at the time, had grilled Braim on what the afterlife was like. Braim had answered the god's questions to the best of his ability, but the Ghostly God still dropped by the school every now and then to interrogate him about it, though Braim had learned how to hide from the Ghostly God whenever he showed up unannounced like that so he wouldn't have to waste time answering more useless questions.

"So you are the Ghostly God, then," said Malock, looking up at the god with curiosity. "Jenur told me about you in a letter she sent to me recently."

"And you are King Malock," said the Ghostly God, "the first mortal to reach World's End and live, if I am not mistaken."

"My crew and I in my youth, yes," said Malock, nodding, though he didn't sound happy about it. "But we never visited your island on our voyage."

"That is because my island is not along the route that your crew took to reach World's End," the Ghostly God said. Then he looked at Braim, despite Braim's best efforts to not draw the deity's attention to himself, and said, "Greetings, Braim. How have you been recently?"

"Fine," said Braim, as tersely as he could. "Is it time for us to go in now?"

"Straight to the point, I see," the Ghostly God said. "Anyway, yes, it is. In fact, I came out here in order to tell you all that you may now enter the main chamber. After all, that is what you are here for."

The Ghostly God gestured toward the doors at the end of the room, which then swung open on their own. It was hard to see what lay beyond the doors, however, due to the fact that Braim stood on the opposite end of the lobby from them.

"Any special instructions or orders we should be aware of before we go inside?" said Darek.

"Simply step through the open doorway," said the Ghostly God, waving one hand in the direction of the doors, "where you will shortly hear the most important announcement that any of you have heard in a long time."

With that, the Ghostly God vanished. Braim looked around to see where the god had gone, but he was nowhere to be seen. Still, Braim felt like he was being watched by an unseen individual, as if the Ghostly God had simply turned invisible rather than vanish into thin air.

King Malock, on the other hand, didn't seem to notice or care. He simply began walking toward the doors, with Hana and Raya by his side, followed by Yorak and Auratus. Jenur and Darek then took after them, so Braim walked to join them as well. He was glad he was at the back of the group. He had a feeling that the other gods would be interested in him as well, and right now he didn't want to be the center of attention of the gods.

When they all stepped through the doors, Braim looked up at their surroundings to see what the chamber they had stepped into looked like.

The Throne Room of the Gods was a massive chamber, much bigger than any room that Braim had ever been in (not that that was saying much, considering how little he remembered of his past life). The room was as wide-open as a field, with a sandy floor and a huge crystal glass dome above, the same dome that Braim had noticed earlier. The dome was so clear that it was like standing outside, and if Braim hadn't know any better, he would have said that there was no dome at all, that the chamber was just open to the blue skies above.

All around the perimeter of the room stood hundreds if not thousands of thrones at varying heights. Upon each throne sat a different god or goddess, all of them talking to each other, the combined volume of their voices almost deafening. As far as Braim could tell, every god in the Northern and Southern Pantheons was present, which was impressive, because it was rare for them all to be in one place like this.

For example, Braim saw the Ghostly God taking a seat next to Ranama, the God of Language, who was one of the other gods that Braim had met shortly after his resurrection. Ranama was recognizable due to his tentacle beard, his glasses that showed two intelligent blue eyes behind them, and the book hanging off his neck. He was currently reading the book, so absorbed in it that he barely paid any attention to the argument between two gods that Braim didn't recognize occurring next to him.

Seeing so many gods and goddesses in one place was an exhilarating experience, especially as a mage, because Braim could feel their power even more so than most non-mages. Yet there was also a deep sense of worry and terror, as if all of the deities gathered here today were trying to avoid focusing on some uncomfortable event that just happened recently.

In fact, Braim noticed how all of the gods and goddesses were pointedly avoiding looking at the massive throne on the opposite end of the Throne Room from him and his friends. While it wasn't the only empty throne in the room (Braim spotted one near Nimiko, the God of Light), it was the largest and most obvious of them.

Braim understood why they were looking away from it, of course. That had to be the throne of Skimif, the previous God of Martir, who had died during Uron's attempt to destroy Martir. The other deities were probably avoiding looking at it because it reminded them of Skimif, whose death had affected everyone on Martir in some way or another.

Then Braim noticed Malock leaning on his cane and staring at the empty throne. It was like Malock was looking at the coffin of a dead friend, which made Braim wonder if the King had once known Skimif prior to his death.

As for the others, they were reacting to the presence of so many gods in one place in different ways. Both Jenur and Hana looked at ease, probably because they had been here before, while Darek, Auratus, Yorak, and Raya were looking around like they could not believe what they were seeing. Darek in particular looked excited about seeing so many gods in one place, while Raya seemed rather put off by it.

It was then that the Ghostly God reappeared next to them, quite without warning, and said, "Oh, yes. I almost forgot. You

25

mortals should be up on the balcony, not down here. Silly me."

The Ghostly God snapped his fingers. A second later, Braim and the others no longer stood on the sandy floor of the Throne Room. Instead, they stood on a balcony well above the thrones of the gods, which gave them a bird's eye view of the entire chamber. The sudden teleportation made Braim feel a little woozy, but he recovered quickly enough and ran over to the railing to look down.

"Wow," said Braim. "We're up high."

He looked over his shoulder at the others. Most of them seemed to handle the teleportation fairly well, except for Darek, whose face was vaguely green and whose hands were on his stomach. Braim recalled that Darek didn't react to heights very well, though Darek was already waving his wand over his stomach, probably applying a healing spell to keep himself from getting too sick.

The others joined Braim at the balcony's railing, looking down at the gods below. Braim noticed that some of the gods were looking up at them. Or rather, they were looking up at *him*. He saw one goddess—who resembled a little girl with mismatched clothes—watching him with curious eyes, while another one, a woman made of water, was also looking up at him, although she seemed less curious and more annoyed at the presence of so many mortals in the Throne Room of the Gods.

Then Princess Raya leaned against the railing to Braim's right, saying, "Are they going to make the announcement soon? I'm getting *so* bored."

"Don't worry, Raya, I am certain it will be soon," said Malock. "While the gods can sometimes be very slow, I was given the impression that this was going to be quick and to the point."

"All right, Father," said Raya, though she didn't sound convinced. "But how much longer, do you think, will we have to wait?"

Malock opened his mouth to say something, but then Jenur—who had been watching the gods below—suddenly pointed at Skimif's empty throne. "What's that?"

Braim looked down at the empty throne. A single ball of light glowed over the throne's seat. In fact, it was growing bright enough to attract the attention of every deity in the room. All conversation died out as the light grew brighter and brighter, before suddenly dimming and then vanishing out right, giving Braim a clear view of the throne, which was no longer empty.

Two beings stood on the throne now. One of them was a skeleton wearing auburn robes and carrying a wand of crystal and gold, with a magic stone wrapped around his upper right forearm. Braim recognized the skeleton as the Mysterious One, a powerful entity from the Spirit Lands who had pretended to be the God of Mystery and Magic for many years, but had since returned to the Spirit Lands in order to lead it. Even though it had only been two months since Braim had last seen the Mysterious One, it felt like it had been much longer.

As for the second being, she was a woman who wore thick, severe-looking glasses and carried a thick tome against her chest, but Braim couldn't read the tome's title because it wasn't facing him. She wore a shapeless a silver robe and her hair was tied in a bun. She could have been pretty if she didn't look so judgmental.

"Father, who is that?" said Raya, pointing at the woman

standing next to the Mysterious One, who was now eying the gods with a rather judgmental glare. "Another goddess? I don't remember Teacher telling me about that one."

Malock leaned forward over the railing, though not too far. He squinted his old eyes, then shrugged. "I do not know. I have never seen her before. Hana, do you know her?"

"No," said Hana, shaking her head. "But I don't like the look of her one bit."

A cursory glance of the other four told Braim that none of the others knew the woman, either. That made Braim wonder if she was even from Martir at all.

Darek pointed at the robed skeleton. "Hey, I think that's the Mysterious One. Was his mission to find the Powers successful after all?"

Braim wasn't sure. According to Darek, the Mysterious One had promised to contact the Powers—that mysterious group of entities that had created all of Martir—to get replacement gods for the deities slain by Uron. That had been two months ago, but Braim had thought that the Mysterious One had given up searching for the Powers well before then, seeing as they had not heard from the Mysterious One since the day he made that promise to them.

"Perhaps he found them after all," said Jenur. She sighed in relief. "Thank the Powers."

"But if that's the case, then why did he bring that one woman with him?" said Yorak. "Is she the new Goddess of Martir? But what about the other four deities we lost?"

"Shh," said Hana, holding one finger up to her lips. "Listen. The Mysterious One is talking."

Hana was right. The Mysterious One was talking. In fact, he sounded like he was standing right next to Braim, even though the Mysterious One was all the way below him on the other side of the room. The Mysterious One was probably using magic to amplify his voice, but whether he was or wasn't, Braim listened intently.

"Welcome, gods, mortals, and katabans," said the Mysterious One, waving at everyone. "I am pleased to see all of you today. I was worried that I might not return in time to help, but it seems that Martir is still functioning even with some of its gods dead. That is good, but Martir still needs both the Northern and Southern Pantheon complete if it is to survive and function as the Powers intended."

Braim wondered if that was part of the reason he felt so off. One of the gods that had died by Uron's hands was a deity known as the Human God, the God of Humans. Braim had not noticed any negative effects toward humans as a result of the Human God's death, but he supposed that the creeping depression that struck him at random might have been partly a result of that god's death (even though he himself had been dead when the Human God died).

"It took me sometime, but I finally succeeded in tracking down the Powers," said the Mysterious One. He lay one bony hand on the woman's shoulder. "And the Powers agreed to give Martir new gods to replace the ones killed by Uron. My mission, I am happy to say, was a success."

Darek shared a fist bump with Auratus, while Jenur, Yorak, Malock, and Hana sighed with relief. Raya, meanwhile, yawned, as if it the Mysterious One had simply announced today's weather. Braim didn't understand that at all, seeing as this was easily the most important piece of news that Braim and everyone else had heard in years.

"I spoke with the Powers and explained to them the situation," said the Mysterious One. He then patted the woman standing next to him on the shoulder. "And this was their solution."

"What?" rang out the harsh voice of one of the gods, the source of which Braim quickly located: A short, green-skinned man with vines for hair and red eyes. "An uptight woman with bad eyesight? How, pray tell, O Mysterious One, is she going to help us? Is she going to scold us for not being well-behaved, maybe threaten to give us a time-out if we don't listen to her like children?"

That lone god's harsh words caused several of the other gods to snicker. Raya actually smirked at the god's words, while Malock glared at that god as if he could cause him to spontaneously erupt into fire by sheer force of will alone. While Braim agreed that the joke was rather tasteless, he thought that Malock had to have some sort of grudge against him, based on how harshly he glared at the god.

The Mysterious One, to his credit, didn't look disturbed at all by the god's joke. He opened his mouth to speak, but then the glasses-wearing woman held up a hand. Much to Braim's surprise, the Mysterious One closed his mouth and gestured for her to speak instead.

The woman adjusted her glasses and then, focusing on the god, said, "You are the Loner God, the God of Solitude, the Jungle, and Animals, correct?"

"Yep," said the deity, who still chuckled at his own joke every now and then. "That's me, though I don't know how you found out my name, seeing as I haven't even introduced myself yet."

"No need," said the woman. "The Powers gave me complete knowledge of the gods of Martir when they created me. I know the names, domains, and abilities of each and every deity in this room. I also know of the Godly War that divided the gods between the Northern and Southern Pantheons eons ago, including the Treaty that the Powers wrote up to govern relations between the two Pantheons."

"Yeah, yeah, so what?" said the Loner God with a sneer. "That's common knowledge by now. Are you just going to keep stating the obvious or is there a point buried somewhere in your blather?"

"I was simply going to say that the Powers had neglected to mention to me how rude you gods can be," said the woman. "Your attitudes and jokes are not very godly, if you ask me."

"We gods are the ones who define what is 'godly' and what isn't," said the Loner God, jerking a thumb at his bare chest. "I don't think you're even a god, anyway, so where do *you* get off telling *us* what is 'godly' and what isn't?"

"It is true that I am not a god or goddess of any sort," the woman said. "But that doesn't mean I can't judge for myself what kind of behaviors should be expected from the deities that rule this world. Gods should be held to much higher standards than mortals ... and I am sad to say that all of you gods must have been held to very low standards for a long time now, if this attitude of your is any indication of your general behavior."

To say that all of the gods, northern and southern alike, appeared offended by her words was an understatement. Half of the gods looked ready to jump out of their thrones and smite her for her blatant disrespect, while the other half muttered among themselves about how disrespectful this woman was. But none tried to attack her, probably because the Mysterious One—who was stronger than any of the other gods in the room—stood next to her.

The woman did not seem to notice the gods' reaction to her words, because she continued to speak like the gods had not reacted at all. "But that is all the more reason for me to raise the low standards to the level at which they need to be. By doing so, I can perhaps make it so that the gods of Martir earn the respect that they claim to deserve."

"Is that the Powers' answer to the deaths of our brothers and sisters?" said the Loner God. "Just raise the standards and that will somehow restore balance among the gods?"

"No," said the woman, shaking her head. She patted the book she held against her chest. "This is what will help us."

"A book?" said the Loner God. "That's even worse."

"It isn't just any book," said the woman. "It is a book written by the Powers themselves. It is the key to bringing new gods into existence in Martir."

"What does the book say?" said the Loner God. "And, forgive me for my 'rudeness,' but you haven't even given us your name yet, woman."

"My name is Alira," said the woman. She then raised the book above her head, though it was still too far for Braim to read its title. "And this book is the Rulebook for the Tournament of the Gods."

Chapter Two

U P UNTIL THIS point, Raya had been quite bored. She had
been bored of World's End—which, despite being the
Throne of the Gods, was not really as exciting or
interesting as the name suggested—bored of the rude katabans
who had greeted her and her parents when they arrived here,
bored of the other mortals that had also been invited to World's
End and who she didn't really care about, and bored of the
Temple of the Gods. Mostly, it had been because Raya didn't like
traveling and didn't like talking to strangers, especially to
strangers who weren't royalty like her.

The only stranger who interested her was the mage named
Braim Kotogs, who had allegedly come back from the dead not
too long ago. Yet even he seemed boring, not to mention there
was something definitely off about him that made Raya want to
avoid him.

The view from the balcony is sort of nice, I guess, Raya
thought. *But the view from my room's balcony back in Carnag
Hall is even nicer.*

But when the severe-looking woman on Skimif's Throne
below—the one who reminded Raya far too much of Teacher—
had mentioned a 'Tournament of the Gods,' well, Raya perked up.
She liked tournaments. In fact, Carnag's Fifth Annual Airship

Tournament had just ended recently and the winner, as per contest rules, had given Raya a free ride in his airship, which had been the most fun Raya had had in a while.

As a result, Raya decided to pay more attention to the announcement. She leaned forward a little bit more, watching the woman named Alira hug the thick Rulebook book to her chest.

"The Tournament of the Gods?" repeated the Loner God. His mocking tone had vanished, which was sad, because Raya had found him to be the most amusing thing about this whole trip. "I've never heard of that."

"That's no mystery," said Alira, "because there has never been anything quite like this in the entire history of Martir."

The Loner God glanced at the strange, green octopus-like god sitting next to him. "Hey, historian, is that true?"

The god—who Raya recognized as the Historic God, the God of History, as he matched the description her father had once given her of him—rolled his eyes, but nodded. "It is, brother. History does not have any records of any Tournament of the Gods being held anywhere in the world before today."

"I guess history doesn't repeat itself after all," said the Loner God with a smirk, earning another eye roll from the Historic God.

"But that still doesn't explain what the Tournament of the Gods *is*," said another god, who Raya immediately recognized as Grinf, mostly because his powerfully built body, square jaw, and large gavel closely resembled the statues of him back in Carnag Hall. "Is it some tournament in which we gods will have to compete?"

"You gods will not need to do a thing," said Alira. "It is in fact a tournament for the mortals. The humans and aquarians, that is. To put it simply, one hundred mortals from all over Martir will be competing for one of the five positions for godhood that are currently vacant."

That caught Raya's interest. She leaned forward even more, ignoring the mutterings between Yorak and Jenur beside her, and the puzzled look on Father's face.

"Hold on," said the Loner God, raising one of his short arms. "You mean that, rather than create new gods out of nothing, we're going to ascend five chosen mortals instead?"

"Precisely," said Alira. "The Tournament is going to have five different brackets for the different gods: One for Skimif, one for Hollech, one for the Human God, one for the Spider Goddess, and one for the Avian Goddess. Each bracket will have twenty mortals competing for the title of each god. For example, the Skimif bracket will have twenty mortals competing for the chance to become the new God of Martir."

Raya's eyes widened. She glanced at Father and Mother. Father stared at Alira with a stunned expression, while Mother looked like she grasped the implications of the Tournament as quickly as Raya did.

I always thought I'd be the Queen of Carnag when Mother passed, Raya thought. Her grip around the railing tightened. *But what if I could become the Goddess of Martir instead?*

"Why didn't the Powers just create a bunch of new gods and send them here?" said the Loner God. "A huge tournament like this sounds like a big waste of time, if you ask me."

"The Powers disagree, Longer God," said Alira. "The Powers believe that creating new gods is less efficient than making mortals who already live here into gods. Newly-created gods

35

would need to be trained by you deities, in addition to learning how to integrate with all of you. They will need to learn the complex social understandings that you gods have created among yourselves, which doesn't even factor in the time learning how to interact with the mortals and understanding Martir itself. Ascended mortals, on the other hand, already have a basic understanding and knowledge of Martir and the gods. Therefore, they will take less time to teach than brand new gods would."

Raya listened to every word that came from Alira's mouth as if it her life depended on it. She kept imagining herself sitting in that throne where the Mysterious One and Alira stood, presiding over the gods as they all bowed down to her.

If I become the Goddess of Martir, it won't just be the gods bowing down to me, but the whole world, Raya thought, unable to hide the smile on her face. *That would be amazing.*

"And finding the mortals who are destined to become gods— who you refer to as 'godlings,' if I understand the term correctly— will not be difficult," said Alira. "If I am not mistaken, Tinkar, the God of Fate and Time, knows which mortals are destined to become gods and which are not."

She was looking at a god as she said that, an old, bald-headed man with a large staff topped with a clock. Raya recalled from her lessons that that was the form that Tinkar typically took whenever he needed a physical form, which meant that the man was indeed Tinkar himself.

Tinkar, however, hardly looked happy about Alira's plan. Nonetheless, he nodded and said, "That is correct, Alira. I know the fates of all mortals on this world. I can help locate the one hundred mortals who are destined to become godlings, as unlike their fellow mortals, the fates of godlings are hidden from me, which makes them stand out quite a bit. It shouldn't take long, especially if some of my siblings help me."

"Yeah, yeah, that's nice," said the Loner God, waving off Tinkar's words like they were irrelevant. "But what are the *details* of the Tournament? I'm normally not the kind of god to worry about the small details, but this seems way too important to gloss over. Like, what are the rules and structure of the tournament?"

"All will be revealed in due time, Loner God," said Alira. She patted the cover of her Rulebook. "We must first decide on a location for the Tournament, as well as gather all of the mortals who are destined to become gods. All of Martir must be informed of the Tournament as well, from the lowest mortal to the highest god."

"Where should the Tournament be held, then?" said the Loner God. "Answer me that, lady."

"I believe World's End would be an excellent spot to host the Tournament," said Alira, "seeing as it is the Throne of the Gods after all—unless anyone here can think of a better place to host the Tournament, that is."

Not a single god objected to that suggestion. Raya had hoped that Grinf would suggest that they host it on Carnag, but Carnag's patron was as silent as the rest of them.

"Okay, but why a Tournament?" said the Loner God. "If we can find one hundred godlings, why not just pick five from among them and ascend them? Surely that would waste less time than setting up a whole Tournament."

"The Tournament is how we will weed out the worthy from the unworthy," said Alira. "Not every mortal with the potential for godhood will attain it. And of those who do, not every one will use their power for good. By completing the Tournament's trials, the new gods will show that they are indeed worthy of that lofty title and the immense power associated with it."

The Loner God said nothing in response to that, although he was clearly grumbling under his breath. He was too far away for Raya to hear him, however.

"If there are no more objections or questions," said Alira, after looking around at the rest of the gods, "Tinkar will lead a team of half a dozen other gods to locate the one hundred godlings who will be competing in the Tournament. Meanwhile, I will inform the rest of the gods about the rules and structure of the Tournament, which will take place exactly one month from now. That should give us plenty of time to find the godlings and organize the Tournament itself."

Alira spoke in a very matter-of-fact voice, which reminded Raya too much of Teacher back home on Carnag. Still, Alira's annoying voice didn't put off Raya from the idea of becoming the Goddess of Martir at all.

I bet that its my destiny to become a goddess,, Raya thought. *I mean, of course I am a godling. I'm the Princess of Carnag. If anyone should be given godhood, it should obviously be royalty like myself.*

"With that, I dismiss this meeting," said Alira. "I will reveal more of the details regarding the Tournament over the next four weeks as we begin the preparations. For now, you gods may leave and do as you wish for the rest of the day."

With that, both Alira and the Mysterious One vanished. As soon as they did, the gods began to leave. Some flew out of an opening in the glass dome above, while others teleported, and still others left through doors behind the thrones that led outside. Raya noticed Tinkar gathering half a dozen other gods around him as he spoke to them, but they were too far away for her to hear anything he was saying to them.

"Wow," said Darek, who Raya was displeased to notice was standing closer to her than she liked. He looked at the other people on the balcony. "A Tournament of the Gods. I have never heard of that before. Has anyone else?"

"No," said Yorak, shaking her head. "In all of my years as the Archmage of the Undersea Institute, I have never heard of such a process of deciding who should become a god."

"What's the *normal* process for ascending a mortal, then?" asked Braim, pushing away from the balcony and turning to look at Jenur and Yorak.

"The actual process is a mystery to us mortals," Yorak said. "It is one of the few mysteries of magic that we mages know very little about. The gods have kept the process a secret from mortals ever since the creation of Martir itself."

"All we do know about it is that only the gods can turn a mortal into a god somehow," said Jenur. "The exact process is unknown."

Braim then looked at Mother. "Say, Queen Hana, you're a katabans, right? Would you happen to know—"

"No," said Mother shortly. "While I did serve the Mechanical Goddess for many years, that was one secret she never saw fit to share with me. We katabans are just as in the dark about the subject of ascension as you humans are, so don't ask me another question about it."

Braim raised his hands defensively. "Okay, okay. No need to bite off my head."

Raya also pushed away from the balcony to stand by Mother. She did not, however, express her desire to become the Goddess of Martir, mostly because she doubted anyone here, except for her parents, would take that wish seriously.

Instead, she said, "Well, I for one am quite excited for the Tournament. I think it will be very interesting, maybe the most interesting thing to have ever happened on Martir."

Darek, who was still leaning against the railing, said, "I just wonder who the participants will be. Alira said that there are supposed to be one hundred godlings, which breaks down into twenty for each god. Any idea who might be chosen to participate?"

"None whatsoever," said Yorak. She then patted Auratus on the shoulder, causing her pupil to look up at her. "But I think that Auratus here would make a good candidate. She is an excellent student and an even better mage."

Raya wrinkled her nose at that. Although she didn't know Auratus very well, she had to admit that she had a hard time imagining an aquarian, of all things, as the Goddess of Martir, or as any of the other godly roles that needed to be filled. True, Skimif had been an aquarian prior to his own ascension to God of Martir, but that was different and Raya wasn't so sure that this Auratus had what it took.

But if Auratus is one of the chosen and we are put in the same bracket, then that means we'll have to compete, Raya thought. *I'll have to keep a careful eye on her in that case.*

Auratus looked a little embarrassed at her mentor's praise,

while Jenur said, "I hope that one of my students is chosen. It would bring even more honor to North Academy than it already has. And I'd just love to put up a picture of that student on the Wall of Mastery among all of our other great students of the past."

Raya, folding her hands behind her back, looked at her parents for their opinions. She expected them to say that she of course would make a great goddess. Not just any old goddess, no, but the Goddess of Martir herself. It was only what she deserved, after all, and as her loving parents, they were obligated to voice their support for her.

But Raya was disappointed when Father said, "It will indeed be interesting to watch. I hope that one of Carnag's mages is chosen. What do you say, Hana?"

"I expect Carnag to have some representation," said Mother, brushing some strands of hair from her face. "After all, the Carnagians are a proud and noble race of humans. I wouldn't be surprised if most of the chosen godlings come from that island."

Raya wondered if her parents might have somehow forgotten about her. So she cleared her throat rather loudly, but no one seemed to pay her any attention.

Instead, all attention was drawn to Braim when he said, "So what kind of challenges do you think that the participants will have to take on?"

"I imagine it will vary from bracket to bracket," said Yorak. "For example, I doubt that the replacement for Hollech will have to go through the same trials as a replacement for Skimif. It is probably wiser to ponder the specific trials that the participants of each bracket will face."

41

"I bet that the people in the Hollech category will have to tame horses, because he was the God of Horses, after all," said Braim. "And maybe steal things, too, because Hollech was the God of Thieves, too."

"That's still not very specific, though," said Darek, shaking his head. "Like, what would Hollechian participants actually steal? Would they have to steal from a king or from one of the gods, maybe?"

Raya found all of this speculation about the actual challenges rather boring. She cleared her throat loudly, but as before, no one, not even her parents, seemed interested in listening to her.

"That would be a very impressive challenge," said Father, tapping his chin in thought. "Steal from a god and try to get away with it. I can't see how any mortal thief could possibly succeed in that, but perhaps that is the point, that if you can successfully steal from a god, then you deserve the title of God of Thieves."

"But what would people who are participating in the Spider Goddess category have to do?" said Darek, a frown on his face as he scratched the back of his head. "Try to pet a poisonous spider and hope it doesn't bite them?"

"I don't know," said Jenur. "But I'm sure that all will be revealed in time. For now, perhaps we should all return to our residences, since the meeting is over and all."

"Good idea, Jenur," said Father. "But before we do that, why don't we all have dinner together? I believe that World's End has many good restaurants that we could patronize, which will be my treat. Right, Hana?"

"Of course it does," said Mother. "Or at least it did, back when I last visited here. I doubt I'll have any trouble locating a

42

good restaurant for us to eat. In fact, I believe I saw a great seafood restaurant on the corner when we were traveling to the Temple." She then turned to Raya. "Raya, what do you think? Do you want to get something to eat before we return to the place we're staying at?"

This wasn't what Raya wanted to talk about at all, but she could see no way to bring up what she actually wanted to talk about in a natural way. Still, Raya was determined to find a way to move the conversation in the direction she wanted it to go.

So Raya said, "Why, yes, Mother, that sounds very nice. I have never eaten at a genuine katabans seafood restaurant before, but I am certain that it will be a splendid place to discuss how great a Goddess of Martir I would make."

Raya was pretty sure that she had succeeded in smoothly and naturally changing the conversation to the subject she wanted to talk about at least, she thought so until Braim snickered, causing her to look at him and say, "What?"

"Oh, nothing, beautiful," said Braim, though he still snickered. "It's just that, well, I kind of doubt that you will be chosen to participate in the Tournament. And even if you are, I doubt you will become the Goddess of Martir."

"How do you know that I won't?" Raya asked. "Can you see into my fate and tell me what lies in the future?"

"Of course not," said Braim. "I just think that it's funny how you think you'd make a great Goddess of Martir."

"Of course Raya would," Mother said, before Raya could respond. She wrapped an arm around Raya's shoulders and squeezed her against her body. "Raya is obviously the best and most qualified mortal to become the Goddess of Martir. Even if she is half katabans, I doubt that will keep her from achieving apotheosis."

"Are you sure that katabans can ascend?" said Braim. "Because I thought that only humans and aquarians can."

"I am *half* human, you know," said Raya. "That, I believe, is enough to qualify for me a chance for the position of the Goddess of Martir. Right, Father?"

Father—who had clearly been trying to stay out of the conversation—nodded hastily and said, "Uh, yes, Raya, of course. And even if you aren't chosen, your mother and I will continue to love you as always."

"Don't talk about *if* she isn't chosen, Tojas," Mother said. "Instead, talk about what we will do *when* she is chosen. On that day, we'll throw an island-wide party on Carnag to celebrate her success. And maybe on Shika as well, if we can get them to celebrate with us."

To Raya, the idea of an island-wide party seemed awfully small for such a momentous occasion. If she became the Goddess of Martir, she'd create a massive worldwide party that everyone, human, aquarian, katabans, and god alike, would participate in. She had never heard of a worldwide party, of course, but she decided that that just meant she'd have to be the first one to do it.

"Uh huh," said Braim, who didn't sound too excited about it. "Well, I guess we'll all just have to see which way the winds of destiny blow, eh?"

"Of course we will," said Raya. "And as we all know, the winds of destiny almost always blow in the direction of royalty."

"If you say so," said Braim, although he didn't sound convinced at all by what she said.

Oh, well, Raya thought. *It's not like I need his support. I have the entire island of Carnag behind me. Who needs the support of a resurrected man, anyway? Especially one as rude as him.*

Chapter Three

MOST DAYS, CARMAZ Korva was certain that the gods hated him. Of course, his grandfather had always told him that it was his own foolishness that got him into all of the trouble that he did, that he should take more responsibility for his own actions and should stop blaming the gods for everything wrong in his life. It was arrogance, his grandfather had said, to think that the gods would single out a poor young man on the even poorer island of Ruwa in the Friana Archipelago just to torment him.

Carmaz was no mage, so he supposed that grandfather was probably right about that. Still, that didn't explain why Carmaz now found himself captured by a tribe of humanoid crustaceans, inside a wooden bamboo cell, with his right arm broken and the side of his head bleeding. It didn't help that the sun in the sky was burning hot, as it always was on the island of Riuja, making him feel even more miserable than he usually was.

But it wasn't like there was literally *no* explanation for how Carmaz got here. Earlier in the day, one of his friends, Saia, had been swimming in the waters on the northern beaches of Ruwa, when he was suddenly kidnapped by the crustaceans—a tribe of humanoid crab-like aquarians known for their tastes in human flesh—who dragged him to Riuja in the north. Carmaz had then taken his grandfather's old raft and rowed all the way out to that tiny island, despite knowing the bloody and violent reputation of the crustaceans who lived here. Due to his poverty, Carmaz had few physical possessions to his name, and so he relied on his friends such as Saia for support and help more often than not.

Unfortunately, when Carmaz arrived on Riuja, his grandfather's old raft—which had been such a reliable and sturdy sea craft for decades—had sprung a leak he couldn't fix, thus stranding Carmaz on the island. Carmaz was sure that the gods must have done that to him, because grandfather's raft had never sprung a leak before, especially not under dangerous situations like this.

Even so, Carmaz decided to save his friend anyway, despite the lack of a ready means of escape. Of course, no sooner had Carmaz taken a few steps onto the beach was he ambushed and captured by the crustaceans (how was he supposed to know that a handful of them would bury themselves in the sand and pop out to attack anyone who stepped on them?).

The crustaceans had then transported Carmaz to what was most likely the only settlement on the tiny island of Riuja. It might have at one point been a human village, as the rundown huts looked like the ones back on Ruwa, but Carmaz saw no sign of any non-crustaceans around, aside from clean human bones scattered everywhere. He didn't even see Saia, though he assumed that the crustaceans were probably hiding him in one of the huts somewhere.

As Carmaz sat there, he watched the crustaceans below start a fire with which to cook him and Saia upon. There were forty or fifty crustaceans in all. Not a large number by any means, but they were such a vicious tribe that even the armies of major nations like Carnag and Shika avoided them when possible. None of the crustaceans wore any clothing and he wasn't sure that they could even speak. All they ever seemed to do was growl and snarl at each other and at anyone else they didn't like. The most notable thing about them was the painted-on markings on their exoskeletons, which resembled stylized flames, but Carmaz had no idea what those meant or if they meant anything at all.

Nor was he much interested in finding out. Carmaz had heard horror stories about these crustaceans and how they ate pretty much anyone or anything that washed up on their shores. No doubt they were planning to eat him and Saia, though the crustaceans must have been smarter than he thought if they were first preparing a fire for the two of them.

I need to get out of here somehow, Carmaz thought. *And save Saia as well.*

Carmaz shook the bars of his cage. They were quite firm, although he wondered how these crustaceans had managed to construct something like this, considering how none of them had fingers with which to construct even the simplest of objects. The cage looked quite old, so perhaps it had been created by the original inhabitants of the island before the crustaceans came and killed everyone off.

In any case, Carmaz was used to getting out of these sorts of situations on his own. Once, as a teenager, he had been kidnapped by a group of pirates whose captain had a taste for boy flesh, and he had escaped using his wits and the captain's own lust against him. In another situation, Carmaz had been chased up a tree in the Swamp of Light by a large toothed lizard, which he had only escaped after pouring salt on the creature, which had burned its skin and forced it to retreat, which allowed him to safely return to his home village of Conewood.

Carmaz kicked the door to the cage, but it was locked tight and his kick only succeeded in causing the cage to sway. Of course, due to the injuries he had sustained earlier, his kicks were not as strong as they could be, but that didn't give Carmaz an excuse to give up.

But even if I do escape, how far will I get before the crustaceans catch me again? Carmaz thought. *And I don't even know where Saia is. This situation seems hopeless.*

But Carmaz banished that thought from his mind. He was well acquainted with feelings of hopelessness—it was impossible to grow up on Ruwa and not feel that way—but right now he could not afford to dwell on it. He would instead focus on how to get out of here, which was within his ability.

Still, his broken right arm made it hard to think, because the pain from it was so awful that it distracted his mind from everything else. With a supreme force of will, however, Carmaz forced himself to forget about it long enough to do what he needed to do to escape.

Then Carmaz jammed his hand on his unbroken arm into his pants pocket and drew out the lock-pick that he had been given by his grandfather many years ago. As quietly as he could, he stuck it into the cage's lock and began fiddling with it. Every now and then he'd stop and watch the crustaceans to make sure they weren't coming to get him for dinner, but most of the crustaceans were either busy preparing the fire or watching two younger-looking crustaceans fighting each other, trying to use their claws to tear each other apart in a frenzy of loud combat.

They're crustaceans, Carmaz thought as he resumed picking the lock. *I doubt even they know why they're fighting. At least it's distracting them from me.*

Then Carmaz heard the lock click, causing him to smile for the first time in several hours. As carefully as Carmaz could, he pushed the cage door open; its hinge, thankfully, did not creak. Once it was open wide enough, Carmaz stepped out of it, though he did so bent over and without making a sound.

Again, the crustaceans were too distracted by the fight and the fire to notice him, so Carmaz made his way around the cage to the thick jungle that surrounded the village. Once he was deep enough in the jungle that he was sure that the crustaceans would not be able to find him if they came after him, Carmaz walked through the muddy ground and thick undergrowth, his eyes on the tiny village itself as he walked.

The question now was where to find Saia. Carmaz's first guess was the somewhat larger hut near the west side of the village. He had seen one of the crustaceans who had captured Saia step out from that hut, and because he didn't see Saia anywhere else, he assumed that that was where his friend was being held. The only problem now was entering the village and freeing Saia, which was currently impossible due to the amount of crustaceans located there.

At least it was impossible until one of the crustaceans looked toward Carmaz's cage and noticed that it was empty. Without warning, the crustacean shrieked and pointed at the empty cage, even hitting one of its friends on the head to draw its attention to Carmaz's empty cage.

All of the crustaceans dropped what they were doing and ran toward the cage. They stopped by the cage briefly to inspect it, before they tore it apart in rage. Then all fifty of of them ran into the jungle behind it, which they seemed to have deduced was where Carmaz had fled.

Maybe my luck isn't so bad after all, Carmaz thought. *But they could be back any minute. Riuja isn't a huge island, so it won't take them long to search it all and realize that they can't find me. Gotta find Saia and then find a way off this cursed island before our 'hosts' return.*

So Carmaz dashed out from the jungle toward the large hut, though he almost tripped over the bones scattered around the village's streets. Soon Carmaz reached the hut door, which was locked, but he broke the rusty old lock off with one kick and then opened the door.

"Saia?" said Carmaz as he stuck his head into the dark hut. He wrinkled his nose at the stink of the hut's interior, which was like a combination of excrement and mud. "Saia, are you there? It's me, Carmaz."

Carmaz spotted his friend immediately. Saia was lying on the dirt floor of the hut, still almost completely naked from his swim, his only piece of clothing the pants with rolled up leggings. Deep, bloody claw marks on his arms and legs marked where the crustaceans had grabbed him, and his dark, curly hair was matted slightly with blood. Still, Saia had enough strength to raise his head high enough to look at Carmaz, his eyes full of both fear and relief.

"Carmaz?" said Saia, whose voice sounded dangerously weak. "Oh, thank the gods. I thought I was a goner for sure."

"Don't thank the gods for what they didn't do," said Carmaz. "Anyway, I am glad to see that you are alive. We need to get out of here before the crustaceans return. They seem to think I'm in the jungle, but it won't be long before they figure out the truth and come back. Then they'll probably skip the fire and just eat us raw."

"I can't stand on my own," said Saia. He gestured at his legs, which were even bloodier and more cut up than his arms. "The crustaceans tore up my legs. You'll have to support me."

Carmaz scowled. *Just what I needed. More bad luck.*

But Carmaz said aloud, "Fine. I'll help you and we'll see how far a couple of cripples can go."

Carmaz dashed into the hut and helped Saia onto his feet. Saia certainly wasn't joking when he said he couldn't stand. He had to lean heavily on Carmaz. In fact, to Carmaz, it felt more like he was carrying Saia with one arm, rather than merely supporting Saia so he could walk on his own.

Saia looked at Carmaz's broken arm that hung limply at his side. "You don't look like you're in much better shape than me."

Carmaz rolled his eyes. "It's fine. Nothing to worry about. You just focus on your wounds, all right?"

Thankfully, Saia was not a very heavy person, so Carmaz managed to get them both out of the hut quickly. A cursory view of the village revealed that the crustaceans still had not returned, but Carmaz wasn't going to press their luck.

"All right, Saia," said Carmaz, breathing hard due to his fatigue starting to catch up to him. He also winced when he felt his broken arm again, although he tried to ignore it. "We head to the beach and then try to swim back to Ruwa."

"Swim?" Saia repeated, looking at Carmaz in confusion. "I assumed you took your grandfather's raft to get here."

"I did," said Carmaz. "But then it sprang a leak and sank."

"I guess the gods really *do* have it out for you, don't they?" said Saia.

"Shut up," Carmaz said. "Anyway, swimming is our best bet. If the crustaceans stay distracted long enough, then by the time they return here, we ought to be back on Ruwa well before they even realize we're gone."

"Just how do you intend to swim across the freezing waters between Riuja and Ruwa with a broken arm?" said Saia, pointing at Carmaz's broken arm. "That's not even counting myself. I don't think I can swim at all in my current condition."

"We'll figure something out," said Carmaz as he led Saia around the hut to the surrounding jungle. "We always do."

"That sounds an awful lot like what Grandma always said," said Saia. "You know, about how the gods will provide and all that?"

"I said *we'll* figure something out," Carmaz said, putting as much emphasis on 'we'll' as he could, though his fatigue and broken arm made that difficult. "I rely on the gods for nothing, and neither does any proud Ruwan."

"Okay, okay," said Saia. "Just saying that that is what Grandma would always say before we went hungry for a week and had to hunt swamp rats for breakfast."

Carmaz rolled his eyes, but before he could respond, he heard the shrieks of the crustaceans behind them. Alarmed, Carmaz looked over his shoulder, as did Saia, to see the crustaceans burst out of the jungle. The crustaceans spotted Carmaz and Saia immediately, causing the lead crustacean to point at them and shriek what might have been an order to its fellow villagers to catch the two of them. Then the entire village stampeded toward them, shrieking and snapping their claws as they did so.

Carmaz tried to run, but Saia could not do much more than limp. The two of them tripped over a bone anyway and fell onto the ground rather ungracefully. The impact wasn't very hard, but falling down for even a moment sealed their fate.

Still, Carmaz rolled over onto his back, despite the pain in his broken arm, and rolled to a crouch. He then drew the rusty, broken knife from his pouch that his grandfather had given him when he was a kid and he held it out in an offensive position, although he knew that there was no way he could fend off so many crustaceans at once with such a puny weapon.

Better go down fighting and defending my best friend than to go down cowering like a scared puppy, Carmaz thought, gritting his teeth as he prepared for the pain of the crustaceans' claws tearing him apart.

But when the mob of crustaceans were not more than ten feet away from Carmaz and Saia, a massive, blinding light suddenly shone between the two groups. The light was so bright that Carmaz had to cover his eyes with his good arm to protect them, but he still heard the startled cries and shrieks of the crustaceans, along with a loud *whoomp* sound that sounded unlike anything Carmaz had heard in his life.

The light, however, lasted only a second. In the next instant, it was gone, making it safe enough for Carmaz to lower his arm to see what in the world had happened.

Standing between him and Saia and the crustaceans was an

elderly, robed man who Carmaz had never seen before. The man was bald and leaned on a tall staff topped with a clock, with clock patterns stitched into his robes.

Carmaz's first thought was that this man must have been a mage of some kind. There weren't too many mages on Ruwa, aside from Herune the Swamp Hermit, the madman said to live deep in the Swamp of Light all by himself. Carmaz didn't know if this man was as crazy as Herune was said to be, but if he was, then that meant that things were going to get much worse before it was all over.

But despite his lack of magical ability, Carmaz sensed that this man was no mere mage, perhaps not even a mortal. The man radiated almost as much energy as the sun, despite his frail and old appearance. The man standing before him and Saia could destroy the entire island and every living thing on it if he wanted, and then remake it to his liking.

Then Carmaz noticed the crustaceans. All of them were where they had been before the old man's appearance, but they looked frozen now. Not frozen with ice. It was more like they had simply stopped, like a man standing still for a painter to do his portrait. They didn't move even one inch. Even their eyes were as still as tree branches on a windless day.

Before Carmaz could wonder aloud what was going on, the man said, "So you want to kill a godling, do you? What arrogance. Let the sand of time consume you, as you rightfully deserve."

The man raised his hand. The crustaceans suddenly began to age so fast that Carmaz's eyes could barely keep up. Their shells became grayer and grayer, until soon they dissolved into dust, leaving their naked bodies before those, too, rapidly dissolved. Soon there was nothing left to suggest the presence of the once-terrifying crustaceans of Riuja save for dozen of piles of dust, but even those aged so rapidly that they vanished as if they had never existed at all.

All of this took place in roughly ten seconds. In fact, it happened so fast that Carmaz was not even sure that it actually had happened at all. It might have been his eyes playing tricks on him or maybe even an illusion cast by the man before him, although with no sign of the crustaceans anywhere, Carmaz had no choice but to believe it.

The man then turned to face Carmaz and Saia. As soon as Carmaz looked into the man's eyes, he knew that this was indeed no man, but a god. He just knew it somehow, despite having never seen a god before. The man's eyes were ancient and authoritative, just as the legends described the eyes of the gods.

"Carmaz Korva," the man said. "Your destiny is at last at hand. The time has come for me to take you away, where you will start the long and difficult journey ahead of you that even I do not know."

"How do you know my name?" asked Carmaz, though he found the words difficult to speak in the presence of such a powerful deity. "I never introduced myself."

"I know the names of all who are destined to ascend," said the man, "for I am Tinkar, the God of Fate and Time. And it is your fate to ascend to godhood. Or it may be, if you work for it."

Carmaz didn't understand what Tinkar meant, but he managed to find enough strength to stand up straight, doing his best to ignore his broken arm. He then looked Tinkar straight in the eye and said, "Are you going to help Ruwa?"

Tinkar looked confused at the question. "What do you mean?"

"I mean, you and your fellow gods," said Carmaz. He gestured all around them with his good hand, even though they weren't on Ruwa. "For years, Ruwa has been a desolate land full of despair and poverty and disease. Why have you gods forsaken us?"

"When was it our job to ensure wealth and health for you humans?" Tinkar said. "Anyway, you are changing the subject. The Tournament of the Gods is starting and you have been chosen to participate in it."

"Tournament of the Gods?" Carmaz said. He looked down at Saia, who looked just as mystified as he felt. "Saia, have you heard of the Tournament of the Gods before?"

"N-No," said Saia, who seemed far more intimidated by Tinkar than Carmaz was. "Never heard of it."

"The Tournament of the Gods is a competition in which the five winning mortals will ascend to godhood and take on the roles of the gods that were slain by Uron not long ago," said Tinkar. "It is my job to gather up the godlings that are destined to ascend at some point, which includes you, my heathen friend."

Carmaz looked at Tinkar again. "You must have me mistaken for someone else. I care not for the gods that abandoned my people. You can take your offer and choke on it."

"You mortals are very good at acting like you have any choice in matters as important as this," Tinkar said. "What makes you think you can reject my offer? It is your destiny to accept it."

"Why should I enter a competition to join a group of beings who have treated my people as if they do not exist?" asked

57

Carmaz. He gestured at Saia. "Besides, my friend here is injured, as am I. We have to return to Ruwa to assure our friends and family that we are still alive."

"We can heal you," said Tinkar. He nodded at Carmaz's broken arm. "I am not a healer like my sister Atikos, but I know some basic healing spells."

Tinkar waved his staff at Carmaz's arm. In a second, the pain in Carmaz's broken arm was gone, causing Carmaz to twist it experimentally just to make sure that it was indeed healed. While it was somewhat stiff, there was no sharp pain anymore.

"I ... thank you," said Carmaz, rubbing his arm. "I—"

"You do not need to thank me anymore than you already have," Tinkar said. "Anyway, I could even take you two back to your friends and family on Ruwa. Under the condition, of course, that you agree to come with me to World's End, where the Tournament will begin, afterward."

Carmaz was about to tell Tinkar to shove off when Saia, who now seemed to be getting over his initial fear of Tinkar, asked, "Uh, Lord Tinkar, you said the winners of the Tournament are supposed to become gods, right?"

"Correct," said Tinkar.

"And one of the open positions is the position as the God of Martir, right?" Saia continued.

"Of course," said Tinkar. "With Skimif dead, the position needs to be filled by someone worthy of the job."

Saia nodded, then gestured for Carmaz to come closer to him. Frowning, Carmaz got onto his knees and leaned close to Saia, wondering what his friend would have to say.

"Carmaz, I got a great idea," Saia whispered, probably to keep

Tinkar from hearing. "You should enter the Tournament."

"Why?" Carmaz asked, keeping his voice as low as Saia's. "Didn't you hear what I said to Tinkar about taking his offer and choking on it?"

"Yes, but think about it," said Saia, the excitement in his voice mixed in with the pain he was probably experiencing in his legs. "One of the open positions is the position of God of Martir. If *you* win the Tournament, you could become the God of Martir, and then use your power to restore Ruwa to its original greatness again."

"Really?" said Carmaz in surprise. He scratched his chin. "Hmm. That never occurred to me."

"Yeah, but it makes sense," said Saia. "I mean, this is the best opportunity to save Ruwa that anyone back home has ever gotten. Even if it means joining the gods, I say you should take it, for Ruwa's sake."

"Saving Ruwa would be great," Carmaz said, nodding. "But the gods—"

"Who cares?" Saia interrupted. "Don't you care enough about Ruwa to make some sacrifices? This is a once-in-a-lifetime opportunity, Carmaz, so I suggest that you *don't* let it pass."

Carmaz didn't want to admit it, but Saia was correct. This did seem to be the best opportunity that Carmaz would ever have to actually help Ruwa return to its original glory. Even though Carmaz didn't want anything to do with the gods, if it was indeed his destiny to join them, even rule them, then maybe he should go ahead and do it. He couldn't really see any reason not to. After all, Tinkar hadn't said that he would die if he lost the Tournament, so he had nothing to lose by trying.

So Carmaz stood back up and turned to face Tinkar. "All right, Tinkar, I accept your offer. But only on a couple of conditions."

Tinkar sighed. "I should have seen this coming, but the fate of you godlings is always denser to my eyes than the fates of normal mortals."

"First, Saia and I want to return to Ruwa to say goodbye to our friends and family there," said Carmaz. "We also need to gather our belongings for the journey to World's End. Second, we want you to heal us. After that, then we'll be more than happy to go with you."

Tinkar raised an eyebrow. "'We'? Your friend is not destined to ascend. Only you are."

"I'm not going if Saia isn't allowed to go," said Carmaz, crossing his arms over his chest. "We're friends. Friends stick together, no matter what."

Tinkar sighed again. "Fine. But he cannot participate in or interfere with the Tournament, and if he does, then we will send him back to Ruwa right away. Do you agree to that condition?"

"Yes," said Carmaz. He looked down at Saia. "What about you, Saia?"

"Sounds reasonable," said Saia, nodding. "I'll support you every step of the way, Carmaz, even if I can't actually participate in the Tournament myself."

"Very well, then," said Tinkar. He held out a hand. "Now, let us go. The Tournament is starting in a month, so we do not have very much time to waste."

Chapter Four

A T THIS POINT, Braim was pretty sure that Princess Raya didn't like him.

She didn't talk to him at all during the dinner that the group had at the seafood restaurant on the corner of the street (the name of which Braim couldn't pronounce due to the fact that it was a katabans word that was essentially impossible to pronounce in Divina). In fact, she didn't even seem to acknowledge his existence, even after he asked her to pass the salt. Nor did she tell him good bye after the group split and returned to their guest rooms at the various inns across the city. He noticed because she said good bye to everyone else except for him, in stark contrast to King Malock and Queen Hana, who told Braim how much they enjoyed chatting with him at the dinner.

Under ordinary circumstances, Braim might have been offended by Raya's rudeness. He didn't like being ignored so pointedly by pretty women, even though he couldn't remember where he gained this dislike of such women. There was a reason he'd called Raya 'beautiful' earlier and that was because he knew a knockout when he saw one.

But Braim didn't feel as offended as he normally would today. That was probably because, despite acknowledging Raya's beauty, he really didn't care much for her as a person. That same shadow from before kept creeping up his spine, into the back of his mind, which made him more apathetic toward this sort of treatment from women.

His mind was distracted, instead, by the Tournament of the Gods. He and Darek spent a good portion of the dinner talking about the Tournament, wondering if either of them were going to be chosen to participate or if they would at least be allowed to stay and watch the events. So far, none of the gods or katabans who lived on World's End had said anything about sending Braim and the others back up north when the Tournament started, so Braim was of the opinion that they were going to at least be allowed to watch the Tournament's events unfold.

But without more facts from Alira or the gods, Braim soon lost interest in the speculation. And when he, Darek, and Jenur returned to the inn they were staying at, he retired to his room immediately and fell on his bed, too tired from the excitement of the day to do much else. Especially with the moon rising in the sky. For some reason, he was always more tired on full moon nights than on any other nights, although he dismissed that as more of a coincidence than anything.

Braim's room was a rather nice, if simple, room. He had a nice, soft bed, with nice silk blankets that always smelled fresh and clean. A dresser and mirror stood on the opposite side of the room, while the door to his bathroom was just to the right of the dresser. Another door opened up to a closet, though Braim had opened the closet up maybe once since he got here. There was a single window that he had closed for the night. Even so, he could see through the thick blue curtains the lights of the city, although World's End was rather quiet for a city at night.

Then again, most of its inhabitants are katabans, and they aren't exactly the loudest people in the world, Braim thought with a yawn. He scratched his stomach, which was exposed due to the fact that he had shed his robes prior to falling on the bed. *Or maybe the gods told them to be quiet so we could get some rest. Not sure if the gods are really that thoughtful, though.*

In any case, Braim decided that he would go to sleep. Not that that would be easy; even though he was very tired at the moment, Braim had found it difficult to sleep thanks to the sense of dread and darkness that always seemed to be hiding just outside of his reach. Still, Braim needed as much sleep as any living being, so he closed his eyes and prepared to doze off by counting baba ragas before he heard something scratch against the floor.

It wasn't a particularly loud sound. It didn't sound like it was coming from the streets outside, however. It sounded, in fact, like it was coming from the closet itself.

Maybe it was just my imagination, Braim thought. *Yeah, that's probably it. I mean, there's nothing in there, right? After all, I didn't put anything in there and no one has been inside this room since I left it earlier today, except maybe the innkeeper Mishak.*

Despite all of that, Braim knew that he had indeed heard a sound in there. That meant that there was indeed something in that closet. What—*Or who,* Braim thought—was in there, he didn't know. He hoped that it was some kind of mouse, something not very big or threatening, although he had no idea whether World's End even had any mice on it.

Of course it does, Braim thought. *There are mice everywhere. Even North Academy has the occasional infestation, and that place is at the very north of the Great Berg.*

Because Braim doubted he could sleep without knowing what was in his closet, he decided to stop fighting fate. He sat up and stretched his limbs, then grabbed his wand off the table next to his bed and stood up. He put his robes back on quickly, then slowly advanced toward his closet.

Not a single sound came from the closet. Even Braim was quiet as he tip-toed across the room. He didn't want whoever or whatever was in there to hear him approaching. Again, he doubted that it was anything that could pose an actual threat to his life, but in case it was, he was determined to get the drop on it.

Braim now stood in front of the door. He laid one hand on the doorknob, but didn't twist it at first. He just listened as hard as he could, hoping to discover its identity by listening to any noise it made.

But no matter how hard Braim listened, he heard nothing else except for the sounds of the city outside his room. He almost believed that there was nothing in his closet at all, but decided he'd rather be safe than sorry.

Bracing himself for whatever was going to happen, Braim pulled open the door and thrust his wand inside.

The closet was empty. Aside from the metal pole that he could hang clothes across, there was nothing at all inside the closet. There wasn't even a mouse. He saw nothing in there that could have made even the slightest sound.

Braim sighed in relief. *Thank the gods. It must have been my imagination at work again.*

Then Braim heard that sound again, that slight scuffling against the wooden floor, and without thinking he jumped to the side. Just in the nick of time, because as soon as he jumped out of the way, a knife flew through the air and struck the inside of the closet.

Startled, Braim turned to see a long, thin sword coming his way. He raised his wand, summoning a magical barrier that blocked the sword, but his shield cracked under the pressure from the mysterious assassin's blade anyway.

As for the sword's user, it was a strange, humanoid being wearing a mask that resembled the face of a baba raga, though the tusks were smaller than the tusks of actual baba ragas. The figure was bulkier than Braim, but he found it hard to describe its appearance because much of its body was cloaked in shadow.

Whatever it was, Braim was not going to let it kill him. He increased the output of his magical energy, but his barrier only seemed to grow weaker and weaker under the pressure that the assassin placed on it, until soon Braim was certain that his shield would break any minute now.

And then it broke, far sooner than Braim expected, and the sword went flying through the air toward him. Braim dodged the blade, allowing the sword to strike the floor where he stood, but almost immediately another sword, similar to the first, appeared out of nowhere and stabbed at Braim.

Because Braim had not expected the second sword, he dodged it much less gracefully than the last one. The sword did not mortally wound him, but it managed to cut through his shoulder, causing pain to shoot through his body as he gasped.

But Braim had enough sense in him to stagger out of the way of the assassin's next blow. He covered his shoulder with his free hand, stemming the blood to the best of his ability, while aiming his wand at the assassin, who turned to face Braim again.

By the dim light streaming through the cracks of the curtains, Braim thought he saw that the assassin had four arms. Two were in the regular spot where arms should go, while the other two sprouted out of the assassin's shoulders. The assassin had two swords, each one glowing with magical energy. The assassin's eyes, however, were blank, which made it impossible to tell what it was thinking or who it might have been.

"Four arms, but two swords?" said Braim, chuckling despite the pain in his shoulder from where the assassin had hit him. "Decided to go easy on me, eh? Or are you just too poor to afford four?"

The assassin paused, as if Braim had just made a good point, and then drew two more swords, similar to the ones it already wielded, from somewhere behind it. The assassin then combined the hilts of each sword pair, creating two double-bladed lances that looked even deadlier than the assassin itself. Then it drew out four more swords and created two more double-bladed lances, effectively giving itself eight swords at once.

"Damn it," said Braim. "It was just a joke. I know that most assassins don't have a great sense of humor, but you didn't need to pull out *all* of your swords on little old me."

The assassin said nothing in response, but whether that was because it could not speak or simply chose not to, Braim didn't know. Nor was it very relevant, because that thing could kill him all by itself whether it could speak or not.

Then it stepped backwards and vanished instantly. It seemed to melt into the shadows, but that made no sense, because Braim couldn't see anywhere it could have hidden itself.

A second later, Braim heard the sound of blades whistling

through the air. He jumped forward, narrowly avoiding getting his head chopped off. Then he looked over his shoulder just in time to see the assassin's arm vanish back into the shadows.

It can shadow travel? Braim thought. *What the hell? I didn't even know that was possible.*

Braim's thoughts were interrupted when the door to his room burst open. Light from the outside hall streamed in as Darek staggered inside, his wand at the ready, his head whipping back and forth as he looked for the threat.

"Darek?" said Braim in surprise. "What are you doing here?"

"Heard what sounded like fighting coming from your room," said Darek, panting as his eyes scanned the shadows of the room. "Were you atta—"

Braim saw the assassin's blades appear over Darek's head, causing him to shoot a burst of light from his wand at them. The burst hit the blades and they vanished, while Darek just looked up at the spot where the swords had been in shock.

"What was that?" said Darek, looking at Braim again.

"The assassin who's been trying to kill me for the past three minutes or so," Braim said. "He vanished into the shadows. Don't know how he did that."

"He must be an adherent of the Thief's Way," Darek said, snapping his fingers. "It's a magical path usually studied by Hollechians, or was while Hollech was alive, anyway. That must be what this guy is doing."

"How do we stop him?" asked Braim.

"Watch," said Darek.

He raised his wand, which immediately became so bright that Braim had to raise his arm to avoid being blinded. And the light became brighter still, until soon all of the shadows in the room had been banished, allowing Braim to see every corner of the room as clearly as on a bright summer afternoon.

This also revealed the assassin, who stood near the window, standing still like it had been stunned by the light itself. Without the shadows to distort its appearance, Braim saw that the assassin was burlier than Darek and he combined. It was clearly not human or even aquarian, though what it was exactly, Braim didn't know, because it wore dark leather clothes that seemed to absorb the light. Its feet, however, were clawed, like the feet of a horian falcon.

The light also showed its eyes through its eye holes. They were almost human, except for the lack of sclera, making its eyes look completely black.

"There you are, you bastard," said Braim, holding up his wand to cast a spell. "Stand still long enough for me to—"

Without warning, the assassin jumped through the closed window of Braim's room. The sound of shattering glass was the only sound that the assassin made as it escaped.

Alarmed, Braim and Darek ran up to the smashed window. Braim tore aside what remained of the curtains to try to catch a glimpse of the assassin as it fled.

But when he stuck his head outside the window, Braim saw no sign of the assassin at all. He only spotted the glass shards of the window on the ground outside, but of the assassin itself there was no sign. All Braim saw was the empty streets outside. It was like the assassin had never existed.

Braim looked at Darek with uncertainty. "Uh, you saw the big, four-armed assassin carrying those double-bladed lances, right? I'm not losing my mind or anything, right?"

"I saw it," said Darek, nodding, a troubled look on his face. "I don't like this. I don't like this at all. Who was that guy and why was he trying to kill you?"

"I don't know," said Braim. "Until today, I didn't even know that I *had* enemies."

"Maybe he mistook you for someone else?" said Darek.

Braim looked at Darek with disbelief. "There are exactly four humans on this island, five if you count Raya. And we all look completely different from one another. I think it's pretty obvious that the assassin was after me."

"But why you?" said Darek. "I'd understand King Malock, seeing as he's the leader of one of the most powerful nations in the entire Northern Isles, but what's so special about you?"

Braim was about to state the obvious when Jenur appeared in the doorway. Unlike Darek, she looked quite tired, with her hair messed up and her robes haphazardly pulled over her pajamas. She waved her wand hither and thither, like she thought that the assassin was still here.

"What happened?" said Jenur, yawning as she spoke. "I heard fighting. What's going on?" She then spotted Braim's bleeding shoulder and gasped. "Braim, what happened to your shoulder?"

Braim glanced at his wounded shoulder, having entirely forgotten about it in the excitement of the moment until just now. "Uh, I should explain to you guys what happened from the beginning."

So Braim briefly explained to Jenur and Darek how the assassin appeared and tried to kill him, including Darek's arrival that saved his life. Because the story was so short, he was able to finish it quickly, and by the time he did, Jenur was wide awake and looked quite worried.

"An assassination attempt in the Throne of the Gods?" said Jenur. She shook her head. "I thought we were safe here."

"Guess we're not," said Braim. "Or I'm not, at least. Did either of you two hear anything unusual before the assassin attacked me?"

"No," said Darek, shaking his head. "In fact, I was about to go to sleep before I heard the assassin fighting you."

"And I was already deeply sleeping during the battle," said Jenur. "That's why I didn't come right away. I only awoke when I heard the assassin smash through the window."

Braim looked at the smashed window and frowned. "Do you think we'll have to pay for the window repair? Because I'm broke as hell, so …"

Darek simply waved his wand at the window and the glass shards flew back into place. In less than a second, the window was good as new.

"I doubt it," said Darek. "Anyway, I'm still troubled by that assassin's attack. It leaves us with far more questions than answers."

Jenur nodded and then raised her wand and pointed it at Braim's shoulder. "Braim, you should let me heal your shoulder. Look at all of the blood leaking out. It's stained your robes."

Again, Braim looked at his shoulder, this time watching as Jenur's healing spell closed up the wound until the skin was whole once more. Though Braim could feel pain much like anyone else, he didn't pay as much attention to it as most people did, even if the injuries were serious like his shoulder. It was probably due to the fact that he had lived a pain-free life as a ghost, so most of the time he barely even noticed his injuries unless they were too obvious to ignore or caused him an unusual amount of pain.

"Thanks," said Braim, looking at Jenur again as she lowered her wand. "I'll wash my robes later. Right now, I'm still confused about that assassin."

"I think we should contact the others and find out if they were attacked as well," said Darek. "I'm especially worried for the Carnagian Royal Family. They're a prime target for any assassin."

"I'll send a gray ghost to Mal later," said Jenur. "And one to Yorak as well, informing them both about what happened. We should also see about contacting the gods and letting them know that someone just tried to kill Braim."

"I think it was a katabans," said Braim. "It didn't look like a human or an aquarian to me, and it probably wasn't a god, either, otherwise it would have killed Darek and me without even thinking. Someone must have hired it."

"Probably a god, I bet," said Darek. "I mean, I don't want to accuse the gods of evildoing, but the katabans only listen to the gods. That means that there is a god out there who wants you dead."

"Again?" said Braim. "But I just came back to life. I'd like to tell that god to wait at least a year before trying to take my life. They're just jumping the gun now."

"That doesn't explain why any god would want to kill Braim," said Jenur, brushing some of her messy curly hair back. "He hasn't done anything to anger the gods. Right, Braim?"

"Yeah," said Braim. "Of course, it's possible that I could have done something to piss this god off in my first life. Maybe he's trying to get revenge for the time I stole his girlfriend or something."

"The gods may be petty at times, but they aren't *that* petty," said Jenur. Her shoulders slumped. "Unfortunately, I don't know how to find out who did it. But I will contact Mal and Yorak as soon as I can and see if they might know anything about this."

"Good idea," said Braim. He glanced at his open closet. "But I'm a little afraid of going to sleep again, because I have a feeling that that assassin is not the kind of guy to give up easily."

"I doubt he'll return," said Jenur. "Now that we know he's trying to kill you, he's lost the element of surprise. Doesn't mean he's not going to try again. It just means that he's not going to try again any time soon."

"You're probably right," said Braim. "Well, you two can go back to your rooms now. I'll wash out the blood from my robes and—"

"Braim Kotogs?" said a voice from the doorway, causing all three of them to turn and see who had spoken.

Standing in the open doorway to Braim's room was a short man with blue, spiky hair. He had said Braim's name with an odd accent, in which he slightly slurred the last syllable of 'Kotogs.' That meant that the man was some kind of katabans, though Braim had never seen this particular katabans before.

The katabans looked quite surprised to see all three of them there, so surprised that he seemed to have forgotten what he had come here to tell them. That was when Braim noticed a letter that he clutched in his left hand.

"Hey, is that letter for me?" said Braim, pointing at the letter that the katabans held.

72

The katabans looked at Braim. His eyes focused on the dried blood on Braim's shoulder with horror before he looked at Braim's face, nodded, and said, in that same odd accent from before, "Yes sir. Letter for you. From Alira."

The katabans threw the letter toward Braim. It glided through the air toward him, allowing Braim to catch it without any difficulty. Frowning, he looked down at the letter's envelope, upon which the word *Invitation* was written in a neat, curly script.

"Thanks," said Braim, looking back up at the messenger. "Tell Alira I—"

But the katabans was gone before Braim could finish his sentence. He looked at Jenur and Darek. "Where'd he go?"

"No idea," said Darek, shaking his head. "He left faster than I could follow. Think he must be scared of humans or something."

"What's he got to be scared of?" said Braim. "Just because you guys are two of the most powerful mages in the world doesn't mean you're scary."

"Just open the letter and see what Alira has to say," said Jenur. "I'm interested in what she's written."

Braim nodded and slit the envelope open with his wand's tip. He then pulled out a folded letter, which he unfolded as quickly as he could.

Reading was another difficult thing for Braim to do ever since he returned, mostly because as a ghost he had never had to do much reading. He could read individual letters just fine, but his mind sometimes had a hard time comprehending full sentences and paragraphs, even after taking several reading lessons from Darek over the past two months. It was probably a side effect of the resurrection process, though that didn't make it any less embarrassing whenever he had to read something aloud to someone else.

But this letter was not very long. It was a single paragraph, which Braim read quickly. And he found its message shocking. In fact, he was so shocked by this message that he wasn't sure if he had read it correctly.

So Braim handed the letter to Darek, saying, "Can you read this for me? I think I know what it's saying, but I'm not sure. It seems to me like it must be a mistake."

Darek took the letter and held it under the city lights streaming through the window. He then read the letter aloud:

"*Dear Braim Kotogs,*

You have been chosen to participate in the Tournament of the Gods, which starts exactly one month from today. Arrangements have been made to allow you to stay in World's End until the start of the Tournament on the first of next month. We will reveal more details about the Tournament to you in due time.

Sincerely, Alira, Judge of the Tournament of the Gods."

Chapter Five

PRINCESS RAYA MANA stared at the letter in her hand, the one with the unfamiliar handwriting upon it. She read the single paragraph over and over again, at first unable to believe what she was reading, but the more and more she read the invitation to participate in the Tournament, the more she believed it, until soon all of her doubt and disbelief was gone, replaced instead by a sense of rightness and fulfillment.

Of course I was chosen to participate in the Tournament, Raya thought with a smile. *I'm the Princess of Carnag. I deserve a shot at becoming the Goddess of Martir. I always knew that I was destined for greatness. I just never knew just* how *great that was.*

Father stood next to her, patting her on the back, saying, "Wonderful, Raya. I am so proud of you. I know you will do better in that Tournament than anyone else. I know you will win."

"Thank you, Father," said Raya, hugging Father tightly for a moment before letting go and looking at the letter again, which she clutched as tightly as if it was the most valuable diamond in the world. "I cannot believe it. I didn't think I'd ever get chosen to participate in such a prodigious event."

"Why does that surprise you?" said Mother, who looked even more excited than Raya at this possibility. "It didn't shock me at all to learn that you will have a chance at becoming a goddess. In fact, it makes perfect sense to me, seeing as you are a very special girl. I will have to send a message back to Carnag informing everyone of this amazing event. We should make this day into an official Carnagian holiday that will be celebrated for generations to come."

Raya smiled again, but then frowned when she read her letter again. "But it doesn't say whether you two are going to get to stay and watch the Tournament or not."

"I imagine the gods will send us home," said Father. "After all, neither of us were invited to enter the Tournament and the gods do not exactly like me very much, anyway."

Raya looked at Father curiously. "They don't? Why?"

"Let's just say that, when I was a youth, I crossed the paths of the gods a few too many times and survived," said Father. He rubbed his disfigured face, a common habit of his that Raya hadn't paid much attention to until now. "Indeed, I am surprised they even invited me back to World's End at all, considering how unpopular I am with most of the gods."

"Even if we have to return to Carnag, rest assured that we will pray every day to Grinf to aid you," said Mother. "And we will send you gray ghosts every day to keep you up to date on recent happenings around Carnag and to find out how you are doing, so it will be like we are still with you even when we aren't."

"You don't need to do that," said Raya. "I will contact you two every day myself. You can just worry about making sure that the Carnagian people are supporting me at all times."

"Of course we will," said Father. "In fact, I doubt that the people will need much persuasion to support you, considering how much the people love you already."

"We need to celebrate tonight," said Mother. "We need to do something special to celebrate this big event."

Raya shrugged and looked out the nearby window at the darkness of the night, which was broken up by the lights from the city. "Oh, Mother, we don't need to throw any major celebrations right away. You two need to rest after your very long day. Father looks like he is just about to fall asleep standing."

"I suppose you are right, Raya," said Father with a yawn. "I am rather tired. But we will make sure to celebrate this momentous occasion first thing in the morning."

"Yes," said Mother. She then rubbed together her hands in a rather diabolical way. "But I need to contact Jenur and tell her about your success. I doubt that *her* son was chosen to participate in the Tournament. I think a little gloating is in order."

Father frowned and yawned again. "Hana, perhaps that can wait until morning as well. I doubt Jenur is even awake right now, as it is rather late."

Mother looked disappointed at having to put off her gloating, but then she nodded and said, "All right. But first thing in the morning, I will send her a gray ghost. Or maybe I'll just make a special trip to the inn that she is staying at and personally deliver the news to her myself."

"Not everything in life is a competition, you know," said Father.

"Who said I was competing with Jenur?" said Mother. "And anyway, if I *was* competing, I clearly won, seeing as Raya was

77

chosen to participate and Darek wasn't."

Father sighed, but then said to Raya, "This is good night, Raya. I wish nothing but the sweetest of dreams for my little girl."

"I wish the same to you, my daughter," said Mother.

Then Father and Mother returned to their room, closing the door behind them as they did so. They left Raya sitting alone on the sofa in the living room of the apartment that the gods had given them. Raya did not hear anymore noise from their room, which told her that they must have fallen asleep rather quickly.

Raya herself was tired, but she was also too excited at the prospect of entering the Tournament to even think about going to sleep anytime soon. She just read the letter over and over again, taking in the words as if she was breathing in the freshest and cleanest air.

This is the happiest day of my whole life, Raya thought, *at least until I actually win the Tournament, which will most definitely be the happiest day of my life for sure.*

That was when Raya's stomach growled. It almost took her by surprise until she remembered that she had not eaten in several hours. She had had a good dinner at that restaurant earlier in the evening, but Raya's body burned through food quickly, so she usually got hungry faster than her parents did even if she had just recently eaten.

Unfortunately, to Raya's knowledge, the apartment they stayed in had no food, and there was no room service, either. That would have meant that she would have to wait until morning to have breakfast, but the idea of having to wait even that short a time was pure torture to her.

So Raya stood up, clutching her letter in one hand, and

returned to her room, which was located opposite her parents' room. She slipped inside and closed the door carefully, then listened to make sure that neither of her parents had gotten up and left their room.

When Raya heard nothing, she relaxed and walked over to the dresser on the left side of the room and pulled open the top drawer. There she found a large piece of rainbow fish—one of the dishes they had had at that restaurant earlier in the evening—wrapped in a paper towel. She picked up the fish, unwrapped it, and started eating, her hunger becoming more and more satisfied with each bite.

The reason for Raya's secrecy was because neither of her parents knew that Raya had taken this fish from the restaurant. She hadn't exactly stolen it. At least, she didn't think of it as theft. She had simply not finished her food and had decided to take some of it with her without first asking the restaurant's owner—a tall, rather handsome male katabans who was excellent with cutting knives—if she could.

Raya knew that most people would see this as theft, but honestly it was just one fish and it wasn't even the biggest rainbow fish served that night, anyway. In fact, Raya saw herself performing an important duty to the restaurant owner. By taking what food she hadn't been able to finish, she saved the owner the time he would have spent in throwing it out.

This was not the first time that Raya had taken something that she technically was not supposed to take. When she had been six, Raya had stolen a paper doll toy from the daughter of one of the male servants who served the Carnagian Royal Family. Of course, Raya had been sure to avoid being caught. She managed to frame one of the other servant girls for her actions, which had resulted in a rather memorable feud between the two servant families that, to her knowledge, was still going on today.

Raya justified this by telling herself that the male servant's daughter—whose name she no longer remembered, as that particular servant had been fired about a year after the incident—already had plenty of paper dolls of her own and didn't need any more. At the time, Raya herself had had about a hundred such dolls, all of them infinitely better than the one she took, but she didn't really want any of them as much as she had wanted that one (which she had then lost in the Royal Garden about a week later).

Then, when Raya was ten, she had taken the pretty diamond necklace of a Shikan noble's teenage daughter. At the time, Raya had been very jealous of the teenaged girl for her beauty, especially the praise and attention the teenaged girl had received from the boys. The diamond necklace had been a particularly praised object that Raya believed to be the source of the girl's beauty. Unfortunately, when Raya stole the necklace, the teenaged girl was still popular with the boys and was married off not long after to the son of a Carnagian nobleman who Raya had had her eyes on at the time. The two were still married today, a thought which made Raya feel sick to her stomach every time she thought about it. She didn't even have the necklace anymore. She had thrown it down the gutter of the streets outside Carnag Hall after taking it, purely out of spite.

And when Raya was thirteen, she had taken the painting of the daughter of a Carnagian nobleman that had been praised by her art tutor for its originality and greatness. By contrast, Raya's own painting had been rather bland and unoriginal.

So Raya had taken the painting and smeared it with paint, messing up the beautifully-done colors and shading that had been the source of the original paint's popularity. It had felt good at the time to see the other girl's hard work ruined and even better to see that girl cry. Unfortunately, the girl had still gone on to become a great painter respected throughout the entire Northern Isles.

But despite her takings not always working out the way Raya wanted them to, she had never been caught. In fact, no one had even suspected her of stealing from anyone. She had managed to deflect all suspicion from everyone by pretending to be as disturbed by these takings as anyone. She sometimes felt a little guilty for deceiving everyone, including her parents, into thinking that she was innocent, but she always banished that feeling by telling herself that she only took things from the people who deserved it.

I'm sure that Grinf would approve, Raya thought. *It's not an orthodox form of justice, but justice comes in many shapes and sizes. There is no reason to believe that any of what I did was unjust. And there is certainly no reason for me to believe that taking this fish will get me in trouble, either.*

That was when Raya heard something behind her. It sounded like someone's foot scuffing the carpet. The sound made her freeze mid-bite, because she knew that there was no one else in this room aside from herself.

Or there shouldn't *be anyone else here,* Raya thought.

To say that Raya felt dread was like saying that the sky was blue. As Princess of Carnag, Raya was well aware that there were many, many people who would like to kill her or her parents for tons of reasons. Just the other day, the Justice Enforcers foiled a plot by a lone assassin who had intended to blow up Carnag Hall with her and her parents still inside it.

The only reason someone would sneak into my room at this time of night without me knowing is to kill me, Raya thought. *He must think that I didn't hear him. Too bad for him.*

Raya whirled around and threw her half-eaten fish across the room. But much to her shock, there was no one else in here with her. Her fish flew over her bed and landed on the floor on the other side, just outside of her view.

Then Raya noticed a green envelope on her bed. It was sitting neatly on top of the blue covers, but Raya was almost certain that the envelope had not been there even ten seconds ago, when she returned to her room to get her snack. The envelope was blank, which meant that it could have had anything in it and she couldn't even tell who left it there.

Raya went over the rather extensive list of assassination techniques that Teacher had taught her last year, as part of her training as royalty. She could not think of any that involved placing an unassuming, blank envelope on the bed of the target and hoping they open it.

Of course, this is World's End, the Throne of the Gods, Raya thought. *The assassins here, if there are any, probably know all sorts of deadly assassination techniques that the assassins up north can only dream of.*

Still, Raya doubted that this envelope was supposed to kill her. If there was an assassin after her, then why didn't he kill her while she was eating her fish and thinking about her past? She was completely unarmed, after all, and not much of a fighter. She had some combat and self-defense training, but Raya knew she wasn't as good at fighting as she was at other things. Any assassin worth his knives would be able to kill her if he tried hard enough.

But if an assassin didn't put that there, then who did? Raya thought. *And why didn't they tell me? Maybe it's another letter from Alira.*

Yes, that made sense. As one of the participants in the Tournament, it made sense for Raya to get another letter, this one probably containing further information and instructions regarding the Tournament. It seemed a little odd, mostly because Raya had not expected to get additional information so soon, but she wasn't complaining. The sooner she knew more about the Tournament, the more time she had to plan and prepare for it.

So Raya walked over to the bed and picked the envelope off the covers. She turned it over once, hoping to find some kind of identifying symbol or seal, but even the seal was a blank red square. She held the envelope up to the magical light glowing from the ceiling and saw that its contents was a single folded-up letter. She saw no dust or poison in it that could harm her.

With all of her fears now abated, Raya opened the envelope and carefully extracted the folded-up letter. Unlike the envelope, this paper was a clean white. When she unfolded it, she saw that the ink was a deep black color that was easy to read.

The letter's handwriting was neat, but generic. Raya had never seen this particular handwriting before, so she had no idea who might have wrote it. She then began reading the letter, which read like this:

Dear Godling,

Do not think that the gods are unaware of your treachery and wickedness. The eyes of the gods are all-seeing and they do not tolerate injustice for long. You are spared only because you have been chosen to enter the Tournament of the Gods. Otherwise, your wickedness would be justly punished as it deserves.

And do not think that you can avoid the fate you deserve for very long. Though justice's journey is long and often tortuous, it always arrives at its destination.

The letter ended there as abruptly as if someone had interrupted the letter writer before he could finish. Or perhaps the letter writer had intentionally chosen to end on such an ambiguous note.

In any case, Raya wanted to laugh at the letter. She had received letters like this before, anonymously sent by her enemies or enemies of the Royal Family making vague threats to her and her parents. Ninety-nine percent of the time, these 'threats' could be safely ignored, especially if they were filled with typos and grammatical errors. In fact, Raya usually saved the most ridiculous ones to read to her friends, who often found them just as amusing as she did.

But it was hard to laugh at this letter. Its mysterious appearance in her room, its lack of a signature, its constant talk of 'justice,' the letter writer's insinuation that it knew all of her darkest secrets … that was different from most threats that she'd received. Most letters typically threatened to kill her or her parents, often in gruesome and nonsensical ways (such as one letter writer who threatened to inflate Raya like a balloon and pop her).

This one, however, made no mention whatsoever of killing her or her parents. It sounded more like the angry words of someone who was pursuing justice. It almost sounded like some of the writings of the old Grinfian monks that she had read about. Once, a long time ago before Father was born, the Carnagian government had been horribly corrupt and completely inefficient at capturing criminals and bringing them to justice. In fact, Teacher had told Raya that at the time many criminals were friends or family members of government officials, who often turned a blind eye to their criminal activities as a personal favor to them.

As a result, injustice ran rampant all over the island until a group of Grinfian Monks, tired of the crime and their inefficient government, formed their own group dedicated to bringing justice called the Judges of Justice. Their modus operandi was to send vague, yet threatening, letters to various well-known and minor criminals alike, written to sound like they had been dictated by Grinf himself, telling the criminals to give up their evil ways, lest they invite the wrath of Grinf himself upon them.

When—inevitably—the criminals would disregard the letters' warning, then the Judges struck. They used a combination of magic and trickery, first to scare the unrepentant criminals, and then to kill them. Often, the Judges wouldn't even bother to hand the criminals over to the authorities, mostly because of their distrust of the government's ability to properly punish lawbreakers.

Eventually, most criminals would cease whatever they were doing as soon as they received a letter from the Judges of Justice, even though the letters were always unsigned and delivered anonymously. The fierce reputation of the Judges themselves caused the crime rate to fall year after year, until a religious reform united the entire Carnagian people under the principles of

Grinf, which led to the government taking the matter of arresting and punishing lawbreakers more seriously. The Judges then disbanded, though many of their letters were in the Carnagian Vault and had been reprinted as Scripture that was still read by many Carnagians today.

That was what this letter reminded Raya of. It was almost like the Judges of old had sent her a letter from beyond the grave. Only, Raya was pretty sure that this letter wasn't written by a bunch of ghosts.

Unless Braim wrote it, but he doesn't seem like the kind of guy to do that, Raya thought.

She considered telling her parents about this letter, but then Raya decided that they didn't need to know. It was probably just a very strange prank. Maybe it was the work of the God of Jokes and Pranks. Or maybe one of the katabans who lived in the city had sent it to her as a bizarre joke that only a katabans would understand.

So Raya walked over to the trash bin near the writing desk on the other side of the room and held the letter above it. She then drew a match from her dress pockets—she always carried a few around—lit it in one stroke and then held it under the corner of the letter.

The flame rapidly ate away at the letter, until soon it was nothing more than a pile of ash in the trash. She did the same to the envelope, thus eliminating all traces of the mysterious letter.

And now it's time for bed, Raya thought as she picked up her thrown fish, which was still wrapped in the paper towel. *After I finish my snack, of course.*

Chapter Six

ONE MOMENT, CARMAZ, Saia, and Tinkar stood in the now-empty village of the crustaceans. The next, all three of them stood in the center of Carmaz and Saia's hometown, which was called Conewood. Not only that, but a cursory look at his body showed Carmaz that Tinkar had somehow also managed to heal him during the teleportation. Saia looked much better as well, so much so that he was able to stand on his own without any trouble.

But Carmaz's stomach immediately rebelled, causing him to grab it with both hands and moan involuntarily. He had no idea where this sudden sickness came from because he hadn't been feeling sick at all earlier. He hadn't even had much to eat today, so what was his stomach trying to get rid of?

"Teleportation can often have unintended side effects on humans who are not used to it," Tinkar said. "I assume you have never teleported before, Carmaz?"

Carmaz looked up at Tinkar with annoyance. "Yes, though I thought you'd know that, seeing as you gods know everything, don't you?"

"Not everything," said Tinkar. "But most things."

Saia, unfortunately, must have had a much weaker disposition than Carmaz, because he actually threw up. It was mostly liquid, but the sight of his friend throwing up made Carmaz's stomach retch, forcing him to look away to avoid joining his friend in illness.

That was when Carmaz noticed that they were standing in the village square of Conewood. It was a village of about three dozen or so huts, with an old well set in the center of town where anyone could gather water (even though the well was dry half the time). Tall jungle stood on the outskirts, surrounding the village on all sides, but Carmaz was so used to seeing the jungle that he didn't have any strong emotional reaction to it except to note that he felt happy and safe being back home, even though Conewood was hardly much safer than the rest of the island.

Right now, Carmaz did not see anyone else in the village out and about. He at first found it odd before remembering that it was in the middle of the afternoon, which was usually the time that the entire village of Conewood napped inside their huts. That was because it was usually too hot at this time of day to do anything else. And indeed, with the sun's rays beating down on him, he wished he could be inside his own hut taking a nap right now.

"Allow me to wake up the people," said Tinkar, raising his hand.

Carmaz was about to ask Tinkar what he meant when the god waved his hand. Not a second later, the doors of the huts opened and all of the villagers streamed out, heading toward the village square as quickly as they could, like they had been summoned by a mysterious force that they could not deny.

In less than five minutes, the entire tiny village of Conewood was gathered in the village square. This was the quickest that Carmaz had ever seen everyone gather like this. It was rare indeed for the villagers of Conewood to gather here. In fact, Carmaz could name only two other times that this type of village-wide gathering had occurred, and both had been several years ago when Carmaz was much younger than he was now.

The villagers were a sorry lot in appearance. Most were quite thin due to a lack of food to eat and very dirty due to a lack of soap and water in which to bathe. One man, who Carmaz knew as Wood-foot, was missing a foot, which had been replaced with a block of wood that was held on by rope. And, although some of the villagers were descended from the old Ruwan Royal Family, none of them looked rich in the slightest.

Yet none of the villagers dared to speak or move toward Carmaz or Saia, even though Carmaz could tell that everyone was both surprised and happy to see that the two of them had returned to the village safely and in one piece. All eyes were on Tinkar, as if everyone knew who this god was but were too afraid to actually talk to him.

The silence was broken when a young girl shouted, "Carmy!" and dashed out from behind the adults. She slammed into Carmaz's legs, almost knocking him over despite her small size, and hugged his legs fiercely as she said, "Carmy, I missed you! I thought you weren't ever going to return."

Despite the serious situation, Carmaz had to smile as he looked down at the young girl clinging to his legs like she thought that she could keep Carmaz from leaving through her childish strength alone. He swept the girl up into his arms, hugged her tightly (much to her delight), and then rested her back on the ground, saying, "I'm glad to see you as well, Frissa. And see, I even brought Saia back with me, too."

The young girl, Frissa, looked up at Saia with her dark, innocent eyes. Saia spread his arms as if he expected a hug from her as well, but then Frissa said, in a rather monotonic voice than before, "I'm glad to see you are alive, too, Mr. Saia."

Saia's smile vanished as quickly as if Tinkar had teleported it away and his arms fell to his sides. "Hey, *I* was the one who was going to be eaten by the crustaceans. Isn't anyone happy to see me?"

Saia looked at the other villagers, but unlike Frissa, none of them came forward to greet them. Even Hazur, the village elder, stood with the others, her old, aged eyes looking at Tinkar with much suspicion and distrust.

Tinkar, meanwhile, was looking at Frissa, though the young girl seemed to hardly notice the god. "Is she your daughter?"

Frissa finally noticed Tinkar when he spoke, but rather than cheerfully greet the stranger, she just hid behind Carmaz. Carmaz wished he could hide somewhere, too, but he knew that it was impossible to hide from the gods.

So he said to Tinkar, "No. Frissa's parents were murdered by some pirates when she was only a year old and so doesn't really have any parents, so to speak. She technically is raised by everyone in Conewood, including me. But you knew that already, didn't you?"

"I know the fates of all mortals," said Tinkar. "I simply asked the question to appear less alien to you, though I doubt I succeeded."

Carmaz found it hard to believe that Tinkar—or any god, for that matter—would bother trying to understand him and the others. He suspected that Tinkar was playing with him, which,

90

considering how the gods in general treated mortals, was not an unheard of thing for a god to do.

Then Carmaz looked back at the villagers. They still didn't seem likely to break the ice, so he decided to explain to the others what was going on and why Tinkar was here.

So Carmaz stepped forward and gestured at Tinkar. "This is Tinkar, the God of Fate and Time himself. He—"

Carmaz didn't even get to finish his sentence before the villagers started to hurl dirt clods, rocks, and even precious shoes at Tinkar. Carmaz, Saia, and Frissa ducked, therefore avoiding most of it, but Tinkar didn't even try to dodge. The clods, rocks, and shoes rapidly disintegrated ten feet from his body. Tinkar's facial expression didn't even change as the projectiles disintegrated, as if he was unimpressed by the villagers' actions.

Once it became clear that throwing things at Tinkar was not working, the villagers stopped doing it, but they still viewed Tinkar with the same distrust from before.

"I will give you mortals credit for being willing to assault a god that is a thousand times more powerful than all of you put together," Tinkar said. "But if this had not been on the north side of the Dividing Line, I would have killed you all for the severe lack of respect you showed toward me."

"Go fuck yourself!" one of the villagers shouted. "We don't want you stupid gods on our island!"

Tinkar didn't even look offended by that. He yawned and said, "Obscenities. Is that the best you mortals can come up with? Wait. Do not answer that question. The future tells me that that is indeed the best that you are able to come up with."

"Are you going to restore Ruwa to its former glory?" another village shouted.

"No," said Tinkar. "I did not come here to help a bunch of heathens."

"Then why did you come here at all?" a third villager shouted. He took off his shoe like he was going to throw it at Tinkar. "Get out of here! No one wants you around."

The villager threw his shoe at Tinkar. His aim, unfortunately, was severely off, because his shoe instead hit Saia directly in the face.

"Ow!" Saia said, rubbing his nose where the shoe had hit. "Barc, what the hell was *that* for?"

"Sorry," said Barc, the villager who had thrown the shoe, sheepishly. "My bad."

Carmaz again rose to his full height and said, "Please, I understand how angry everyone here is at Tinkar and the gods, but you must understand that Tinkar rescued Saia and me from the crustaceans and has offered us hope for Ruwa."

"Hope for Ruwa?" Frissa repeated, looking up at Carmaz with her large eyes. "What do you mean, Carmy?"

Smiling, Carmaz scooped Frissa into his arms again and then addressed the villagers once more, saying, "According to Tinkar, there is an event starting next month on World's End known as the Tournament of the Gods. It is an event that will pit one hundred mortals against one another to determine who will ascend to godhood to replace the gods that died in Uron's attack on Martir two months ago."

"I have never heard of this 'Tournament of the Gods' before," said Hazur, her old voice full of suspicion.

"That is because, elder, it is the first of its kind," said Tinkar.

"The Powers themselves created the idea as an efficient way of replacing the deities lost by Uron's hand. It is no lie."

"What's so great about this stupid Tournament?" Barc said, folding his arms over his chest. "Sounds like a glorified game to me."

"It's great because I have been chosen to participate," said Carmaz, gesturing at himself. "That means I have a shot at becoming the God of Martir. And if I become the God of Martir, I can use that power to help Ruwa."

"Really?" said Frissa. She hugged Carmaz's head in excitement. "Yay! You can help Ruwa. Can I help?"

"Sorry, Frissa, but you have to stay here," said Carmaz, pushing her hands off of his head. "Saia and I are going to World's End alone. We only came back here to explain the situation and say good bye to everyone."

"But don't you worry, Frissa," said Saia, giving her the thumbs up. "I'll make sure to keep Carmaz here out of trouble for you while we're away."

Frissa giggled, but Carmaz paid her no more attention. He was now looking at the other villagers, waiting to see what their reactions would be. He saw no reason for any of them to be against it. After all, everyone here knew him well enough to understand that he really would use the power given to him as God of Martir to help fix Ruwa if he won the Tournament. He expected complete support from everyone.

But the longer he waited for a reaction, the less likely it seemed he would get one. Or at least, the less likely it seemed that he would get a *positive* reaction. The general facial expression he saw was a mixture of disappointment and betrayal. Barc even looked away and made a noise of disgust.

Carmaz's smile fell. "What is the matter with you all? Aren't you happy for this rare opportunity I could use to actually improve the lives of us all?"

Still no smiles.

Then Hazur looked Carmaz straight in the eye. Her gaze was one of betrayal and sadness, which actually hurt Carmaz more than he thought it would.

"Why should we be happy that you have a chance to join those who have ignored us?" said Hazur. Though she spoke softly, her words were impossible not to hear. "We remember the last God of Martir, Skimif, who did not improve our lives in any way. I recall when he first ascended thirty years ago. I was a much younger and more hopeful woman then than I am now."

"But I'm not an aquarian like Skimif was," said Carmaz. "I'm one of you. I would never forget you, no matter how big and powerful I may get."

"Skimif did nothing for us," said Hazur, as if Carmaz hadn't said a word. "He only ever seemed preoccupied with higher things. Or perhaps it was his aquarian bias against humans that prevented him from helping us. In any case, we have learned not to rely on any higher powers to help us, because the higher powers have shown that they do not *want* to help us, even when they are able."

"I understand your distrust and hatred of the gods," said Carmaz. He tried to keep his voice calm, but it was hard, even with Frissa in his arms. "But you have to realize what a grand opportunity this is. I am not asking you to trust Tinkar or any of the other gods. I am asking you to trust *me*, which I know that

94

everyone here already does."

"We trust you only because you are one of us," said Hazur. "But one thing I have learned in my life is that power changes people, often in bad ways. And I can think of no position with more power than that of the God of Martir."

"Are you saying that I will go mad with power?" said Carmaz. "Elder, you have to know me better than that."

"I did not say that you would go mad," said Hazur. "But I believe you will forget. You will stop thinking of us as your equals. You will come to view us much like the rest of the gods, as minor annoyances who you are under no obligation to aid or protect."

Carmaz did not know what to say to that. He looked at the other villagers, searching for any who might disagree with Hazur, but none did. Even Frissa was quiet, though that may have been more due to her lack of understanding of what they were talking about more than anything. Saia looked as uncomfortable as Carmaz, but like everyone else, he kept his mouth shut.

Then Hazur turned and walked back toward her hut. The rest of the villagers did as well, until soon the entire village square was empty once more, save for Carmaz, Saia, Frissa, and Tinkar.

Carmaz lowered Frissa back onto the ground. She looked up at him with worry and confusion on her childish features.

"Carmy, are you really going to forget us if you go away?" asked Frissa. She sounded close to tears.

Carmaz smiled, though it felt fake, and mussed her hair. "Of course not, Frissa."

"But Hazur said—"

"Elders can be wrong sometimes, despite their immense

wisdom and experience," said Carmaz. "Just know that, whether I win or lose the Tournament, I *will* come back. I will not forget anyone here, even the people who refuse to support me. You can count on that."

"Okay," said Frissa in a much happier voice. "But I want you to take this with you before you leave."

Frissa jammed her hands into the pockets of dress and then pulled out a shiny, solid gold coin that Carmaz had never seen before. She then held it out for him to take, which he did. Turning the coin over, Carmaz saw that it was one of the old Ruwan coins that had been the primary currency of the island nation before its downfall centuries ago.

Carmaz looked down at Frissa again. "Where did you find this?"

"In the jungle when I was out gathering wood for the fire," said Frissa. "It was shiny and pretty, so I took it. But you can have it. I think you need it more than me."

Carmaz did not have the heart to tell Frissa that the gold coin was completely worthless, so he simply closed his hand around the coin and said, "I will treasure it always, Frissa. Thank you."

Frissa gave a great, big smile when he said that. "That makes me happy."

"Now I think you should go," said Carmaz, gesturing at the rest of the village. "It's time for Saia and I to leave now. But we will definitely return, no matter what."

"Okay," said Frissa. She waved at him and Saia. "Bye Carmy, bye Saia. I hope you both become gods!"

With that, Frissa turned and ran off into the village. Carmaz watched her go, feeling a little better about himself now, knowing that he had at least one supporter here who cared about his success.

"Well ..." said Saia, causing Carmaz to look at him. Saia had his hands in his pockets, looking rather uncomfortable. "That was not how I expected the announcement to go. At all."

"Think nothing of it, mortals," said Tinkar, shaking his head. "Few mortals are intelligent enough to see when they will benefit from something like this. Most are so caught up in jealousy and the trivialities of day-to-day life that any possibility of improvement becomes a myth to them that must be shot down at all costs."

"You knew they would react this way, didn't you?" said Carmaz, looking at Tinkar with disgust. "Why didn't you tell me?"

"As the God of Fate and Time, I have made a point of not interfering with either," said Tinkar. "I am not like the other gods, who regularly interfere with their domains as they see fit. Fate and time are too fragile to alter without causing devastating consequences for everyone, including the gods."

"What about the things that my people said to you?" said Carmaz. "When they accused you and the other gods of not caring about us? What did you think about that? Didn't it bother you?"

"You act like I hadn't already known they would say that," said Tinkar. "Besides, why should I be angry at the truth? Skimif really did fail to improve Ruwa's condition while he reigned. And the rest of us have not done much, either."

Carmaz's fists shook. "Is that all, then? No apologies for ignoring us? No justifications for your lack of action?"

"Justify? To whom and why?" said Tinkar. "It is not the gods'

97

job to make everything comfortable for you humans. Our job is to watch over the domains that the Powers assigned to us, and to defend Martir when necessary."

Carmaz didn't say anything to that. He just looked down at Frissa's coin, which was cold in his hand.

"I imagine, then, that your village's rejection of you has caused you to rethink your previous plan for helping Ruwa if you win the Tournament," said Tinkar.

Carmaz looked up at Tinkar in surprise. "'I imagine'? I thought you knew the actions of every mortal before even they do."

"Not if you are a godling like yourself," said Tinkar. "Most of your actions come as a surprise to me. It makes you godlings annoying to deal with, but even gods like myself have our limitations."

"Well, to answer your question, no," said Carmaz. He held Frissa's coin up to his chest. "If I win this Tournament, I am still going to use my power to help Ruwa."

"Despite their obvious lack of support toward you?" said Tinkar, now sounding genuinely surprised. "Why?"

"Because they are still my people and my friends," said Carmaz. "And I know that if I don't help them, then no one will."

For once, Tinkar looked at a loss for words. Then he shrugged and said, "I guess you humans still have a few surprises up your sleeve. Anyway, let us leave right away. There is not much time before the Tournament begins and there are still many other godlings to gather before the fateful day."

"Then take us there, Tinkar," said Carmaz, gesturing at himself and Saia. "We're both ready to go right away."

Tinkar nodded. He then snapped his fingers and Ruwa faded away around Carmaz, until he and Saia found themselves standing in the largest city he had ever seen in his life.

Chapter Seven

One month later ...

BRAIM KOTOGS STOOD before the massive, domed stadium known as the Stadium of the Gods, looking at it with interest. It was a brand new building, having only just been finished about a week ago. Neither Braim nor any of the other godlings had been allowed to watch its construction while it was in progress. In fact, the godlings had all been separated entirely, kept in their own apartments or inn rooms to avoid meeting each other until the day of the Tournament. The reasoning behind that, according to Alira, was so that the godlings would not be able to formulate strategies to use against each other in the Tournament itself, though Braim thought it was actually because neither Alira nor the gods wanted the godlings to interact with each other unsupervised.

Whatever the case, the Stadium resembled the Temple of the Gods, except its exterior was made of pure gold and its doors were crystalline. It was located on the far west side of the city, on one of the few places on World's End that had been open enough to build on. Even then, Braim knew that the gods had had to tear down a handful of buildings that were already there in order to make room for the large structure.

The Stadium had a huge frieze built above the entrance that

100

displayed the thousands of gods already in existence. It was so intricately made that Braim sometimes wondered if it was just an illusion, as he doubted even the gods could make a frieze so intricate. On either side of the entrance were two stone statues of Alira, flanking the entrance like guards, holding up the Rulebook of the Tournament in their stone hands.

Braim shook his head. He was already pretty late as it was. He had slept-in this morning—despite knowing that today was the first day of the Tournament—and was certain that he was the last godling to arrive, because he had not run into any other humans or aquarians on his way to the Stadium. He had, however, literally run into a rather large, menacing-looking katabans who had threatened to rip out his spine and beat him with it before the katabans realized who Braim was and let him go with his spine intact.

Braim had no idea if there were any consequences for arriving late, though he bet there were. Alira had struck him as a very disciplined, by-the-book kind of woman. She probably did not tolerate tardiness or lateness for any reason. Even if the entire city had been burning down, Alira would likely not have accepted that as a valid excuse for not being on time.

Then again, there was a reason that Braim had woken up later than usual. Ever since his first night on World's End, after that katabans assassin had tried to kill him, Braim had found it almost impossible to sleep through the night anymore. Anytime he heard anything—the scurrying of the mouse, the fluttering of a bird outside his window—his eyes would snap awake and he'd prepare to shoot a spell, only to realize that he was completely alone in his room. Even so, Braim had come to sleep with his wand under his pillow at night, with one hand firmly grasping it at all times. He had cast a few spells to protect his room, but he was not much of a teichomancer and believed that any determined assassin could break in with only a little effort.

As for the identity of the assassin, that was still a mystery to Braim. Jenur, as the Magical Superior, had gone to the gods and informed them of the assassin's attack on Braim, but the gods all claimed ignorance about the attacker and his identity and the identity of his employer.

Nonetheless, the gods had assigned a group of katabans known as the Soldiers of the Gods with the task of locating and arresting the assassin. The Soldiers of the Gods were supposedly some of the best trackers in the world, yet to Braim's knowledge, they had not found even one hint as to the current location or identity of the assassin.

Darek and Jenur had both wanted to stay on World's End to help protect Braim, but the gods had insisted that the two go home because they were not supposed to participate in the Tournament and were not needed here. Besides, the two of them had their own responsibilities anyway and thus could not stay away from their important jobs for very long.

But Braim had kept in contact with both of them, sending them gray ghosts every day to let them know how he was doing. Even so, Braim didn't feel safe about being on World's End by himself and so he went to bed each night figuring that he'd wake up in bed with all eight of the assassin's blades in his chest.

Maybe I shouldn't worry as much, Braim thought, shaking his head. *The assassin hasn't even been seen since the night he tried to kill me. He's probably given up. Anyway, I should head into the*

Stadium now. Hopefully Alira won't be too angry at me for being late like this.

So Braim walked across the street to the massive Stadium doors. He was just about to push them open and enter the building when he heard someone behind him shout, "Wait for us!"

Pausing, Braim looked over his shoulder and saw two young men—both maybe a few years older than Princess Raya, at most—running toward him as fast as they could. Their curly, dark hair and pale skin immediately pegged them as Ruwans, although he could tell that they were not brothers or related in any way. Both wore identical silk tunics, although the taller one wore a green tunic and the shorter one wore a blue tunic. Both tunics had built-in hoods on the back, just like Braim's did.

The two skid to a halt before Braim, panting as if they had just run a mile (and depending on how far they had run, they very well might have run such a length in order to get here). Braim had never seen either of them before, so he had no idea who they were, though he guessed that they were both godlings like himself.

"Looks like I'm not the only one who is going to be late after all," said Braim, smiling at the two younger godlings. "Slept-in?"

"Even worse," said the shorter of the two, wiping the sweat off his forehead as he thrust a thumb over his shoulder. "Stupid katabans innkeeper who can't speak Divina tried to get money out of us, even though Tinkar *told* him that the gods are the ones paying our tab. Idiot tried to swindle us."

"Yeah, the katabans in this city aren't exactly the most trustworthy, especially the ones who run their own businesses," said Braim. "Anyway, I don't think we've met before. What are your names?"

"Carmaz Korva," said the taller one. He nodded at his friend. "And he is Saia Qurea. We're from Ruwa. Ever heard of it?"

"Yeah," said Braim, nodding. "I actually know someone who grew up on Ruwa. Or, well, I used to know her and only got to know her again recently."

"Oh," said Said. "So you went on a long trip or something without communicating with her for a while and only just returned recently?"

Braim cracked a smile. "Something like that."

"Now that we've introduced ourselves, who are you?" said Carmaz. He glanced at Braim's wand, which was in the wand holster tied to his waist. "A mage?"

Braim noted a surprising bitterness in Carmaz's words when he said that, even though Braim had done nothing to annoy or anger him. He figured that Carmaz was probably not very fond of mages for some reason.

"Yep," said Braim, nodding. "I'm from North Academy. Ever heard of it?"

"Of course," said Saia. "It's the most famous magical school in the world. Are you a student there?"

Braim thought about it, shrugged, and said, with a smile, "It's complicated."

"Okay," said Carmaz. Then he started and looked at the Stadium. "Almost forgot. We have to enter the Stadium. They're probably starting without us."

Braim—relieved that he wouldn't have to tell them his name (as he suspected they knew it, seeing as everyone seemed to know it nowadays, even people he had never met before)—nodded and opened the door. He stepped inside, but held the door open for Carmaz and Saia. Once they entered, he closed the door and looked around at their surroundings.

He, Carmaz, and Saia had stepped into the lobby of the Stadium, which was rather wide-open and had lots of standing room. At the end of the lobby were five large steel doors, each one emblazoned with the symbol of the five gods that had been killed, though they were currently closed.

Much to Braim's surprise, however, the lobby was full of people, who were undoubtedly the other ninety-seven godlings. Most of them were human, but there were a fair few aquarians as well, and all of the godlings were talking amongst each other, introducing themselves, speculating about what challenges they would have to undertake, what brackets they would go into, and so on. None of them seemed to notice Braim, Carmaz, and Saia enter, which was fine by Braim, as he was not in the mood to talk to a bunch of strangers about his resurrection.

Even so, just seeing those people caused that dark feeling to creep up his spine again. Braim tried to ignore it, but as always, that feeling sneaked up on him wherever he went. It always became worse when he was with other people or was trying to sleep at night, which explained why it had come back here all of a sudden.

Then Braim heard a familiar shrill voice say, "Hello, Braim!" and a young Carnagian woman, wearing a practical black tunic with the hood down, stepped out of the crowd of godlings. Her hair was in a simpler style, like a ponytail, but she still somehow managed to make herself look fabulous.

Princess Raya walked up to Braim, Carmaz, and Saia with a

rather arrogant step, as if they were her peasants that she was graciously allowing in her court. Braim noted how Saia's eyes ran up and down her body, though he didn't dwell on that because the darkness was still trying to cloud his mind.

"Hey, Raya," said Braim, waving at her as she approached. "Haven't seen you in a while. You look different."

Raya threw back her hair. "Well, of course I do. I am dressed for success. If I am going to become the Goddess of Martir, then I need to be dressed to take on whatever challenges Alira presents to me. Not that it will be terribly difficult for me, of course, because I *know* that it is my destiny to win."

"You sure seem confident, silver spoon," Carmaz said, causing Raya to look at him (unlike Saia, Carmaz was looking at her face with dislike), "despite the fact that no one here even knows what the challenges in the Tournament will be. Tell me, are you just bragging or do you know something we don't?"

"How do you know I'm a princess?" said Raya in surprise. "I don't recall ever introducing myself to someone as uncouth as you."

"You're an actual princess?" said Carmaz. He looked at Braim worryingly. "Is she telling the truth or pulling my leg?"

"She's telling the truth," said Braim. He gestured at Raya. "Beautiful here is Princess Raya, the Princess of Carnag."

"The one and only," said Raya. She then put her hands on her hips. "But how could you *not* have heard of me? Everyone in the Northern Isles, even those who don't live on Carnag or Shika, knows my name, if not my appearance."

"We're from Ruwa," said Carmaz. "The only royalty we know of has been dead for at least five hundred years, the rumors of the ghosts in Castle Ruwa notwithstanding. Afraid we don't keep track of international politics very closely."

"Ruwa?" Raya repeated. "I have never heard of the place. Is it some backwards island somewhere in the west?"

"Friana Archipelago, actually," said Carmaz, whose tolerance for Raya's rudeness, Braim could see, was growing thinner and thinner every second. "Ever been there?"

"Oh, I visited Friana once on holiday," said Raya with a bright smile. "Absolutely beautiful weather and geography. Loved the Crystal Mines, though the food was awful and the people ranged from mediocre to rude."

"Gee, I wonder what it's like to talk with a rude person," said Carmaz dryly.

"It's awful, I tell you, just awful," said Raya, shaking her head. "And I am royalty. I just can't imagine how they would have treated me if I was a peasant."

"Probably worse," said Carmaz.

"Indeed," said Raya, "although I've always wondered what it would be like to live life as a peasant. I've sometimes considered putting on some of my rattier clothes and going among the people of Carnag without telling anyone my name, but I think I'd be instantly recognizable no matter what I wore or how I styled my hair."

"I think your attitude and word choice would give you away more than your face," said Carmaz. "It is very … distinctive."

Raya, as usual, didn't seem to notice Carmaz's implications. "Yes, yes, I agree that I am very unique. Father always tells me that there is no girl like me in the whole world. Even among the princesses of other nations, I am unique. After all, I have learned that I am the only member of royalty among the godlings, aside from that aquarian man named Foroz, who claims to be a descendent of some ancient aquarian king from the Primordia Era or something like that."

"I suppose that does make you ... unique," said Carmaz. He looked at Saia. "Right, Saia?"

Saia blinked several times and then looked at Carmaz suddenly, like a dozing student suddenly called on by the teacher to answer a question during a lesson that he had paid no attention to. "What? Yes, I agree that Raya does have a very unique body."

Carmaz elbowed Saia in the side, causing Saia to say, "I mean, yes, Raya is a unique woman, which includes her body, because the body and mind are one whole that can't be separated from each other."

"Yes indeed," said Raya, folding her arms across her chest with a smug smile on her face. "But I don't believe you two have introduced yourselves to me yet. What are your names?"

"I'm Carmaz and I am what you would call a 'godling,' I suppose," said Carmaz. "And this is Saia, my friend. He's not a godling, but the gods allowed him to come and support me while I'm participating in the Tournament."

"What?" said Raya, looking at Saia in shock. "The gods sent my parents away and told me I couldn't bring any of my servants to stay with me here. I've had to learn to fend for myself without my servants to dress and feed me. It's been so horrible, and yet they've allowed a commoner like you to bring a friend along who isn't even a godling?"

"Sounds like you have had such a *tough* life, silver spoon," said Carmaz. He had completely dropped all pretense of politeness now. "Having to dress and feed *yourself*. However did you survive a month on your own? I can't imagine what that must have been like."

"It was the toughest month of my life," said Raya. She sniffled. "Fortunately, the gods provided me with a katabans servant to attend to some of my needs, but he was so rude and didn't serve me nearly as well as my servants back in Carnag Hall. But I believe that this month on my own has only reinforced my belief that I would make an excellent Goddess of Martir. If I can survive this, then ruling the world should be no problem for me whatsoever."

Carmaz looked like he was at a loss for words now. Saia, on the other hand, was nodding along, but it was pretty clear, based on the position of his eyes in relation to Raya's body, that he wasn't actually listening to a word that Raya said.

"Anyway, Braim, do you know what bracket you've been put in yet?" said Raya, looking at Braim again. "I know we're not supposed to know until Alira arrives and tells us here, but I wanted to know if the list might have leaked to you."

"Sorry, beautiful, but I'm just as in the dark about this as you are," said Braim with a shrug. "I haven't even seen Alira since the day she announced the Tournament. So it's going to be a surprise for me, too, whenever she comes out and announces it."

"Braim?" Carmaz repeated. He was looking at Braim with curious eyes now. "As in, Braim Kotogs?"

"Braim Kotogs?" Saia said, finally looking away from Raya to look at Braim instead. His mouth gaped. "The man who came back? Is that really you?"

The darkness creeping up Braim's spine almost made him

growl at Carmaz and Saia for some reason, but he instead said, in a casual tone of voice, "Yeah, that's me, all right."

Raya pouted. "Oh, come on. Neither of you have heard of the Princess of Carnag, but somehow you've heard of *him*?"

"We heard about Braim because a pirate from up north brought back word of him two months ago," said Carmaz. "I honestly didn't believe the pirate, though, because it sounded like another far-fetched pirate tale to me, but I guess he must have been telling the truth when he spoke of a man who came back from the dead."

"Yep," said Braim, nodding. "I really did come back from the dead. Took me thirty years, but I did it."

"What does being dead feel like?" asked Saia. "Does it hurt?"

Braim shrugged, not sure how to answer the question. "Well, uh—"

He was thankfully spared from having to answer that question when a sudden hush fell over the entire Stadium lobby without warning. All of the godlings, including Braim, then looked up at the ceiling. It felt like some kind of indescribable magical force was drawing their attention to that direction.

Then a portion of the ceiling slid to the side, allowing a thick metal platform to descend from the hole. Upon the platform stood Alira, who looked exactly the same as she had a month before, carrying the thick Tournament Rulebook in her arms. The platform floated over to the front of the lobby, above the five doors, allowing all of the godlings to see her.

"Is that Alira?" Carmaz whispered to Braim, who nodded in confirmation.

"Never seen her before?" Braim whispered back.

"First time," said Carmaz.

The judge of the Tournament adjusted her glasses and then looked down upon all of the godlings. She said, "Welcome, godlings, to the Stadium of the Gods, where you will spend the majority of your time as participants in the Tournament over the next few months. I am pleased to see that everyone is present and ready to start participating."

Braim breathed a sigh of relief. So he hadn't been late after all. He had thought that he was, but if Alira was telling the truth, then he had clearly arrived on time. And based on the facial expressions of Carmaz and Saia, they also looked quite relieved that they were not late as well.

As for Raya, she was staring at Alira with such intense concentration that she seemed to have forgotten everything else. Braim had a feeling that he could poke her in the back of the head with his wand and she still wouldn't take her eyes off of Alira.

"For the past month or so, you have all been kept in the dark regarding the finer details of the Tournament," said Alira. She patted the thick Rulebook in her arms. "Today, however, I will finally explain the basic rules and structure of the Tournament so that everyone here understands what the rules are and how the Tournament works."

Finally, Braim thought. *I've been wondering about this since the Tournament was announced.*

Alira flipped open the large Rulebook and then let go of it. But rather than fall to the floor, the Rulebook floated open in midair, as if being held by a large, invisible hand. Alira placed one finger on the page, as if pinpointing the spot where she had left off.

"First, we will start with the structure of the Tournament," said Alira, in her usual matter-of-fact tone. "The Tournament of the Gods is divided into five brackets, one bracket for each deceased god: Skimif, the God of Martir; Hollech, the God of Deception, Thieves, and Horses; the Spider Goddess, Goddess of Spiders and Sleet; the Avian Goddess, Goddess of Birds; and the Human God, the God of Humans."

Braim already knew who each of the dead gods were. Nonetheless, he found himself wondering which position he'd get. Because he didn't really want to be in the Tournament, he had no actual preference for any of the positions.

He glanced at Carmaz, who perked up at the mention of Skimif, and Raya, who also had perked up at the mention of that deceased god's position. In fact, Braim thought that most of the godlings in the lobby appeared very interested in Skimif's position, seeing as it was the highest and most prestigious of them all.

"Each bracket will contain twenty godlings, all competing for the position of god of whatever bracket they are assigned to," Alira continued. "For example, the Skimif Bracket will have twenty individuals competing for the position of God of Martir, as will the other four. And each bracket is further divided into ten sub-brackets, which have two participants each competing against each other in a task that is relevant to the position they are trying to win.

"The winner of each sub-bracket will then move onto the main bracket, where they will compete against the other nine sub-bracket winners for whatever divine position they are competing for. As an example, the Skimif Bracket will have a sub-bracket and the winners of the Skimif Sub-Bracket will then move onto the Skimif Bracket, where they will compete with the other nine Skimif Sub-Bracket winners for the position of God of Martir."

Braim folded his arms across his chest and looked at Carmaz again. He couldn't read the Ruwan's facial expression due to not knowing him very well, but Carmaz hardly seemed put off by the possibility of so much competition. Raya looked positively giddy, like she thought that this Tournament was going to be a piece of cake.

"The winner of each bracket will then be ascended into godhood, with all of the power and prestige that that title implies," Alira finished. "To keep things orderly, all sub-bracket and bracket challenges will take place in a specified order over a certain period of time. The exact order and time period for each bracket will be revealed later on, after each godling has been sorted into their own bracket."

"What about the rules?" asked Carmaz, his voice rather loud in the quiet and open lobby.

Carmaz's question caused all of the other godlings to look at him, while Alira looked almost taken aback by his question. She quickly regained her composure, however, and said, "The what?"

"The rules for the Tournament," said Carmaz, who didn't seem taken aback by all of the attention from the other godlings. "If this is a competition, it's got to have rules, right?"

"Why yes, of course," said Alira, though she sounded rather annoyed by his interruption. "I was just about to get to the rules, but thank you for asking. Yes, the rules for this Tournament are rather varied. You do not, however, need to know all of them. I will only cover the ones that will absolutely get you thrown out if

113

you break them. Others may be read on the posters on the lobby walls."

That was when Braim noticed tons of posters—each full of walls of text—plastered on the lobby walls. He wondered why he hadn't noticed them before, though based on the reactions from the others, he guessed that he wasn't the only one who had somehow failed to notice them. In fact, he was now wondering if the posters might have appeared just as Alira mentioned them. It was a real possibility, after all, given what the gods were capable of doing with their magic.

"The first, and most important, rule is 'Do not murder your competitors,'" said Alira. "It is rather self-explanatory: Killing your fellow godlings will result in an instant disqualification from the Tournament. Not only that, but participants who break this rule will also be locked away deep beneath World's End, where they will receive a terrible punishment from Grinf, the God of Metal, Fire, and Justice, himself for their crime. Accidental killings may be forgiven, but it is still advised that all godlings avoid putting their fellow participants into mortal danger."

That seemed like a no-brainer to Braim. He certainly had no plans to kill any of his fellow Tournament participants. And he doubted that Carmaz, Raya, or any of the others here had plans to do that, either, though considering how few of the participants he actually knew personally, he couldn't be sure about that.

"The second most important rule is, 'Don't cheat,'" Alira continued. "That, too, is rather self-explanatory. If you are going to prove yourself worthy of godhood, then you must play fairly and by the rules. It is fine to use wit, cunning, and creativity to complete whatever tasks have been placed before you, but you cannot blatantly break the rules and expect to get away with it. Any blatant or willful breaking of the rules is grounds for instant disqualification from the Tournament, though the cheater in this case will simply be sent back home, rather than thrown beneath World's End for all eternity, unless their cheating also broke the first rule."

Now Braim could see some people—he was looking at Raya when he thought that—cheating. Even so, Braim wondered why anyone would risk cheating if it meant instant disqualification. It seemed rather illogical to him, but he supposed that people didn't always make sense.

"The third most important rule is 'Do not enlist the aid of a god or goddess to help you complete a task,'" said Alira. "That means that you must solve each task on your own. Conversely, no god or goddess is allowed to aid any of you in completing any task, even if they want to. You must earn your godhood by yourself. Like with the second rule, this one is also grounds for instant disqualification and returning the offender home."

Now there was something Braim could certainly never see himself doing. It would never have even occurred to him to ask for help from one of the other gods or goddesses. He didn't really like most of them anyway, considering how they tended to treat him due to his status as a dead man brought back to life.

"Those are the top three most important rules that every godling should know before entering the Tournament," said Alira. "As long as you remember to follow these three rules, you should have no trouble in the Tournament at all, aside from whatever troubles the challenges may present to you."

"Who will judge the Tournament?" Carmaz asked, again

drawing the eyes of the other participants toward him.

This time, Alira took his interruption in stride. She gestured at herself and said, "Why, I will, of course. That is the entire purpose of my existence. If I did not judge the Tournament, then I would quite literally have no other reason to live."

"Okay," said Carmaz. "And what about people who lose honestly in the sub-brackets and main brackets? What happens to them?"

"They are sent back to their homelands, assuming they lost without cheating," said Alira. "Any other questions, Carmaz?"

Carmaz shook his head, but Braim could tell that Carmaz was thinking hard about Alira's words. Braim heard nothing strange in Alira's answers, so he decided not to think about them.

"Very well," said Alira. "With all of that out of the way, I will now distribute these cards to each godling."

Alira drew a stack of cards from her breast pocket. The cards were shining and silvery in the light. Indeed, from a distance, they looked like they were made out of actual silver. She raised the deck high for everyone to see.

"Upon each card is written the name of each individual godling, along with the bracket they were assigned to," said Alira. "Some of you may be surprised with the bracket to which you have been assigned, but rest assured that it is no mistake and that you have been assigned to the correct bracket."

Alira threw the cards into the air. Braim at first thought that that was a stupid thing to do, because the deck was going to get scattered everywhere and it would probably take a long time for all one hundred godlings to find their own card (unless *that* was the first challenge, in which case the gods really *were* crazy).

But the deck—rather than scattering into every corner of the room like Braim expected—floated in midair for a moment before each card shot out from the deck one by one. The cards flew all over the room, flying into the hands of each godling to whom they belonged.

Three such cards flew toward Braim, Raya, Carmaz, and Saia. Because Raya was slightly closer to Alira than the others, she got her card first, which she eagerly began reading.

Braim and Carmaz caught theirs at exactly the same time. Saia drew closer to Carmaz to see what his card said, while Braim tilted his head down to look at the tiny, silver card in his hand, which read thus:

BRAIM KOTOGS
BRACKET: SKIMIF BRACKET

Braim turned the card over, wondering if there was more to it than that, but the card was completely blank aside from those words. Even so, Braim sensed a warmth in the card that was not natural. He suspected that it was caused by a spell cast by Alira, probably in order to identify the card's owner.

So Braim turned the card over again to read the words written upon it again. His eyes focused on the second line—*BRACKET: SKIMIF BRACKET*—and he found himself dreading it greatly.

Damn it, Braim thought, frowning. *Probably should have expected it, but damn it.*

Then he looked at Carmaz. The Ruwan was squinting at his card with a frown on his face.

"What does yours say?" said Braim.

"I ..." Carmaz scratched the back of his head, looking somewhat embarrassed. "I can't really read it. I never learned how

117

to read."

The idea that Carmaz was illiterate confused Braim until he recalled that Carmaz was from Ruwa, an island with a rather high rate of illiteracy. He had quite forgotten that, seeing as Carmaz had behaved more like someone who could.

"Let me look at it and I can tell you what it says," said Braim.

Carmaz still looked embarrassed, but he held out his card for Braim to read. Braim leaned forward and read the card, which had a layout and font similar to his:

CARMAZ KORVA
BRACKET: THE HUMAN GOD BRACKET

"It says you're in the Human God Bracket," said Braim, pulling back and looking at Carmaz.

Carmaz's face fell. He looked at the card again himself, as did Saia, who was now looking over his shoulder, and he said, "That can't be."

"It is," said Braim. "Sorry, man, but that's what it says. Did you want to be in a different bracket or something?"

Carmaz looked at Braim with desperation in his eyes. "What bracket are you in?"

"The Skimif Bracket," said Braim. "Why?"

Carmaz looked like he was about to crumple his card in his hand. He then glared up at Alira, who was looking down at everyone from her platform as if to make sure that everyone had received the correct card.

Braim, who was not entirely sure why Carmaz was upset, decided to find out which bracket Raya had been assigned to. He turned to her and said, "So, Raya, what bracket did you get?"

Raya was so still that Braim almost believed that she had

somehow become a statue. She didn't even seem to hear him at all. Worried, Braim reached out to lay a hand on her shoulder, but then Raya said, without looking at him, "Don't touch me."

His hand freezing partway between him and Raya, Braim said, "What?"

"I said, don't touch me," Raya repeated. Her tone was flat.

Braim lowered his hand and smiled. "Let me guess, you didn't get put into the bracket that you wanted."

"I got put in the *worst* bracket," said Raya, still without looking at Braim.

"Which one is the worst again?" said Braim. "Is it the Spider Goddess's bracket? Because I don't like spiders much myself, either."

Raya thrust her card up into Braim's face. He leaned back slightly so he could actually read the card, which read—again in a similar layout and font to his and Carmaz's cards—thus:

RAYA MANA
BRACKET: HOLLECH BRACKET

Chapter Eight

RAYA DIDN'T EVEN wait for Braim's response. Nor did she care to hear it. She marched straight into the crowd of godlings, her eyes fixed solely on Alira. The other participants—some of whom, she realized in the one part of her mind that wasn't consumed by rage, were also going to be in the Hollech Bracket—parted as she made her way through, as if her anger alone was generating enough force to move everyone out of her way.

About halfway across the room Raya realized that Carmaz was walking beside her. He was quite a bit taller than her, a fact that she had not realized when she first saw him, but she could not remember asking him to come with her. A quick glance at him showed that Carmaz was just as angry as she was. She had no idea what bracket he was in—she had stopped paying attention to everything when she read her card—but she found that she didn't care. Maybe he was even angry about her placement, though considering how rude Carmaz was, she doubted that greatly.

Alira didn't seem to notice either of the two coming toward her until they were halfway across the lobby, at which point Alira's cold, objective eyes looked down on both of them. To Raya's surprise, Alira's platform actually lowered down closer to them, but then it stopped several feet above their heads, although she didn't need to be face-to-face with Alira to make her displeasure known.

Raya and Carmaz stopped ten feet away from Alira's platform. Alira adjusted her glasses and, with a sigh, said, "What may I help you—"

Raya held up her card and said,"What is the meaning of this? Why am *I* in the Hollech Bracket? Do I look like a deceiver, thief, or equestrian to you? Is this some kind of joke?"

Carmaz raised his card as well and said, "How am I supposed to help my people now? What kind of power does the God of Humans have, anyway? What's the deal?"

Alira didn't look even slightly disturbed by Raya or Carmaz's harsh words and tone. She looked rather unimpressed, actually, as if they were nothing more than a couple of annoying brats that she was stuck babysitting.

"Well, I *said* that the results might surprise you," said Alira. "Did not these results surprise you?"

"That's not what we're angry about," Raya said. She waved her card in front of her. "What we're angry about is the fact that we were not placed into the brackets that we *deserve*, the one that we were *destined* to be placed in. This is righteous anger, the kind that Father always taught me was an appropriate response to injustice."

"For once, I agree with silver spoon," said Carmaz. "I only agreed to enter the Tournament under the belief that I would get a shot at becoming the God of Martir. This is not what I signed up for, not at all."

Alira peered over the top of her glasses at Raya like she couldn't believe what she was saying. "Oh, so you two genuinely feel entitled to enter whatever bracket you want, rather than accepting what you were given. I now see why the gods tend to have a rather divided opinion over allowing the continued existence of humanity."

"It's not entitlement, only logic," Raya said. "As the Princess of Carnag, I am the most fit and qualified person for the position of Goddess of Martir, not for the position of Goddess of Deception, Thieves, and Horses. It offends me, as a Grinfian, to even be considered for that position, as deception and theft are both highly unjust actions."

"I'm not entitled, either," said Carmaz, folding his arms over his chest. "I want to help my people most of all, and the best way to do that would be as the God of Martir. I might be able to help as the God of Humans, but the truth of the matter is that I need more power than that to fix Ruwa."

Much to Raya's surprise—and anger—Alira chuckled. "Humorous, the both of you. I see I must not have explained the Tournament clearly. You were not chosen for these brackets based on what you *wanted*, but instead based on what you are *suitable* for. And I believe that your current brackets are the most appropriate categories for you two. I do not believe either of you would make a good God or Goddess of Martir, in other words."

"I am going to tell my parents," Raya said. "And I will ask them to come here and make you change your mind."

"Well, if that's the case, then I want out of this Tournament," said Carmaz. He threw his card onto the floor and stepped on it. "I never really liked the gods anyway. I'd rather go home to Ruwa and continue to eek out an existence there than live in this city as a god who can't solve the problems of my people."

"And now the two of you are throwing tantrums," Alira said in a sardonic tone. "I suppose I must have also forgotten to tell you that when you enter the Tournament, you can't quit. You must either progress through the Tournament's brackets until you win or lose or break one of the rules and get disqualified. Quitting is not an option."

Carmaz's card reappeared in his hand. He looked at it in surprise, though Raya ignored it. She just glared at Alira with all of the hate she could muster.

"This is not fair," said Raya. "You don't even know me. How can you know that you put us in the right brackets?"

"I need not know you on a personal level to know what bracket each of you needs to be in," said Alira. "It is a mixture of my own research and what the gods have told me regarding your character and abilities. Your own god, Raya—Grinf—was the one who recommended you for the Hollech Bracket, as he did not think you were an appropriate fit for any other."

"Liar," Raya said. "Lord Grinf would never recommend me for such an unjust bracket. He should know better than anyone that, with my royal training, I would make an excellent Goddess of Martir."

"Actually, I believe it is *because* he knows you so well that he recommended I assign you to this one," said Alira. "But please, if you have any complaints or issues with this decision, feel free to blaspheme Grinf. Of course, I have heard that he is not a particularly kind god, but I am sure he will patiently listen to your complaints and understand your anger."

Raya gulped. The idea of complaining to Grinf ... well, that was almost enough to defuse her anger completely. She remembered too many stories about how Grinf dealt with those who questioned his judgment to know that complaining to him was not a very wise move to make even for royalty such as herself.

Carmaz, on the other hand, said, "Then who recommended me for the Human God bracket? I demand to know so I can find that god and tell him what I think about his judgment."

"That is not information you need to know," said Alira. "I have no reason to tell any of you anything, anyway. You are supposed to accept the role that I have given you. You may not like it, but your own personal tastes about the bracket you were assigned do not matter in the long term."

Raya shook her head to get herself to stop thinking about her fear of Grinf and said, "Can't you change it? If you are the one who actually assigned us to our brackets, then logically you should be able to change it, yes?"

"As Judge of the Tournament, when I make a decision, it is *final*," Alira said, putting as much emphasis on the word *final* as if she were chanting a secret incantation. "Even if I could change it—which I cannot—I would by necessity be forced to reorganize all of the brackets. That would be far more work than is necessary. Besides, not everyone is whining about their placement in the Tournament, though I believe that would change if I submitted to your pathetic wishes."

Raya looked over her shoulder, suddenly remembering all of the other godlings in the lobby. All of them were staring at Carmaz and her. Some of them looked annoyed at their argument with Alira, while others looked like they were happy that someone was standing up to her.

Then Raya looked at Alira again. She folded her arms across her chest and said, "What if I promised to give you all of the money you could possibly want? My father is the King of Carnag, after all. I can ask him for anything, and he will give it to me without question."

"Your father has nothing that would interest me," said Alira, though she sounded more confused than anything now. "Besides, I have no need of anything. I desire one thing and one thing only: To ensure that the Tournament advances smoothly and that any rule breakers are promptly punished for their crimes. And that is all."

At this point, even Raya could see that there was no point in arguing with Alira any further. There was something final and authoritative in the Judge's voice, like the authority that Raya had heard in the voices of some of the gods back in the Temple. Alira was not a god herself, but Raya now saw that the Judge clearly held at least as much authority as the gods, at least regarding the Tournament and its rules.

Raya looked at Carmaz pleadingly, hoping that he might somehow be able to come up with an argument to persuade Alira where Raya had failed.

But Carmaz—though he looked at least as angry about Alira's stubborn refusal to reconsider her decision as much as Raya was —nodded and said, "Very well, Judge. If you won't reconsider your decision, then maybe we just need to learn to make the best of a bad situation."

"Learn to make the best of a bad situation?" Raya said. She slapped his arm, causing Carmaz to glare at her in annoyance. "Carmaz, I was *counting* on you to come up with a persuasive argument to make Alira rethink her decision, not for you to defer to Alira's judgment."

Carmaz shook his head. "Just because I may not be royalty doesn't mean that I am one of your peasants to be bossed around. If you want something done, silver spoon, then I suggest you do it yourself."

Raya's mouth fell open. She tried to come up with some sort of comeback, but Carmaz's sarcasm stabbed deep and nothing came out of her mouth.

Instead, she said, "Hmph!" and turned and walked away from Carmaz and Alira back into the crowd of godlings. As before, they parted to allow her through, but Raya barely paid them any attention. She just marched through the crowd to the back of the lobby, past Braim and Saia (who also parted as though they were afraid that she might bite their heads off), and out the doors into the city.

Far more time must have passed since Raya had entered the lobby than she had thought, because the sun was lower in the sky now and its dying rays were reflecting beautifully off the windows and surfaces of World's End's skyscrapers. Yet Raya hardly paid attention to that. Instead, she picked a random street in a random direction and marched down it, grumbling under her breath all the while.

Stupid Judge, Raya thought, scowling as she kicked at the street as she walked. *Stupid Alira. She doesn't know me. And I doubt Grinf told her to put me in the Hollech Bracket anyway. She just said that to take the blame off herself for making a stupid decision.*

Somewhere in the back of her mind, in the small part that was not touched by her anger, Raya was aware that she was probably going to get into trouble for just walking out of the Stadium lobby like that. She hadn't told anyone where she was going, when she was going to get back, or anything like that. She had simply left and had no particular idea of when she would return.

But Raya didn't see this as a big deal. She was rightfully angry, in her view, for being denied what she felt was her birthright. She just couldn't see how she could possibly make a good Goddess of Deception, Thieves, and Horses anyway. She never lied, certainly never stole (her takings didn't count), and she didn't even know how to ride horses anyway. It was the most unfair thing that had ever happened to her in her life and she just wasn't going to take it.

Not like I can leave *World's End anyway,* Raya thought, allowing her anger to simmer. *Don't have a ship or an airship, can't teleport, can't ask any of the gods or katabans to take me away, and definitely can't swim all the way back to Carnag. I'm stuck on this stupid island until I win or lose the Tournament. Feels more like Rock Isle than World's End right now, if you ask me.*

Still, Raya looked over her shoulder anyway, wondering if any of the other godlings or Alira were coming to fetch her. She saw no one. In fact, she didn't even see any katabans on the street that she walked upon. She wondered if the city's inhabitants had gone to sleep already, though she didn't care if they had or had not. Despite being part katabans herself, she didn't feel any real affinity with the katabans that lived in World's End.

I want to be alone right now anyway, Raya thought, scowling as she turned her attention back to the streets before her, though she wasn't really seeing where she was going, mostly because she was too distracted by her emotions and thoughts to focus on anything else. *I don't want to be around other people. I don't even want to be around the gods. All I want to do is walk forever and ever.*

A sudden rumbling in the sky caused her to look up. Dark clouds were moving in, which was odd, because no one had told Raya that it was going to rain tonight. In fact, Raya had thought that it couldn't rain on World's End at all. She had assumed that its position at the very end of the southern seas meant that it never rained here, yet there was no mistaking that rumble of thunder or those dark clouds rolling through the sky like an unfurled carpet.

And now it is going to rain, Raya thought as she turned a corner into a wide-open area. *Bet it was the Rain God who did it. Probably trying to make me go back to the Stadium so I can participate in a bracket that is probably made up of a bunch of deceivers, thieves, and horse-lovers.*

Then Raya bumped into something solid and fell backwards onto the streets on her behind. Shaking her head, Raya thought that she might have accidentally walked into a building before she looked up and saw that she had actually walked into a person.

She had never seen this being before. He towered above her, far taller than any human or aquarian she had ever seen, his entire body cloaked in shadow. Though humanoid in appearance, he had two extra arms sprouting from his shoulders, which made Raya think he had to be a katabans of sort. His mask resembled a baba raga's face, although Raya saw nothing but darkness through the eye holes. His overall appearance creeped Raya out. In fact, she was so creeped out by him that she thought that he shouldn't have

128

existed at all.

But even Raya's creeped out feeling didn't stop her from rising to her feet, and poking him in the chest with one finger, scowling at him all the while. "Are you even going to apologize for not getting out of my way and knocking me over? And what's with your mask? Is this some sort of stupid katabans cultural practice that I am unaware of or are you just crazy?"

The figure said nothing. Above, thunder roared more ominously and Raya felt a few tiny raindrops fall on her hair, which caused her anger to dissipate almost instantly.

"Oh, dear," said Raya, raising her hands above her head to protect her hair from the rain. "If it rains, it will mess up my gorgeous hair and my clothes. Sorry, stranger, but I have to return to the Stadium of the Gods."

Again, the figure did not speak, did not even move, but Raya paid little attention to that, because the drops were coming in more frequently now and Raya could not afford to waste any more time on mute, rude idiots like this guy.

So Raya turned to leave, but then paused. She didn't recognize this part of the city at all. True, Raya was not a native of World's End, so it made sense that she didn't know every little nook and cranny as well as a native. Still, Raya had thought that she knew enough about its layout to be able to retrace her general path back to the Stadium at least.

The problem was that Raya just couldn't recognize any of it. She saw the tall, colorful buildings, the smooth white streets, the stoops leading up to the entrances of the skyscrapers, as well as cafes and restaurants that were currently closed, but it was like she had stepped into another world entirely. That it was starting to rain only heightened her confusion about this strange part of the city that she did not recognize, that she could not recognize, as if her mind was unable to comprehend what she was looking at.

Raya turned to face the stranger, saying as she did so, "Mister stranger, I—"

But he was nowhere to be seen.

Then Raya felt a creeping presence behind herself and turned around in time to see the stranger raising four blades above his head. The blades were thin and long, but looked sharp enough to dice Raya into tiny pieces with little effort on the part of their owner.

Raya could not help but scream when she saw the stranger and his swords, especially when he brought them down on her with frightening speed.

Chapter Nine

FOOLISH GIRL," SAID Alira, shortly after Raya left the Stadium lobby. "She is foolishness incarnate."

For once, Carmaz agreed with Alira. While he had somewhat empathized with Raya's anger at Alira's decisions (even though he found her reasoning for it incredibly selfish and immature), he still thought it was stupid for Raya to march out of the lobby like that without telling anyone where she was going. At the very least, it was immature, though Carmaz thought that calling Princess Raya immature was also redundant.

As for the other godlings, none of them seemed to want to acknowledge Raya's tantrum, or perhaps they simply didn't know what to do. Carmaz couldn't see Saia or Braim, due to the fact that they were at the back of the crowd, but he doubted that either of them had gone after Raya, either.

Alira sighed and pushed her glasses up the bridge of her nose. "Carmaz, can you go and find Raya? We cannot begin the Tournament unless all godlings are present and accounted for."

Carmaz looked up at Alira and frowned. "Why me? Can't you send a katabans to find her?"

"Because I think it is a suitable punishment for your disrespect for my judgment," said Alira. Then she added, under her breath, "Besides, the katabans never listen to me anyway.

They only ever listen to the gods."

Carmaz sighed, but nodded and said, "All right. I'll track her down as quickly as I can."

Depositing his card into the front right pocket of his pants, Carmaz made his way through the crowd of godlings to the back of the lobby. Here he found Braim and Saia standing awkwardly together, but he said nothing to them. He just nodded at Saia, indicating that he should follow him, and his friend understood and walked behind him to the lobby's exit.

The two emerged onto the street just outside of the Stadium. Much to Carmaz's consternation, it was starting to rain. He always hated the rain, even though it rained fairly frequently on Ruwa. Thankfully, his clothes had a hood, so he pulled it up over his head to keep his head dry.

So did Saia, who was now looking at Carmaz from under his own hood. "Where do you think Raya went?"

Carmaz frowned and looked down the street both ways. "I have no idea. Maybe we won't have to find her at all. She struck me as the kind of girl to come running back as soon as she gets a little wet. Maybe she'll return when the rain really picks up."

Saia looked down at the street and pointed at something. "Hey, is that Raya's card?"

Saia quickly bent over, picked up the card, and showed it to Carmaz. Carmaz still couldn't read it. He figured that it had to be Raya's, seeing as all of the other godlings were still in the Stadium lobby and still had their cards with them.

"She must have dropped her card while going in this direction," said Saia, pointing down the street. "Let's see if we can find anyone who might have seen where she went."

Carmaz nodded and the two walked down the street even as the rain began to increase in intensity. It wasn't quite as heavy as the torrential downfalls of Ruwa, but it was still loud and wet enough to shut off all potential conversation between the two friends as they walked quickly down the street, keeping their eyes open for any sign of Raya.

Even though Carmaz tried his best to keep his mind focused on the task at hand, he still couldn't help but feel a little annoyed at this recent turn of events. He had wanted to be the God of Martir, not the Human God. He didn't see any reason or logic in Alira's decision or in the decision of whichever god had recommended this position for him to Alira in the first place.

But maybe it won't be all bad, Carmaz thought as the rain beat against his head and shoulders, soaking through his hood and making him feel more miserable than ever. *I would still be a god. Not as powerful as whoever becomes the God of Martir, maybe, but I will still have far more power and influence than I do now. Maybe I will even be able to help my people somehow.*

The problem was, of course, that Carmaz had no idea what being the God of Humans even meant. He certainly had not heard of the Human God until recently. Did it mean that he had control over all of the humans on Martir? Did it mean that all humans were dependent upon his power and rule? It was all too vague for his tastes. Perhaps he'd find out more about what the position actually entailed during the Tournament itself.

Taking his mind off the Tournament, Carmaz tried to focus on the present. He looked everywhere as he and Saia walked, but he didn't see any sign of Raya at all. He didn't even see any katabans, though that made sense, seeing as the rain was falling hard now and any katabans with sense in their heads were undoubtedly inside their homes keeping warm and dry.

One thing Carmaz did notice about the street was how it did not get very slick despite the rain. The odd white stone that made up the street upon which he and Saia walked felt as dry as ever, as if the stone was somehow absorbing the rain. Carmaz was no mason, but he found that to be more than a little odd, though he dismissed it as being the work of the gods' magic, which he found even less comprehensible than mortal magic.

Then, over the roar of thunder and the thundering rain, just as Carmaz was beginning to wonder if it might be wiser to head back and wait until the rain let up before continuing, a high-pitched, girlish shriek shot through the air.

It was so loud that both Carmaz and Saia stopped and looked at each other in surprise.

"Was that Raya?" Saia shouted over the rain, his words barely comprehensible to Carmaz.

"I think it was!" Carmaz shouted back. "But where did—"

His question was interrupted by another loud shriek. This time, Carmaz knew where it came from: On the other side of one of the smaller buildings on the other side of the street.

"There!" Carmaz shouted, pointing toward that building. "I heard her over there!"

Without hesitation, Carmaz and Saia dashed across the street, through the alleyway between the smaller building Carmaz had noticed and the taller one to its right, and into a back street on the other side.

Carmaz saw Raya walking backwards, away from a large, hulking figure that seemed to wear darkness like a cloak. It had four arms, each carrying a sword, and it wore a mask like a baba raga, but that was all Carmaz could make out of the strange figure. In addition to the darkness around it, the heavy rain made it hard to see clearly, but Carmaz didn't need to see the assassin perfectly to understand that it was trying to kill Raya.

"What the hell is that?" said Saia, his eyes widening under his hood. "A katabans?"

"No idea," said Carmaz. "But we have to stop it before it kills her."

Saia looked at Carmaz in alarm. "How? You and I are unarmed, you know."

"Then we rescue Raya and run away from it," said Carmaz. "But we need to distract it first."

"Great idea," said Saia. "So how do we do that?"

Carmaz bent over and picked up a rock on the street. He then handed it to Saia and said, "You throw the rock at the creature. Insult it and then run once it starts chasing you. I'll grab Raya and all three of us will make a break for the Stadium, where we will be safe."

"Hold it," said Saia, looking up from the rock Carmaz had given him. "When did I volunteer to be the bait?"

"You're a better runner than I am and you have better aim, so the creature is less likely to capture you than me and you will be far more likely to hit it with this rock," Carmaz said. "So it is unlikely that it will kill you."

"Unlikely?" said Saia. "How 'unlikely'? Are we talking 'the gods actually giving a damn about Ruwa' unlikely or 'Tinkar appearing out of nowhere to save us from the crustaceans' unlikely?"

Carmaz just patted Saia on the shoulder and said, "Just do it. I promise you'll be safe. The creature clearly wants Raya anyway, so it will probably give up chasing you when it realizes it's been tricked."

Without waiting for Saia to answer, Carmaz ran back into the alleyway between the buildings and made his way through the other alleys until he found himself watching the creature stomping toward Raya from behind her. The creature didn't seem to have noticed either Carmaz or Saia just yet, but then the rock that Carmaz had given Saia from earlier flew through the air and struck the creature in the side of the head.

But the creature didn't even look at Saia as it walked. It continued stomping toward Raya with single-minded obsession, as if it hadn't even felt the rock hit its head.

Plan B, then, Carmaz thought.

He dashed out from the alley as fast as he was able. The creature was upon Raya now and raised its swords again. Raya looked too afraid to move. She just stared up at the blades through the hair plastered to her head as though she were facing an executioner about to behead her.

Desperate, Carmaz jumped the last few feet and tackled Raya to the ground. The two rolled across the pavement until they stopped and Carmaz found himself on top of Raya, way too close for comfort.

But then Carmaz heard the sound of the street cracking and looked up to see that the creature had brought all four of its blades down on the street. The street was now cracked and broken, which was an impressive feat, because Carmaz had not seen any cracks or wear in the streets of World's End since he got here. He had been under the assumption that the streets were made of some kind of unbreakable stone, but if this thing could crack the streets, then Carmaz was pretty much certain that there was no way any of them could beat it in a fair fight.

Carmaz scrambled off Raya and hauled her to her feet. She practically collapsed against him, shivering and cowering. It seemed like the creature's attack on her had traumatized her, making her even more useless than ever, though Carmaz found that he oddly liked the way she clutched him so.

Then Saia ran up to them and said, "Sorry the rock didn't work! I threw it as hard as I could, but—"

"Doesn't matter," Carmaz cut him off. "Just help me get Raya out of here. We can't beat the monster, but I think we can outrun it if we try."

Saia nodded and without another word grabbed Raya's other arm. The two hauled her between them as fast as they could, but it was slow-going. Raya could hardly stand on her own and could walk even less well, perhaps only walking every two or three steps. The rest of the time Carmaz and Saia had to drag her and, while she was not a particularly big or heavy woman, it still felt like dragging a large bag of rocks between them anyway. That it was raining, thus making their clothes heavy and obscuring their vision, only made everything worse.

Just when they were halfway to the alley from which they had emerged, Carmaz heard a whistling in his ears and the monster was in front of them. Raya screamed when she saw it, while Carmaz and Saia looked up at it with pure fear. It raised its swords again and then swung them as ferociously as a swamp tiger swiping with its claws.

All three of them dropped to the street, narrowly avoiding getting their heads cut off by the monster's blades, which whistled by over head. Then Carmaz, seeing an opening, stood up and punched the creature in the stomach as hard as he could.

But it was like punching solid brick. As soon as he hit its stomach, the pain in his hand exploded, causing him to cry out and fall back down next to Raya and Saia. His hand felt broken, though he had no way of healing it at the moment.

The monster grunted, as though amused by Carmaz's pathetic attack, and raised its blades again. This time, Carmaz was absolutely certain that it was not going to just kill Raya, but him and Saia as well, but he wasn't going to let that happen.

As fast as he could, Carmaz grabbed Raya and then kicked Saia with his foot. The blow sent Saia rolling across the wet street away from them with a cry of shock, while Carmaz and Raya slid across the slick stone street underneath them.

None of them slid or rolled very far, but it was enough to put them out of the reach of the creature. Only this time, the creature seemed to realize that they had escaped, because it stopped itself from smashing its swords down on the street and turned to face Carmaz and Raya, completely ignoring Saia, who was now cowering on the street behind it.

Carmaz got to his feet, ignoring his broken hand and using his good hand to haul Raya back up to her feet. He tried to pull her along, to make her run away with him, but she was so traumatized by the monster's attack that she just stood there as frozen as a statue. Raya seemed to have lost all will to live, which almost made Carmaz want to just leave her and run.

But he didn't. He stood by her, pushing her behind him, as the monster stomped toward them again. This time, even Carmaz could tell that the monster was losing its patience, as if this attack was taking far longer than it had planned.

Then, out of nowhere, a burst of light hurtled through the air and struck the monster in the side. The monster let out a yelp, the first sound it had made so far, while a familiar voice nearby shouted, "Hey, ugly, long time no see!"

Carmaz and Raya looked in the direction from which the light had come. Braim stood in the alleyway from which Carmaz and Saia had emerged, wand in hand, soaking wet from the rain but clearly ready to fight. He tossed his wand from hand to hand, his large, confident grin visible from under his hood even through the thick rain.

"What, did you miss me?" said Braim. "Because I didn't miss you, you know, since you tried to murder me the last time we met and all."

Much to Carmaz's surprise, the monster turned away from him and Raya and began making its way toward Braim. Almost as soon as it did so, however, Carmaz felt the wind whistle by him and then heard the sound of metal tearing through flesh and the monster actually screamed.

A second later, Carmaz saw an aquarian man, with a shark-like head, standing to the right of the monster. The aquarian man —who Carmaz had never seen before—carried a sword of his own, but it was a strange one, resembling the fin of a shark more than anything, though it glowed with energy, which meant that it was probably not an ordinary sword.

The monster staggered forward, strange gold blood leaking out of a wound on its side where the aquarian's sword had cut through its skin. The gold blood melted through the stone underfoot, hissing and sending steam into the air.

As for the aquarian, he stood up and turned around, holding his blade in both hands. The monster also turned to face its assailant, making growling noises as it did so, but it didn't even get another two steps before Carmaz saw motion out of the corner of his eye. Something small landed on the monster's back and stabbed it with two short swords.

Again, the monster cried out in pain, only this time it tried reaching for whatever had landed on its back. The small thing, however, jumped off before the monster's four arms could reach it, and landed next to Carmaz and Raya.

Now Carmaz saw that the 'thing' was a person, a very short, middle-aged woman, who carried twin short swords that glowed like the aquarian's sword. She wore a tunic similar to theirs, except gray. She stood up to her full—albeit not very considerable—height and looked up at Carmaz and Raya with a concerned, almost motherly look on her face.

"How are you two, my dears?" asked the woman, as if she had not just stabbed a strange shadow beast in the back with her two swords. "Did that monster hurt you at all?"

Carmaz and Raya—both utterly speechless at this sudden turn of events—shook their heads in response.

"Oh, how wonderful," said the woman with a kind smile. "I was worried that I'd have to tear that thing apart with my swords if it hurt a handsome man and beautiful woman like you two. Though that thing is a lot tougher than I thought."

The woman was right. The monster, despite now having two small but rapidly bleeding holes in its back to go along with the sword cut in its gut, whirled around to face them again. It now looked finished with this entire situation, but it still stepped toward them again anyway, as if it was not yet ready to give up.

Not that it got very far before a chunk of the street rose up in front of its feet. The creature tripped over the protruding bit of street and fell flat on its face, causing more of that strange gold blood to leak from its wounds and melt the street beneath it.

A sudden laugh caused Carmaz to look to the right. He saw yet another godling—this one a young man who didn't look much older than Raya, perhaps even younger due to his baby fat—pointing a wand at the monster, clearly trying (and failing) to hold in his laughter. He waved at them with a large, rather mischievous grin on his face, as if he was sharing a great joke with them.

"Hey, wasn't that funny?" the young guy shouted. "First he tried to kill you, but then he tripped and fell over himself. All thanks to little old me."

"This is not the time for joking, young man," the aquarian swordsman shouted over the rain, the irritation in his voice obvious. "This is the time to kill this monster before it can kill any of us."

The young man looked offended by the aquarian's admonishment, but before he could respond, the monster rose back to its feet. Only this time, Carmaz noticed that it struggled to rise, no doubt due to the pain caused by the immense amount of blood it had lost already. That it could still stand at all was an impressive feat, though Carmaz doubted it would be standing up much longer.

"Let's stop playing around, guys," Braim shouted, causing the three newcomers to look in his direction. "Let's finish this off so we can get the Tournament started already."

"At least someone around here is taking the threat seriously," said the aquarian swordsman loud enough for the young mage to hear him, who only scowled in response.

Then Braim fired another burst of light from his wand tip, while the young mage waved his own wand and caused two stone chains to rise up from the street and wrap around the monster's waist. The light blast struck the monster in the back, right where the motherly woman from before had stabbed it, causing the monster to howl in pain again.

Then the aquarian swordsman and the motherly woman jumped toward it with their blades above their heads. The monster struggled to escape the stone chains holding it down, but the blood loss must have weakened it considerably, because the chains didn't even budge under the stress it was no doubt putting on them.

But just as the swordsman and the woman came within stabbing reach of the monster, it melted into a puddle of shadow, leaving the stone chains still standing where it had been moments before. The swordsman and the woman landed on top of the stone chains and then looked around rapidly, as if trying to find the monster.

Carmaz also looked around while Raya clutched him as if she was afraid that he, too, would melt into shadow like the monster. The rain was letting up now, making it easier to see the street around them, but Carmaz saw no sign of the monster anywhere, save for the melted parts of the street where its blood had been.

Before Carmaz knew it, all four of their saviors—Braim, the young mage, the aquarian swordsman, and the motherly woman

—were gathered around them. Saia, too, was with them, but he looked rather intimidated by all of the godlings and seemed hardly able to speak in their presence.

"You two okay?" said Braim. "How about Raya? Is she all right?"

Carmaz looked at the quivering Raya at his side. He didn't see any wounds on her, so he nodded and said, "I think so. She just got scared is all."

Then Carmaz's hand—the one he had used to punch the monster—flared with pain, causing him to grunt. But the motherly woman then touched his painful hand with one of her swords and the pain vanished instantly.

"There you go, dear," said the woman. "Just a tiny bit of panamancy to make your hand all better."

"Uh, thank you, er …" Carmaz trailed off uncertainly, because he did not know her name.

"Malya," the woman said as she sheathed her short swords. "I'm a godling just like you. I'm from Friana and I am also in the Avian Goddess Bracket, in case you were interested."

"My name is Tashir," said the aquarian swordsman, who unlike Malya kept his sword unsheathed. "Spider Goddess Bracket. I come from the country of East Yudra in the Undersea. Graduate of the Undersea Institute."

"And I'm Yoji," the young mage said. He puffed out his chest. "Student from the Itrijan School of Magic. Graduated top of my class, since I'm a child prodigy. Also in the Hollech Bracket."

"I see," said Carmaz. "But how did you four find us? *Why* did you even come search for us?"

"Because you three were gone for too long and Alira was

getting impatient," Braim said. "Said that the start of the Tournament is going to have to be put off until tomorrow thanks to Raya storming off like that. As for how we found you, Yoji here knows some topomancy, so it was easy to locate you guys that way."

"It was really hard, though," said Yoji. "It was like you guys just disappeared off the face of the earth. And when we did locate you, I thought it was a fluke, but I guess I'm just that awesome."

"Disappeared?" Carmaz said. "What does that mean?"

"No one could locate you," said Tashir. "It was like something was blocking our magic. Perhaps that monster had something to do with it."

Yoji looked toward the stone chains that still stood where he had summoned them, a frown on his face. "Just what *was* that thing, anyway? I've never seen anything like it in my life."

"I've seen it before," said Braim. "First night on World's End, the thing tried to kill me in my sleep. I just barely survived thanks to some help from a friend of mine. I haven't seen it at all since then. Thought it had decided to leave and not bother anyone anymore."

"Was it a katabans?" said Carmaz. "Because it certainly didn't look human, or aquarian for that matter."

"Who knows?" said Braim with a shrug. "The gods are *supposed* to be investigating this to find out who he is and what he's trying to do, though I have no idea how well that investigation is coming along."

"Find out what he's trying to do?" Saia repeated in disbelief. He brushed back some of his wet hair and pointed at himself and Carmaz. "You mean the fact that he tried to murder us doesn't imply that maybe he's just a psycho murderer who likes to kill people?"

"There has to be a deeper reason as to why he's only targeting us godlings, though," said Braim. "As far as I know, he hasn't targeted any katabans or gods. Just us godlings."

"There likely is," said Tashir, nodding. He looked around the area briefly, like he thought that the monster might still be around. "But I think we should return to the Stadium now. I dislike being out in the open like this, especially in a place where that monster just tried to kill us."

Before anyone could respond to that, a loud voice shouted, "Halt!"

The loud voice caused Raya to start and clutch Carmaz so tightly that she actually hurt him. Nonetheless, Carmaz looked in the direction that the voice had come from, as did the other godlings, to see who had shouted at them.

It was a katabans wearing the crystalline armor of the Soldiers of the Gods. But he wasn't alone. Six other Soldiers walked behind him, each one clad in armor similar to his, carrying swords and spears by their sides. Despite the rain, none of the Soldiers looked even the slightest bit wet, as if they had been inside until just recently.

The lead Soldier—who must have been their Captain—was rather thin and scrawny under the armor, but he walked with far more confidence than Carmaz thought someone like him should have. The leader Soldier gestured at his underlings, who walked out from behind him and started examining the scene of the battle using strange tools that looked like magnifying glasses made of gold, though what they actually were, Carmaz had no idea.

As for the lead Soldier himself, he walked up to the group of godlings and stopped. He didn't salute them. Instead, he said, "Which of you godlings was attacked by the mysterious assassin?"

"Raya was," said Carmaz, nodding at the princess who still clutched him as if her life depended on it. "And you are?"

"Captain Garvan, Captain of the Soldiers of the Gods," the Soldier said, tapping a star on his right shoulder that must have proved his position in the Soldiers. "When we heard about the attack from reports we received from katabans living in the area, we came as soon as we could. Was anyone hurt or killed in the attack?"

"Hurt, yes, but not killed," said Carmaz. "Thankfully."

Garvan frowned, as if he was actually disappointed that the monster had failed to claim any lives. But then his frown vanished and he said, "Where is the assassin now? Is he still in the area?"

"No," said Braim. He pointed at the stone chains that Yoji had made, which some of the other Soldiers were now inspecting with those strange magnifying glasses. "Bastard ran off after it became clear that he couldn't beat us. Just melted into shadow and vanished."

Garvan looked even more disappointed now, but then he shook his head and put on a more professional expression. "Well, we shall use all available methods to us to track him down, then. Once we do, we will make sure to let you know."

"Right," said Carmaz, who wasn't very impressed by the slowness of the Soldiers in arriving to fight the assassin. "Tell me again why it took you guys so long to actually get here?"

Garvan either ignored or had not heard Carmaz's question,

because he then asked, "Did you learn anything about the assassin during his assault?"

"Yes," said Tashir. He held up his sword, which was still glowing with energy. "The beast can be harmed with a sword channeling magical energy. It also bleeds gold blood, similar to what the gods are said to bleed, and the blood melts anything it touches that is not protected by the gods' divine energy."

"Gold blood?" Garvan said. "How odd. Are you certain of that?"

"As certain that the sky is blue and the Undersea is deep," said Tashir.

Garvan stroked his chin. A worried look appeared on his somewhat human features, a look which told Carmaz that Garvan was not sure what to make of this new bit of information.

Finally, Garvan ceased stroking his chin and said, "Well, if that is all, then I will have some of my Soldiers escort you all back to the Stadium. We certainly do not want any of you to be assaulted on the way there by our assassin, who I sincerely doubt has given up trying to kill you yet."

"It probably bled to death," said Yoji with a chuckle. "You should have *seen* all the blood it lost. Crazy."

"Even so, you still need as much protection as you can get," said Garvan. "I will assign to you the best Soldiers in the squad to protect you."

"As long as they don't escort us *after* we head back to the Stadium, that sounds good to me," said Carmaz.

The way Garvan glared at Carmaz told him that he was probably Garvan's least favorite godling at the moment. Not that Carmaz really cared. He had a rather low opinion of katabans in

147

general, so whether one liked him or not was of no concern to him.

Then Garvan shook his head again and said, "Your escort should be here shortly. Once they arrive, it will be safe for all of you to return to the Stadium where you belong."

Chapter Ten

U PON RETURNING TO the Stadium, Braim and the others learned that Alira had decided to postpone the start of the Tournament's first challenge—which was in the Hollech Bracket, they learned—until the next day. The reasoning behind this decision was due to Raya's absence, especially when it was discovered that Raya was too traumatized by the assassin's attack to do anything. Still, Raya expected to recover and it was believed that she would be ready to participate in the Hollech Sub-Bracket challenge the next day.

As a result, the godlings were sent back to their rooms in the city, because it was now believed that the assassin, whoever he or she was, was after godlings in general, rather than Braim in particular. That both reassured and yet worried Braim. Reassured him because he now felt safer knowing that he was not being targeted in particular. Worried because that now meant that the others, including Carmaz and Raya, were at risk as well.

But the godlings were actually not totally segregated from each other anymore. For example, Braim learned that Raya had insisted that Carmaz stay in her apartment with her for her protection, which Carmaz had grudgingly agreed to, although several Soldiers were still placed outside the front door to keep them both safe. Saia had to go back to wherever he and Carmaz stayed and without protection. As far as Braim could tell, Saia's life was considered less important than Carmaz's, as his status as an ordinary mortal meant that it was unlikely that the assassin would come after him.

As for Braim, he was content to take a warm shower and take a nap, because all of that excitement and action had worn him out. Besides, there was that same creeping feeling of darkness following him again, which he tried his best to ignore, though he found that nearly impossible at this point.

It was only when Braim lay down on his bed, however, that he suddenly felt ravenously hungry. It was then that he also realized that he had actually been hungry all day, but had forgotten to pay attention to it because he was still getting used to the desire to eat. When he had been a ghost, after all, Braim had not needed any sort of food or sustenance to survive at all.

So Braim sat up and looked around his room for any food. Unfortunately, he saw nothing edible, so he decided to contact Mishak, the innkeeper, to have some food delivered up to his room when, without warning, a plate with a sandwich on it materialized in his lap.

The sudden appearance of the sandwich—which had some sort of meat between it that Braim didn't recognize—caused Braim to knock it off his lap onto the floor. The plate shattered upon crashing, while the sandwich's bread and meat scattered.

But nothing bad happened. No one attacked Braim or anything, though Braim hardly relaxed, because a sandwich magically materializing in his lap like that had set off his survival instincts. He would have blasted it with magic if he had been holding his wand at the time.

"Why did you throw the sandwich onto the floor?" said a voice above him that caused him to look up. "I thought you mortals liked sandwiches."

A familiar, pale face appeared near the ceiling, followed by an even more familiar armored body with a ghostly tail. The Ghostly God looked down at Braim with a genuinely confused expression on his face.

"Wait," said Braim. He pointed at the sandwich on the floor that lay amid the broken plate. "*You* made that for me?"

"Yes," said the Ghostly God. "I confess that I've never done it before, but if you mortals can do it, then I can as well, and better, because I am a god."

"You're joking, right?" said Braim.

"Of course I'm not," said the Ghostly God. "Why would I be joking? I was merely trying to help you meet one of your needs. That you threw my plate off your lap, however, shows just how little respect you hold for me."

Braim rubbed the back of his head. "It's not that I disrespect you, per se. It's that I've kind of been in danger of being killed by some four-armed freak over the last month or so and so I'm kind of on edge all the time. You could have at least warned me ahead of time what you were planning to do."

The Ghostly God folded his arms across his chest. "Very well. I guess I ... probably should have told you about it before I gave you the sandwich. It was ... not the wisest move I could have made."

Braim was under the impression that the Ghostly God was doing everything within his power to avoid saying 'I made a mistake.' Not that that shocked Braim, seeing as the gods in general rarely ever admitted to their mistakes, even on minor issues such as this.

As a result, Braim did not expect to get an honest admission of error from the Ghostly God, so he changed the subject. "Why'd you give me a sandwich anyway? I didn't ask for it."

"I was merely trying to meet one of your needs, as I stated before," said the Ghostly God. "While I generally dislike serving mortals, you are a godling, which makes you a little bit more important than other mortals. One day, you will be one of us. In fact, you might even rule over us. So why shouldn't I treat you perhaps a bit more kindly than how I normally treat mortals?"

"Did you deliver sandwiches to the other godlings?" asked Braim.

"Of course not," said the Ghostly God. "What do I look like, a sandwich maker? They can do that on their own if they get hungry. I am not responsible for meeting their every want and need, like some kind of *katabans*."

The Ghostly God said the word *katabans* the same way that Raya would say *peasant*.

"Uh huh," said Braim. "Let me guess: The *real* reason you tried to feed me is because you needed an excuse to study me more, right?"

The Ghostly God looked even more offended than before. "Why would I ever do that?"

"Because I know that you've been trying to study me for as long as I've been alive again," said Braim. "You want to figure out how I came back to life and how you can use that knowledge to your advantage. Right?"

Braim expected the Ghostly God to deny it, but to his relief, the Ghostly God nodded and said, "Very well. I can tell that no amount of deception on my part will convince you otherwise. Yes, indeed, that is what I came here to do."

"Sorry, but I can't help you there," said Braim, lying back in bed with his hands behind his head. "I know about as much as anyone else about how I managed to come back to life. All I remember is stabbing Uron in the Spirit Lands and then waking up naked in the graveyard outside North Academy. Weird way to come back to life, but there it is."

"That is because you are a mortal who doesn't even remember what your first life was," said the Ghostly God. "But I, with my centuries of experience and study of ghosts and the dead, might be able to understand better how you came back, if you gave me a chance to study you."

"Nah," said Braim. "I'm not interested in becoming your experiment, sorry. While I'm for the advancement of magic and all that, I'd rather do it with my freedom intact."

"Whoever said anything about denying you your freedom?" said the Ghostly God. "You can still be free, you know, even if you let me study you."

"Right," said Braim. "Are you going to trick me into becoming your servant for ten years, like you did to Darek?"

"I didn't trick Darek into doing anything," said the Ghostly God. "He was the one who came to me with that offer, not the other way around. Is he trying to play the victim again?"

"The point is, I don't really want to be associated with you," said Braim. "Or any of the other gods, for that matter. Hell, I don't even want to win the Tournament."

"Then what *do* you want to do?" said the Ghostly God. "Drift around the world aimlessly?"

Braim shrugged. "Dunno. Haven't figured it out yet. I just came back to life, after all. I thought I'd go back to doing what I was doing in my first life—being a student at North Academy and next in line to become the Magical Superior, or so I've been told —but even that doesn't interest me anymore."

"Would you like to be free of the darkness that creeps up on you when you least expect it?" asked the Ghostly God. "The darkness that has made it almost impossible for you to sleep?"

Braim looked at the Ghostly God suddenly. "How did you know about that? I haven't told anyone about that, not even Darek or Jenur."

"Because you mortals are not as good at hiding your secrets from us gods as you like to think you are," said the Ghostly God. "I have seen your thoughts in which you worry about this darkness that follows you wherever you go."

"So what?" said Braim, trying to hide his feelings of unease with an indifferent tone. "Maybe it's depression or something. It's probably nothing serious."

"Oh, but I think it is," said the Ghostly God. "It is serious enough that you would like someone to get rid of it for you."

"And if I do?" said Braim. He looked at the Ghostly God hard. "Are you going to get rid of it?"

"No," said the Ghostly God, shaking his head. "Or rather, I can't, seeing as I have no idea what it may be and how to get rid of it. But I do have a theory about your body that may help shed some light on the subject."

Despite himself, Braim said, "Shoot. I'm listening."

"All right," said the Ghostly God. He sounded like he had

been waiting to share this theory with someone for a long time. "I believe that the darkness lingering in your body is from Uron's possession of it. Uron was one of the Almighty Ones, remember, which makes him far more powerful than even us gods. Although Uron no longer exists as an entity independent of the universe, I would be severely surprised to find out that his possession of your corpse did not leave at least some lasting scars that will take either years to heal or will never heal at all."

"So you think there might still be a little bit of Uron left in me?" said Braim with a gulp.

"Not exactly," said the Ghostly God. "Consider a forest fire that has recently been put out. While the flames that once burned the forest may no longer be causing any active damage, the fire has left behind ash and smoke and burnt wood in its wake. It will undoubtedly take years before the forest will grow again to its original strength. Uron is that fire and your body is the forest."

Braim frowned. "But forest fires can start again. Does that mean that I am in danger of being possessed by Uron again?"

"Of course not," said the Ghostly God. "By all accounts, Uron has been utterly destroyed. There is no chance at all that he will ever return, much less to possess your body. You are taking the analogy too far. Typical human behavior."

"Hey, bud, *you* were the one who said my body is a forest, not me," said Braim. "So what do you think that all means, then?"

"I have absolutely no clue," said the Ghostly God. "It might mean nothing. Perhaps you will simply go on to live a normal mortal life and then die of old age later on. Or maybe it will have a lasting effect on your personality that will leave you utterly changed. You're unique, so no one knows for sure."

"If it changes me, will it be in a good way or a bad way?" asked Braim.

"Again, I do not know," said the Ghostly God. "That is why I wish to study you. I don't even know if you can actually die. Your resurrection might have granted you immortality for all I know."

"Immortality, huh?" said Braim. "Well, I guess that's plenty of time to figure out exactly what is wrong with me. *Without* your help."

"But why reject the aid of someone as experienced and knowledgeable on the subject as I am?" said the Ghostly God. He made a sound of disgust. "Wait, don't answer. I know how you humans think, behaving as if you know better than us gods. You are all the same."

Braim shrugged. "Whatever. Anyway, do you know anything about that assassin that tried to kill me? You know, the guy who just tried to murder Raya and Carmaz about an hour ago?"

"No," said the Ghostly God. "We have been working alongside the Soldiers of the Gods to find out who he is, but so far they have not found any evidence to point towards the assassin's identity or the identity of his employer."

"Is it one of you guys?" said Braim. "Because if he's a katabans, then that means he's working for one of you, right?"

"You are assuming that that is what he is even when you have no proof to justify that belief," said the Ghostly God. "More typical human behavior. But no, the evidence doesn't suggest that our assassin is a katabans at all."

"Well, he's clearly not human or aquarian, either," said Braim. "And I kind of doubt he's a god. Otherwise, we'd all be dead by now. That still doesn't explain what he is, though."

"The answers, I am sure, will come in time," said the Ghostly God. "Both the gods and the Soldiers are working hard to discover who he is. It is shameful that this assassin has struck twice on World's End and has yet to be caught."

"Yeah, I was wondering about that," said Braim. "Thought that World's End was supposed to be the safest island in the world, because it's also the home of the gods and everything."

"It is still quite safe in comparison to other islands," said the Ghostly God. "In any case, it is only a matter of time before the assassin is found, caught, and exposed. I know that Grinf in particular has been searching for him everywhere. He cannot stand the idea of a criminal running loose on World's End. It isn't 'just,' as he put it."

"I think we'd all sleep a little safer if that guy was behind bars," said Braim. "But one thing I noticed about him was how he bled gold blood when Tashir and Malya attacked him. You gods bleed gold blood, right?"

"Typically, yes," said the Ghostly God.

"But our assassin is clearly not a god," said Braim. "So what's up with that?"

The Ghostly God opened his mouth to answer, but then a sudden realization came over his features. He closed his mouth and tapped his chin, like his brain was putting together all of the pieces of the puzzle.

"No, that can't be," the Ghostly God was rapidly muttering under his breath. "But yes, it seems logical and certainly fits all of the evidence. But that only opens up more questions, though they may be far easier to answer than this one was."

Braim raised an eyebrow. "Ghostly God? What are you

muttering about?"

"You will find out in time, assuming my theory is correct," said the Ghostly God. "For now, I must contact my fellow gods and share with them my theory. If it is correct, we should have an idea of what we are up against. If it is not, then you do not need to know it and thus fill your mind with more wrong information that will not help you survive if the assassin comes after you again."

With that, the Ghostly God vanished as suddenly as he came, leaving Braim all alone in his room. While Braim was glad that the Ghostly God was gone, his stomach grumbled again, causing him to look at the sandwich on the floor sadly.

"He could have at least gotten me a new sandwich before he left," said Braim under his breath.

Chapter Eleven

RAYA LAY IN her bed in her apartment in World's End, shivering every now and then, despite the warmth of her blankets. She was certain that she must have come down with pneumonia, even though the katabans healer who had seen her had told her that she would be fine with some bed rest and food and water. Raya didn't believe the healer. She felt so awful and sick that she knew she had to have come down with *something*, even if she didn't yet know what.

I just want to go home now, Raya thought, tightening her grip on her blankets and trying to keep the tears from flowing. *I don't want to be in the Tournament anymore. I don't want to be on World's End. I just want to go back to Carnag. If that means I'll only become the Queen of Carnag when I get older, then so be it.*

Raya was used to assassination attempts on her life. She was royalty, after all, which meant that she had always been the prime target for assassination even from the day she was born.

But this one had been different. This was the closest that Raya had ever come to actually being killed in cold blood. And she *would* have been killed had it not been for the aid of the other godlings. There was no ifs, ands, or buts about it. Had things been even slightly different—had the others come even slightly late—Raya knew for a fact that she would not be lying here in her bed, thinking about how she could have died if things had turned out differently.

It brought to mind that letter that she had found on her bed on her first day on World's End, that letter that had claimed that justice always reaches the destination to which it travels. Raya had blown it off as nonsensical and without teeth, but now she was starting to think that it had been very serious. Might the letter have been placed on her bed by that four-armed assassin? But if so, why did he wait so long to attack her? And just what *was* he doing out on the street in the open like that anyway?

Despite going over these questions in her mind, Raya found that she didn't really care about the answers. What mattered was that she should have been dead and that World's End was no longer quite as safe as she used to think that it was.

But I can't leave until I win or lose in the Tournament, Raya thought. She brushed the tears out of her eyes. *And I am not even sure I want to compete at all. I mean, if I do win, then I'll become the Goddess of Deception, Thieves, and Horses.* Thieves! *What would Father say about that?*

But Raya had not yet tried to contact either of her parents and tell them about this recent assault on her life. It wasn't that she thought they wouldn't believe her—her parents always believed her about everything—but she just didn't want to worry them at the moment. It was an odd internal conflict. On one hand, she wanted to tell her parents all about what she just experienced, but on the other hand, she also didn't want to tell them for fear that they might become too worried about her ability to participate in the Tournament.

Raya put her hands over her face. This was all too much for

her. Raya hadn't expected to be feeling such stress before the Tournament started. All she wanted to do was sleep and forget about it all, but she knew that she couldn't even do that much, because she remembered what Braim had said earlier, about how that same assassin had tried to kill him in his sleep not long ago, which meant that he might try to do the same thing to her if she wasn't careful.

Despite how tired and worn out she felt, Raya sat up and swung her legs over the side of her bed. She then stood up and made her way to the door of her room, which she cracked open slightly and peered through to look at the living room of her apartment.

She saw Carmaz lying asleep on the sofa with one arm draped over his body and the other hanging over the side of the sofa. He looked like he was sleeping deeply, his chest rising and falling with his breath, but he was completely silent. He didn't snore at all, which Raya found made him a lot better than some noblemen she had once known.

Raya wasn't sure exactly why she had asked for Carmaz to stay in her apartment with her. As a matter of fact, Raya couldn't remember much about the actual attack at all. The trauma must have messed with her memories. She just remembered Carmaz and his friend (whose name she honestly could not remember at the moment, probably because his friend hadn't especially impressed her and wasn't even participating in the Tournament) saving her from the assassin, but even they would have gotten killed if Braim and the others had not arrived in the nick of time.

Raya didn't understand why Carmaz had bothered to try to save her. Perhaps he had been sent by Alira to fetch her when she stormed away from the Stadium, but even so, he had put his own life at risk just to save hers. And the two of them didn't even know each other that well. Of the few interactions they had had so far, they had all been fairly antagonistic. She had never met anyone from Ruwa before. In fact, until she met Carmaz, Raya had assumed that anyone from that island was an uncivilized savage who didn't even know how to count beyond ten.

But Carmaz was completely different from the stereotype that she knew. While hardly as handsome as some of the princes and noblemen that she had known back on Carnag and Shika, Carmaz still looked far better than someone from Ruwa had any right to look. He was also a lot smarter and stronger than most of the handsome princes she knew, though a lot less respectful than most.

More strangely, though, was why Carmaz had agreed to protect her at all. It was possible that Carmaz had explained his reasoning for staying in her apartment with her at some point, but that had probably happened while her mind was traumatized and so she had probably missed it. Still, Carmaz had not seemed like he liked her all that much, so why would he agree to stay here with her, especially since she already had some guards outside?

Whatever Carmaz's motives may have been, Raya found that she liked the idea of him protecting her. Maybe there wasn't much that Carmaz could do against the assassin, should that assassin ever attack her again, but just the knowledge that he was here with her made Raya feel much safer than she had since the attack.

She considered going out and waking him up, but then decided that Carmaz needed to sleep perhaps even more so than she did. Even so, Raya stood there watching him for a few minutes longer before closing the door and returning to her own bed, having found that she was actually tired enough to rest after all. And she slept well that night, in spite of all of that had happened recently.

Chapter Twelve

CARMAZ AWOKE WHEN he heard a loud knocking at the door to Raya's apartment. It sounded like someone was trying to bash down the door with a battering ram and Carmaz was too tired at first to get up and answer it.

Go away, Carmaz thought, closing his eyes and hoping that whoever was knocking at the door at this awful hour of the morning would give up and find someone else to bother. *I'm sleeping.*

Then he heard a familiar voice on the other side of the door shout, "Hey, Carmaz, it's me! Open up."

That was Saia's voice. Of that, there was no doubt. That made Carmaz sit up, brush back his messy, curly hair, yawn, and then stand up. His body ached all over and, despite the warmth of the room, he shivered like he had come down with a cold. His stomach growled and his throat was dry. Carmaz had expected to feel the pain in his body when he awoke this morning, so he didn't complain, especially when he remembered how awful he used to feel upon waking up on the floor of his hut on Ruwa what seemed like a lifetime ago now.

Still, Carmaz took his time crossing the short gap between the sofa and the door, muttering, "Coming, coming," as he did so, though he doubted Saia heard him, because his friend was still hammering on the door like his life depended on it.

Then Carmaz grabbed the doorknob, took a deep breath to ready himself for whatever Saia had come to talk with him about, and then opened the door.

Saia stood in the doorway, but unlike Carmaz, he looked like he had rested well and was up and raring to go. Carmaz did not see any of the guards that had been placed outside of Raya's apartment to protect him and her, but he was too tired to ask where they might have gone.

"Hey, brother, what's up?" said Saia, his tone too cheery and loud for this time of the morning. "How'd your night with Raya go?"

Carmaz shook his head and looked at Saia in confusion. "What?"

"You know, your night with her," said Saia. He leaned forward and whispered, probably to make sure that Raya didn't hear this, "It's not every night you get to sleep with the princess of one of the most powerful nations in the Northern Isles, after all."

"Sleep with—?" Carmaz repeated. His anger woke him up better than any cup of coffee could. "I slept on the sofa all night. Raya slept on her bed, in her room, with her door closed. We only talked for a few minutes before she went to sleep. Nothing happened between us."

"It's okay, Carmaz, I won't judge," said Saia, putting a hand on Carmaz's shoulder like he always did when he wanted to reassure Carmaz that he could trust him. "Sometimes trauma brings people together and they do things they don't always—"

Carmaz slammed the door shut and turned away, intending to go back to the sofa and sleep in for the rest of the morning, before

Saia's insistent knocking on the door caught his attention again, along with Saia's slightly muffled voice saying, "Hey, man, it was just a joke. Sorry if I offended you. Could you let me in? Please?"

Carmaz considered telling Saia to go away and never come back, but he had forgiven Saia for far worse offenses than this in the past. So he turned around and opened the door to see Saia— who, he was pleased to see, looked far more sheepish than he had a few seconds ago—standing there.

"Come in," said Carmaz with a yawn, stepping aside. "But don't you dare insinuate anything between me and Raya while you are here. Understand?"

"Perfectly, sir," said Saia, stepping inside as he said the word *sir* with sarcasm. "But seriously, if you and Raya got together—"

"Say one more word, and I'll drop kick you off the top of this building," said Carmaz as he closed the door and glared at his friend. "Personally."

Saia gulped and immediately changed the subject. "So, brother, I just came by to see how you were doing. Haven't heard from you or anyone else since that assassin's attack last night. Any updates?"

Carmaz yawned again and shuffled toward the sofa, trying to ignore the pain caused by every step. "No. I just woke up. Haven't heard from the gods or anyone else."

"Huh," said Saia. "I don't like that. What I heard is that some of the gods have actually been leading the search for our mysterious assassin personally, though they haven't found any clues yet as to his real identity, obviously."

Carmaz did not respond to that. He just sat down on the sofa again, stretched out on it, and pulled his blanket up to his chin before looking at Saia again. "How did you even get here? I thought we were all supposed to stay in our apartments while the assassin was still at large."

"Maybe you godlings are, but no one seems to care about me," said Saia with a shrug. "I just walked out of my apartment, asked around and got directions to yours, and then came here. I think the gods and katabans living here put less value on my life than on yours because I'm not a godling. Why, I could vanish off the face of Martir and I doubt any of them would notice."

"But what about the guards who are supposed to stand guard outside the door?" said Carmaz, rubbing his eyes to get the sleep out of them. "Where are they?"

"I told 'em that Alira sent me to pick you two up," said Saia. "I also told them that the hot bread cart down the street was having a special discount for Soldiers of the Gods. They must like hot bread, because they left almost as soon as I told them about it."

"Did you think about what they might do when they reach the hot bread cart and find out that there *isn't* a special discount for Soldiers of the Gods?" asked Carmaz.

Saia shook his head. "Nope. But I doubt they'll get too angry. I mean, they must know that I'm your friend. Obviously, they will just think that I wanted to see my best friend in the world badly enough to lie to them."

Carmaz didn't think so. The Soldiers of the Gods seemed to take their job with the utmost seriousness. He doubted they would be very happy to learn that a human had fooled them, especially a human who technically shouldn't even be on World's End at all. He dreaded having to convince the Soldiers to not kick Saia into the Crystal Sea and force him to swim all the way back to the Northern Isles himself.

Saia glanced toward the door to Raya's room and opened his mouth, but Carmaz said, "What did I say about talking about my relationship with Raya?"

Saia held up his hands defensively. "Hey, I wasn't going to ask about that. I just wanted to know how Raya is doing is all."

"She's fine, as far as I know," said Carmaz. "Slept straight through the night and hasn't come out of her room once. She probably isn't even aware that you're here or that it's morning yet."

"Okay," said Saia. He scratched the back of his neck. "That assassin sure was scary, wasn't it? Much scarier than anything the Swamp of Light has. Makes me glad it's gone."

"For now," said Carmaz. "I imagine it will attack again at some point, though when, I don't know."

"But maybe it won't," said Saia hopefully. "Everyone is looking for it now, which means it will be harder for it to attack again. Maybe it will even give up entirely."

Carmaz shook his head. "Do you honestly believe that? That thing clearly isn't like you or me, so it will probably strike again soon, though when and who its next victim will be, I don't know."

"I sure hope it's not me," said Saia with a shudder. "I don't think there's anything I could do against something like that if it wanted to kill me."

"It probably won't," said Carmaz, "since you're not a godling, after all. Based on what Braim said, it sounds like it is targeting godlings for some reason. If it kills you, it will only be because you got in its way."

"Yeah," said Saia, "I know, but it still freaks me out. If it kills you, then that will definitely destroy any hopes of resurrecting Ruwa to its former glory."

Carmaz frowned and looked away. "Don't talk to me about Ruwa."

"But why not?" said Saia. "Sure, you aren't going to become the God of Martir, but surely you can still do some good as the God of Humans, right? I mean, I don't exactly know what a God of Humans even does, but that is still a ton of power that you as a mortal don't even have."

"Maybe, but ..." Carmaz tried to put his feelings into words. "I'm just disappointed. I don't see how I can do all of the good that I want to do with such a massive decrease in power and influence. It messes up my plans."

"Look on the bright side," said Saia. "You can probably still do a lot of stuff. All of the gods are obscenely powerful, after all, even if the God of Martir is more powerful than all of them."

"Yeah, but what if whoever becomes the God of Martir tells me not to help Ruwa?" said Carmaz. "That is a possibility, you know."

"Well, what if the new God of Martir is Braim?" said Saia. "Yeah, I know that neither of us really knows him all that well, but Braim seems like a swell guy to me. I'm sure he'd allow you to help Ruwa as much as you want if he became the God of Martir."

"You're assuming that he will," said Carmaz. "There are nineteen other godlings also competing for that spot. If it went to any of them, and the winner turns out to have different goals from mine, then we might as well give up."

169

"Well, you can't give up anyway," said Saia. "Remember, Alira said that you only get out of the Tournament if you win or lose or are disqualified because you broke one of the rules."

"When did I say I was giving up?" said Carmaz, looking at Saia again. "I'm still going to participate in the Tournament and I am still going to win. I will figure out how to make this sudden turn of events work even if I didn't plan for it."

"Great," said Saia. "For a moment there I really *did* think you were going to give up, but I should have known better. After all, you never give up on anything, no matter how hard it gets."

"Stubborn as a mule, Grandmother always used to say about me," said Carmaz with a smile. "Wonder what she would say now if she could see me here, with a real chance at becoming a god?"

"She'd probably just tell you to stop moping and win the Tournament," said Saia with a chuckle. "She'd probably also tell that assassin not to kill her kids unless it wanted to die an early and painful death at her hands."

Carmaz chuckled also. Then he yawned and said, "Okay, now I can't get back to sleep. Might as well get up."

He threw the blankets off his body, sat up again, and stood up. Stretching his limbs, Carmaz said, "Saia, could you check the pantry for any—"

Carmaz was interrupted by the door to Raya's room bursting open and Raya herself staggering out. She looked a lot better than she had last night. Her hair was done in simple but attractive braids, her clothing was dry, and there were no bags under her eyes at all.

Nonetheless, she stopped and then moaned as if she was in extreme pain, prompting Saia to say, "Raya, what's wrong?"

"Ooooh ..." Raya moaned. She rubbed her arms and shuddered. "So much pain ... most pain I've ever felt in my whole life ..."

That did not surprise Carmaz in the slightest. Raya was probably experiencing all of the pain her body taken the night before. It was no shock to him that she was taking it badly. As the prim and proper Princess of Carnag, Carmaz figured that the worst pain Raya had ever felt was getting a paper cut from turning the gilded pages of an expensive and heavy book.

Then, without warning, Raya staggered forward toward Carmaz. She fell into his arms, forcing him to catch her so she wouldn't fall onto the floor and hurt herself, and moaned again. She looked up at Carmaz with a smile and said, "Oh, thank you for catching me, Carmaz. You are a true gentleman, despite your humble origins from such a backwards island."

Carmaz looked at Saia, who shrugged as if to say *I'm not a princess, don't look at me.*

Then he looked back at Raya and said, "Er, you're welcome, Raya, but perhaps you should go back to your bed and rest a little while longer. You seem tired."

"Perhaps you're right," Raya sighed. Then she grabbed Carmaz far more tightly than she had last night and said, "And you can give me a massage to help get the pain out of my bones. Your hands are the perfect size for the job. I should know, since my personal massage therapist back on Carnag has similar-sized hands to yours."

Carmaz glanced at Saia again. This time, Saia gave him the thumbs up, as if to say, *You just struck gold, my friend. Keep up the good work.*

171

Carmaz decided not to look to his friend for advice in dealing with this situation any longer. Instead, he raised Raya to a standing position and said, "Well, Raya, I don't have any experience massaging anyone, so I doubt I'd do a good job."

"That's fine," said Raya, whose pain seemed to have magically disappeared all of a sudden. "I can teach you where to touch me, you know. It's something I have a lot of experience in. I think it will be fun."

Carmaz immediately let go of Raya. Raya—who had been leaning on Carmaz for support—fell on her bottom with a "Hey!" She then glared up at Carmaz, who stepped away from her with what he hoped was an apologetic look on his face.

"Oh, sorry, silver spoon, looks like I accidentally let go of you," said Carmaz, his tone apologetic. "It must be because I just got up and am so, so tired. I didn't sleep very well last night, you know, so I'm not as focused as I usually am."

Raya stood up and brushed off her clothes. She then glared at Carmaz again, said, "Hmph!" and stomped off back into her room, slamming the door shut behind her as she entered.

As soon as she was gone, Saia walked over to Carmaz and said, in a low voice, probably so that Raya wouldn't hear him, "What did you do that for, man?"

"What was—" Carmaz sighed before he lost his temper. "What do you mean? Are you talking about Raya?"

"No," said Saia, shaking his head. He poked Carmaz in the chest. "I'm talking about *you*. She clearly is interested in you, so why'd you blow her off like that?"

"Because frankly, I don't have time for romancing silly princesses like her," said Carmaz. "My focus is on my people. I would think that Raya, as the future ruler of her own people, would understand that, but I guess she doesn't."

"Yeah, but that doesn't mean you can't have some fun every once in a while," Saia said, slapping Carmaz on the shoulder. "I mean, not only is she as beautiful as a goddess, she's the princess of an entire nation. If you play your cards right, you could become King Carmaz, King of Carnag, in the future."

"Why would I want to become the king of a foreign nation?" Carmaz asked. "Carnag isn't much of an ally to Ruwa, you know."

"Yeah, I know, but don't you think that being the ruler of one of the most powerful nations in the Northern Isles could still benefit you?" said Saia. Then he put his hands on his hips and sighed. "But now you blew it. I bet she probably hates you now. She'll probably start to spread nasty rumors behind your back about you. Seems like the kind of girl who'd do such a thing if she got rejected by a guy she liked."

"If that's the kind of woman she is, then that makes me want even less to do with her," said Carmaz. "Anyway, who even has time for that kind of romance when the Tournament is going to start today? I bet there are rules against godlings romancing each other during the Tournament anyway."

"I don't see why there would be," said Saia. "You two aren't even in the same bracket, so how could having a little fun possibly interfere with your competitiveness?"

"I don't know," said Carmaz. "And I don't care. I will think about getting a wife and kids later, assuming I don't win the Tournament, in which case I won't marry at all."

"But don't you see?" said Saia. "If you romance Raya, then

you will win no matter what. If you win the Tournament, you can become the God of Humans and use your powers to help Ruwa. If you lose, but get married to Raya, you can use Carnag's vast resources and wealth to send aid to Ruwa. And if you do both, then you can become the first ever god-king of Carnag, who can use his powers along with Carnag's wealth to make Ruwa into a great nation, maybe even the greatest nation on Martir. Doesn't that sound fantastic?"

"I'd rather spend a week with a boulder tied to my head than marry her," said Carmaz.

Saia sighed. "Very well, then. I see that you are clearly not going to listen to anything I say. I suppose it is up to me, then, to romance Raya and marry her at some point. For the good of Ruwa, of course."

Carmaz looked at Saia skeptically. "She hasn't even shown any interest in you. How, then, do you expect to romance her?"

"By using my obvious charms as a seducer," said Saia. "Remember Homal and how I successfully seduced her?"

"You mean that girl who ended up in our village and then stole a week's worth of food from everyone, which no one even realized until she had skipped town and caught a ride with a pirate ship heading who knows where?" said Carmaz. "And, correct me if I am wrong, but she also manipulated you into helping her by promising to marry you if you'd only give her the keys to the food supplies, yes?"

"The point is," Saia said, not hiding the annoyance in his voice, "you and I are both working toward the greater good, just in different ways. That's all."

"Different ways," Carmaz repeated. "Sure."

"Anyway, we need to get ready to leave," said Saia, looking out the window at the city, which was growing brighter and brighter due to the sun rising in the east. "The Tournament is going to start soon, so Raya needs to head on over there to get ready for the first challenge."

"I'll go check on her to make sure she's ready," said Carmaz.

He walked over to the door to Raya's room and knocked on it several times. "Raya? Are you ready to go? The Tournament is about to start and I just wanted to remind you in case you forgot."

"I am getting ready!" came Raya's shrill, offended voice on the other side. "Just leave me alone. You don't need to baby me, you know."

Carmaz looked over his shoulder at Saia, who shrugged as if to say *Don't look at me. It's your fault for offending her.*

Carmaz rolled his eyes, then said to Raya, "All right. Just wanted to make sure."

"Do you want to help me dress?" came Raya's voice again, this time sounding more seductive than offended. "Because I'm used to my servants back home dressing me and I think that—"

"No," said Carmaz. "You yourself said you didn't want me to baby you, after all, and I can't think of anything more babying than dressing someone for them. You'll do a fine job of it, I'm sure."

An offended "Hmph!" came from the other side, but Carmaz didn't care. He just turned and headed over to the kitchen area to get something to eat for breakfast, while Saia was scratching his chin and looking at the door to Raya's room as if he was thinking about how he could convince her to let *him* dress her.

What am I going to do with these two? Carmaz thought,

shaking his head as he opened the pantries of the kitchen for anything edible. *Anyway, time to eat. I'll think more about this later, after I've had a good breakfast of whatever I can find in here. I have a feeling I'm going to need extra energy today, even though I'm not going to be participating in this challenge.*

Chapter Thirteen

BRAIM WOKE UP this morning feeling groggier than usual. He dragged his body out of bed, stepped into the shower to wash off, threw on his Tournament uniform, had breakfast provided by the innkeeper (some type of cooked, greasy meat Braim had never had before that the innkeeper called *halar* that had no direct translation to Divina, along with eggs and some kind of juice that tasted like strawberries and oranges), and then left the inn to head for the Stadium. He had three Soldiers of the Gods accompanying him in order to protect him from that assassin from last night, each one armed to the teeth, although Braim had no idea how effective they might be at protecting him.

But Braim didn't focus too much on his bodyguards. There was that darkness again, floating in the back out of his mind just out of reach of his conscious thought. It reminded him of his conversation last night with the Ghostly God, as well as the Ghostly God's theory about why Braim felt that way.

Braim did not really remember Uron all that well. True, he had regained his body by stabbing Uron with the ghostly sword that he used to have (the sword that had vanished when he returned to the physical plane, unfortunately), but like most things from his time as a ghost, Braim didn't remember that too well, either. The others had told him that Uron was a wicked, evil being

177

who could not be trusted, which he figured was true based on the few memories he had of the being who also went by the alias 'Great Snake.'

But it seemed logical that the darkness that seemed to follow Braim everywhere was simply the remnants of Uron's previous possession of his body. It was the only explanation that made any sense. Even so, Braim wondered if there might be another explanation that made even more sense.

Could Uron even somehow still be influencing my thoughts? Braim thought. *Nah. Uron's gone. He's never coming back. Like the Ghostly God said, his consciousness is no longer independent of the universe, so there's no way he could influence me now.*

Despite that, Braim wished he had some way of getting rid of the darkness that followed him everywhere. It made enjoying life harder, because he felt a constant sense of impending doom wherever he went and whatever he did. It may have simply been one of those things that would go away on its own, given time, but whether that was true or not, Braim didn't know and would not know for some time.

In any case, Braim arrived at the Stadium without running into the assassin or any other problems on the way there. His bodyguards insisted that Braim go in by himself, because they had not been given authority to follow Braim into the Stadium and that he was probably safe from the assassin in there anyway. Braim supposed that that was probably true, but he still didn't like seeing his three bodyguards walk off and leave him alone.

I can take care of myself, Braim told himself, patting his wand in its holster at his side. *After all, I've had two encounters with that assassin guy so far and have survived both. I've got nothing to worry about.*

So Braim pushed open the doors and entered the Stadium lobby, which he discovered to be full of godlings once again. It looked like everyone was present, but they were not all mixed together again as usual. Instead, a good chunk of them stood in line on one side of the Stadium, going into a door on the right side of the lobby. On the left was another, much smaller line of about twenty people, which was going into another door. Braim saw both Raya and Yoji in that line, which told him that that was probably the line for the participants of the Hollech Sub-Bracket Challenge.

Then Braim heard someone say, "Hey, Braim, over here!" and he looked over to see Carmaz and Saia in the first line, standing at the back of it and waving at Braim to join them. Braim walked over as quickly as he could and soon stood behind the two of them in the line, which gradually grew smaller as the godlings ahead of them stepped into the open door at the end.

"Hey, guys," said Braim to Carmaz and Saia. "How did your night go? Any news on the assassin?"

"None so far," said Carmaz, shaking his head. "We haven't heard any news from the gods, so we're assuming that the assassin is still out there."

"Uh huh," said Braim. "Well, I'm glad to hear that you guys weren't murdered in your sleep, at least. So where does this line go, anyway?"

"To the Stadium's box," said Saia. "You missed Alira's explanation. She said that the rest of us godlings who aren't participating in the Hollech Bracket are supposed to go to the Stadium's box and watch the Hollech participants compete in the

179

challenge."

"That includes Raya and Yoji, right?" said Braim. He looked at the line, where he saw Yoji and Raya talking.

"Yes," said Carmaz. "Raya didn't want to participate, but she went ahead and did it anyway because there's no backing out of the Tournament at this point."

"Surprised that Raya didn't try to bribe a katabans to take her home," said Braim. "Guess she's resigned to her fate by now, huh?"

"More or less," said Carmaz. "It wouldn't surprise me if she intentionally throws the Tournament so she'll get disqualified. She spent the entire trip to the Stadium complaining about being in the Hollech Bracket."

"And trying to seduce Carmaz," Saia said. "She was trying to elicit sympathy from him, but Carmaz didn't show her any. I did, but she didn't seem to appreciate it much coming from me."

"What?" said Braim. He looked over at Raya, who he now noticed was glancing at Carmaz not-so-furtively, apparently not paying attention to whatever Yoji was saying. "She was trying to seduce Carmaz?"

"Let's not talk about it, please," said Carmaz, almost begging Braim to drop the subject. "Raya is crazy. Let's leave it at that."

Braim was not quite sure what to think about this new piece of information, but he decided to respect Carmaz's wishes and not bring it up again. He just followed the rest of the godlings through the doorway, which lead to a set of stairs that took them up higher and higher with every step. It was slow-moving, however, due to the eighty godlings that had to go in an orderly line up the stairs, but soon the top of the stairs came into view, an open doorway that, as Braim soon discovered, led into a large box with about a hundred seats in neat, rising rows that were in front of a thick gray stone wall with no windows or holes in it, which made Braim wonder how they could see the field where the challengers were.

There was apparently no particular order to the seating, so everyone sat pretty much wherever they wanted. Braim, Carmaz, and Saia took up some seats near the back, but they weren't alone. Tashir, the shark-headed aquarian godling from last night, also took a seat next to them. He still had his sword, even though there was no reason for it, seeing as it was unlikely that a fight of any sort would break out in here.

"Hey, Tashir," said Braim, smiling at the aquarian, despite not knowing him very well. "How are you?"

"Fine," said Tashir. Like most aquarians, he had that strange gurgly accent whenever he spoke in Divina, though it wasn't as bad as some aquarians that Braim had heard. "You?"

"Great," said Braim. "Heard anything about that assassin from last night?"

"No," said Tashir, shaking his head. "I stayed up all night listening for it, but it did not come after me, so I managed to get a few hours of sleep before breakfast."

"You mean you aren't tired at all?" said Braim.

"Of course not," said Tashir. "I have trained my body to require the absolute minimum amount of sleep in order to function at its maximum. I sleep no more or less than I need to, and as a result, I am rarely tired."

Saia, who sat on the other end of the seats away from Braim, leaned forward and pointed at Tashir's sword. "What's up with your sword? It was glowing last night. I've never seen a glowing sword before."

Tashir rested his hand on the handle of his blade. "I am a practitioner of the magical style that you humans call makhimancy. In essence, sword magic."

"So you're a mage?" said Saia, who seemed very interested in Tashir's abilities. "But where's your wand?"

"My sword acts as my wand," said Tashir. "My sword is made out of a special type of metal that is capable of handling the magical energy I channel through it."

"I think we offer makhimancy classes at North Academy," said Braim, stroking his chin, "though I've heard it's one of the toughest magical disciplines to learn."

"It is," said Tashir, nodding. "The art of makhaimancy requires its user to be both physically and mentally fit, whereas most ordinary magic simply requires mental fitness from its users. Makhimancers must master swordplay and magic, which is a much tougher combination to learn than you might think."

"Is Malya a makhimancer as well?" said Saia, glancing down at the other godlings in the seating rows below them. "I saw that she had two swords that glowed like yours."

Tashir folded his arms over his chest and scowled. "I suppose she is, but her form of makhimancy is nowhere near as efficient as mine. It is the dual sword style, which is far less effective than my single sword style. Though that doesn't surprise me, seeing as I've noticed that you humans tend to go for style over substance in many areas of your lives."

Braim was pretty sure he should be offended by Tashir's generalization about humans, but he was frankly too distracted by the darkness settling in his mind to care. Carmaz, on the other hand, did look rather offended, while Saia said, "So there is one-sword style makhaimancy and dual sword style. Is there a three-sword style version of makhaimancy?"

"Three-sword style?" Tashir repeated incredulously. "How would you hold the third sword? Between your teeth, perhaps? How ridiculous."

"Just checking," said Saia. "Anyway, where do you come from? Are you from the Undersea?"

"Considering that I am an aquarian, yes," said Tashir. "I come from the country of East Yudra. Have any of you heard of it?"

Braim, Carmaz, and Saia shook their heads.

"Well, it is a beautiful country, set in the middle of a vast coral reef that is famed throughout the Undersea for its sheer beauty," said Tashir. "It is in that country that I was born and raised, though I learned makhaimancy after I went to the Surface."

"Can you fight well on both the Surface and the Undersea?" said Braim.

"Yes," said Tashir, nodding. "I have spent years training in both environments. I prefer to fight underwater, but I can fight just as well on land."

"Interesting," said Braim. "Changing the subject, does anyone know what is supposed to happen next?"

"In the Tournament?" said Tashir. "Well, Alira explained that we will be able to watch the other godlings below as they participate in the Hollech Sub-Bracket Challenge, which should be starting any minute now."

"So what's the Sub-Bracket Challenge, then?" said Braim.

"She didn't say," said Tashir with a shrug. "I imagine it must have something to do with deception, thieves, or horses, though I don't know for sure."

"I hope Raya wins against her opponent," said Saia, folding his hands behind his head and resting his feet on the back of the chair before him, causing the godling sitting there to glare at him, though Saia apparently didn't notice. "I think she'd make a great goddess."

"Why?" said Tashir. "She certainly doesn't seem very special to me. She may be royalty, but she stomped off after she was assigned to a bracket that she doesn't like and almost got herself killed as a result. She seems like a very foolish girl to me."

"What about Yoji?" said Carmaz. "You know, the kid mage? Anyone know anything about him?"

"I spoke with him because he showed interest in my sword," said Tashir. "He told me that he's a child prodigy and student of the Thief's Way. Hollech was his favorite god, so of course he was ecstatic after learning which bracket he was put into."

"Didn't he mention being in the Itrija School of Magic?" said Carmaz. "I've never heard of that school."

"I have," said Braim. "They're known as the second best human magical school in the world. They don't really like North Academy all that much, mostly because they've been trying to take our position as best human magical school in the world for decades, with little luck."

"Wonder how well he will do," said Carmaz, scratching his chin. "If he's a mage, that gives him a pretty large advantage over Raya, seeing as she doesn't know any magic at all. I wonder if they will have to compete in the same challenge at some point."

"Always a possibility," said Tashir. "I, personally, would like Yoji to be the winner. He is a bright and eager young lad who seems less spoiled than Raya."

"The idea of making a kid like that into a god, though, kind of scares me no matter whether they're a 'child prodigy' or not," said Braim with a shudder. "I've seen some of the kids his age at North Academy. While they're not stupid by any means, they're still kids, with all of the positives and negatives that that entails."

"How is Yoji a 'child prodigy,' anyway?" said Saia. "Sounds suspicious to me."

"Yoji told me that Skimif visited his mother when she was pregnant with him and blessed him prior to his birth," Tashir said. "That's what he thinks gave him his natural magical talent. I have no idea if that is true or not, but he does seem to have an advanced understanding of magic for a kid his age, considering how he briefly discussed with me the Five Principles of Elemental Magic and how humans and aquarians apply said principles differently."

"So he's smart and magically-inclined, then," said Carmaz. "Clearly, that gives him an edge over Raya."

"Raya will probably do well," said Saia. "I don't know how, but I'm sure that she will."

"Anyone know anything about the other participants in the Hollech Bracket?" said Braim, because he saw that Carmaz was going to voice his disagreement over how well Raya would do and he didn't want these two arguing about the matter with the first challenge about to start.

"Nay," said Tashir, shaking his head. "I have tended to avoid that group, aside from Raya and Yoji, because they have struck me as an untrustworthy group of individuals."

"Gee, you think that a group of beings who are competing for the position of God of Deception and Thieves might be *untrustworthy*?" said Carmaz, the sarcasm dripping from his words. "Wow, I would never have guessed that."

Tashir looked more than a little irritated by Carmaz's sarcasm, but before he could talk, Alira appeared at the front of the seats where everyone could see her. She clapped her hands, causing all conversation among the spectators to die off immediately as everyone looked at her.

"The Hollech Sub-Bracket Challenge is about to begin," said Alira. She gestured at the blank stone wall behind her. "From this place you will be able to see all of the participants in the Challenge as they attempt to conquer it."

"But Judge, how will we be able to see them with that wall in the way?" asked one of the godlings sitting in the front rows. "It's not like we can see through solid stone, after all."

"A good point that I was just about to address," said Alira. She waved behind her. "This is how you will be able to see how everyone is progressing."

As Alira waved her hands, ten shimmery bubble-like squares came into existence behind her until they filled up the entire wall. Each bubble-like square showed nothing on their surfaces, which made Braim wonder what those were supposed to do.

"These are your viewer bubbles," said Alira. "Each bubble will focus on two challengers at once, so you can view whichever individual pairing you want without having to strain your eyesight. As each challenge is completed, the bubbles will vanish, until the entire Sub-Bracket Challenge is over."

That's convenient, Braim thought, reclining in his chair as his eyes darted from bubble to bubble, wondering which one would show Raya and which one would show Yoji.

"But the challengers will not be able to hear you through the bubbles," Alira continued. "You can talk all you want, but they won't hear a word you say. They will not even be aware that you are watching them. They will behave as if they are entirely alone within the Stadium."

"I have never heard about this kind of magic before," Tashir muttered to Braim. "How about you?"

Braim shook his head. "Me neither. Maybe it's exclusive to Alira?"

Tashir shrugged as Alira continued speaking.

"The gods are also viewing this match from the Temple," said Alira, "and I, of course, will also be watching the bubbles so that I can intervene in the unlikely event that any godlings attempt to cheat."

Alira waved her hand to the side and a throne that looked much like the thrones that the gods sat on back in the Temple materialized to the left of the seats. "And so, without further ado, let the first challenge of the Tournament of the Gods begin."

Chapter Fourteen

LTHOUGH RAYA WAS still angry at Carmaz for rejecting her every advance, she hadn't yet given up him. He reminded her of a story that she had once read, in which a handsome prince repeatedly rejected the advances of the equally beautiful princess who had fallen in love with him. The princess had chased the prince for years until he finally gave in, at which point the two were married, had ten children, and went down in history as the most loving married couple that had ever walked the face of Martir. Their relationship was even said to have been blessed by Yashira, the Goddess of Love herself.

Now Raya sincerely doubted that that story had ever happened, but she liked its overall message: Never give up on your dream man, even if he doesn't know that he wants you at first.

Even so, Raya had spent the trip from her apartment to the Stadium without speaking a word to Carmaz. She had no problem with admitting—to herself, at least—that she was upset at Carmaz's constant rejections of her advances, but even when she was stewing in her anger, a part of her was busy figuring out a way to woo him anyway. She knew there had to be some way to do it. Carmaz might have *thought* that he was not interested in her or in romance, but she knew better.

But upon arriving at the Stadium, Raya had to put her plans on hold, because Alira told her to get in line with the other nineteen participants in the Hollech Sub-Bracket Challenge. Thus, Raya found herself standing in line with Yoji, the young mage from yesterday who had helped save her, Carmaz, and Saia from the assassin.

Yoji, for reasons known only to himself, took this opportunity to brag about how he was the smartest student in his school, how he was even better than some of the teachers, and how he had originally been intending on graduating this year before he had learned about his destiny as a godling. Raya at first thought that Yoji might be attracted to her (a horrifying thought) and was trying to impress her with his accomplishments, but the more she listened to Yoji's endless bragging, the more she realized that he just liked to talk about himself and how awesome he was. He barely complimented her on her beauty or said anything else to even hint that he might find her attractive.

Thus, Raya felt safe in ignoring most of his bragging, especially when it became clear that Yoji didn't even notice that she wasn't listening. She had a feeling that she could walk away for a few hours and then come back to find Yoji still bragging about his accomplishments to empty air.

As as result, Raya had plenty of time to think about the Tournament. She still didn't want to be here anymore, now that she was no longer in the running for the position of Goddess of Martir, but during the night she had come to a change of heart. She had originally planned to intentionally throw this first challenge so she could go back to Carnag, but when she awoke this morning, it was like her subconscious had devised a

189

counterargument to that idea that had convinced her to give it her all.

Think about it, Raya, she had told herself earlier. *Maybe you won't become the Goddess of Martir, even though you obviously deserve that position more than anyone else—especially more than Braim Kotogs—but if you give up now, then you won't ever become a goddess at all. If you try to win the Hollech Bracket, then you have an opportunity to rise higher still. You never know. Maybe down the line you will get an opportunity to become the Goddess of Martir.*

Of course, Raya didn't know for sure if she would ever get an opportunity to become the Goddess of Martir. But she figured that it was the gods themselves who had a higher chance of ascending to that position than anyone else. So—while she still found the position of Goddess of Deception, Thieves, and Horses to be horribly unfit for royalty such as herself—she decided that she would 'work her way up,' as some of her lower class servants put it, even if it took her a long time.

Besides, being a goddess of any sort is still better than being queen, isn't it? Raya thought. *I will still have more power than I know what to do with.*

The problem now was that Raya had no idea what the first challenge was going to have in it, so she couldn't adequately plan for it. Nor did she know who her challenger would be. It might be Yoji, or it might be any of the other eighteen challengers, most of whom she did not know except by sight.

But Raya decided that she would give it a shot. Worse case scenario, she lost and had to go back to Carnag, which was really where she wanted to be anyway. Best case scenario, however, she won and would be that much closer to achieving godhood, which was also what she wanted, despite not wanting this position in particular.

Yoji only let up on his bragging when the twenty Hollech Bracket participants went through the door into a room that was different from the lobby. First, it was much smaller. Second, it appeared more like a circular tunnel than an actual room, because there were entrances on either end that seemed to stretch on forever.

In front of the group were two normal-sized doors that had a stylized horse on them. Raya vaguely recalled Teacher, in her studies about the relations between gods and humans, telling her that the Hollechians often used the image of a stylized horse to represent Hollech. In fact, when Raya looked more closely, she saw that this wasn't just a stylized horse, but an image of a man with the head of a horse, which was the usual form that Hollech had been said to take prior to his death at Uron's hands.

There was no one else in the tunnel-like room besides Raya and the others, which made Raya wonder what they were supposed to do until Alira appeared before them without warning. The Judge still held her Rulebook in her arms, clutching it like it was the most important book in the world.

"Greetings, godlings," said Alira, adjusting her glasses as she spoke. "Welcome to the Hollech Sub-Bracket Challenge, the first sub-bracket challenge in the Tournament of the Gods. In this challenge, participants will be divided into pairs and the winner of each pair will then go onto the Hollech Bracket Challenge later on."

None of the godlings said anything in response to that, but

Raya was annoyed at Alira repeating information that they already knew. She felt like Alira was talking down to them, like the Judge thought that they were stupid children who had forgotten what they were supposed to do.

"As for what the first challenge is, you must compete with whoever you have been paired up with to be the first to tame one of Hollech's original Steeds," said Alira, "of which there are twenty."

Raya frowned. She looked at Yoji, who was nodding along like he understood what Alira was referring to. "What are Hollech's Steeds?"

"Well," Yoji said, in a tone that clearly said he had been waiting for someone to give him an opportunity to share his vast knowledge of the gods with them, "at the beginning of time, when the Powers finished laying the foundations of Martir, Hollech was given the order to make horses. So he created twenty horses, which he called his Steeds, from which every single horse in the world is descended. The Steeds are said to be immortal and undying, but very few mortals have ever actually seen them."

"What happened to them when Uron killed Hollech?" asked Raya.

"No one knows," said Yoji, "but obviously, they must have survived, otherwise Alira couldn't have set up this challenge for us. A challenge, I might add, that I will easily sweep. I know everything there is to know about the Steeds, in addition to the knowledge I have on general horse behavior and attitudes, so I shouldn't have any trouble at all winning this."

Raya knew very little about horses. Carnag didn't have very many, and of those few that it did have, Raya never rode them, mostly because their job was to pull along the royal carriage. She had always thought that horses were large, ugly, and disgusting creatures, which made her wonder why anyone saw any beauty or majesty in them.

But there was no way that Raya would ever admit her ignorance of horses to Yoji or anyone else. She just said, "Ah, yes, I, too, will have an easy time doing this. I ride horses all the time on Carnag, so taming these ones should be easy."

"The Steeds are a little different from most horses, though, from what I've read," said Yoji. "For example, they're almost as smart as humans and are stronger than most horses. One story I read said that one Steed alone is as strong as ten thousand raging stallions."

"You don't think they'll kill us, do you?" asked Raya, keeping her tone calm and disinterested in order to hide the very real fear now starting to creep up her spine.

"Nah," said Yoji, shaking his head. "Well, unless you anger them. All the old stories say that the Steeds don't tolerate stupid or disrespectful people. Like in the story of Abacos, the First Steed, who kicked off the head of the arrogant human who tried to tame him. His head went flying all the way over a mountain, or so the story goes."

Unconsciously, Raya rubbed her neck, right where it connected to her head. "Really? Well, that is certainly a ... painful way to go."

"It's just a story," said Yoji dismissively. "Only children believe in those stories. Still, all of the research I've done—which is quite a bit, more so than even the most respected Hollechian scholars—states that the Steeds are not to be taken lightly, but of course *I* won't, seeing as I know more about them than they know about me, even if you take into account that not all of the stories about them are true."

Raya didn't know what to say to that, but thankfully, she didn't have to say anything, because Alira continued speaking, causing the other godlings to stop talking among themselves.

"After I pair you all together, you will then go through these doors," said Alira, gesturing at the two doors behind her. She then pointed down either tunnel. "Along the tunnel walls at regular intervals are doors that each pairing will have to step through. But each pairing must enter the Stadium's field at the exact same time as the others. I will let you all know when to enter the field.

"Now it is time to pair you all up."

Alira pulled another deck of cards from her robes and tossed them into the air. Raya had just enough time to see that there were about twenty cards in all, in a variety of colors ranging from blue to red to yellow and beyond, before the cards flew among the godlings. One of the cards flew toward Raya, causing her to catch it to avoid so it wouldn't fly into her face.

Looking down at the card she'd caught, Raya saw that her card was purple and had no text or pictures on it at all. Beside her, Yoji had a red card, which he was studying as if he thought that it would reveal the secrets of the universe to him (which, based on his bragging, he probably already knew, of course).

"Each card has a twin that shares it color," said Alira. "To find your challenger, you must find the godling with the same color card as you."

Yoji immediately leaned over to look at Raya's card, leaned a little too close to Raya for her liking, before he pulled back and said, "Darn it. Our cards have different colors, so it looks like we'll not be competing against each other today."

Raya nodded, but before she could say anything, an older man came up to her and said, "Do you have a purple card?"

Raya looked at the older man. He was probably middle-aged, though he looked a lot younger than that. He was quite muscular and fit, with a graying mustache which made him look a little odd to her. He wore a black tunic, similar to hers aside from the color and size. While he wasn't the largest man Raya had ever seen, he still looked like he could go toe-to-toe with an adult baba raga if he wanted.

"Um, yes," said Raya, holding up her purple card for the man to see. "What about you?"

The man held up his own card, a smile appearing under his thick mustache. His card was the same purple hue as hers. "Yep. Nice to meet you. My name is Zaos."

The man held out a large hand, which Raya's own, rather tiny hand disappeared into when she shook his. His hand was rough and dirty, like he was the kind of person who worked outdoors.

"Princess Raya Mana of Carnag," said Raya, looking up at the large man who was smiling at her as if she was his own daughter. "And you are from …?"

"Zinza," said Zaos. "You've probably never heard of it. It's a tiny, though wealthy, island located in the Friana Archipelago. Born and raised there."

"Ah," said Raya. "No, I have not heard of it, but now that you have told me about, I guess that I have."

Zaos nodded. "But I've heard of Carnag, even visited the island a few times in my youth. They make the best boots there.

In fact, I'm wearing some Carnagian boots right now."

Zaos raised one of his tall, thick legs to show that he was indeed wearing a genuine Carnagian leather boot. "Fits better than any boot I've worn in my life, which is hard to do, believe me, because we Zinzans tend to be big people, so finding clothes and footwear that actually fits is always a challenge."

"Well, on Carnag, you can find high quality, affordable boots in a variety of sizes and styles," said Raya. "We make only the best."

"And I believe that," said Zaos, lowering his boot onto the floor. "But you're the first princess I've ever met. Zinza doesn't even have royalty. It's such a small island that we practice a democratic government, where we vote in the Mayor of the island along with a Council to help him govern."

Raya made a face. "Ah, yes, democracy. I've heard of that, but it's not quite as good as a monarchy, if you ask me."

"Eh, both types of government have their upsides and downsides," said Zaos with a shrug. "Each nation needs to go with what works best for them. But in truth, I've always admired the great kings and queens of the Northern Isles, even though I'd never actually want to live under them. King Malock, your father, is someone who I have particularly respected, mostly because he was such a mischievous, adventurous sort in his youth, unlike some princes, who just sit around in their palaces all day waiting on their servants to meet their every whim."

"Yes, Father is certainly a great king, and I am proud to be his daughter," said Raya. "Anyway, what gods do you worship on Zinza?"

"All of them, more or less," said Zaos with a shrug. "Unlike most other nations, we Zinzans aren't united under one religion. You got your Grinfians, your Xocionians, your Kanonites, even a few Tinkarians here and there. In the last decade alone, we've had a Grinfian Mayor, a Tinkarian Mayor, and a Kanonite Mayor, in that order."

"How interesting," said Raya. "What kind of work did you do on Zinza prior to coming to World's End?"

"I was just a simple day laborer, is all," said Zaos rather humbly. "There are a lot of rich people there who don't like getting their hands dirty but still need physical labor done, so they hire me to do it. Sometimes I get some of my friends to help, but most of the time it's just me. Been doing it for forty years now, ever since I left home and decided to make my way in the world."

"Very interesting," said Raya, though in truth, she found herself losing interest in Zaos when he said he was a day laborer, because she had found the day laborers back in Carnag to be very boring conversationalists. "How have you taken to World's End?"

Zaos smiled. "It's huge. Bigger than Zinza or anywhere else I've ever been. But I am quite honored to be in the Throne of the Gods, you know. Never thought I'd live long enough to get a chance to come here, but I did, and now I even have a shot at becoming a god, of all things."

Despite Raya's general dislike of day laborers, she found something infectious in the older man's excitement. He seemed so genuine and sincere, which she found a rather refreshing difference from the stiff and formal way most royalty tended to behave.

So Raya said, "I guess you don't mind possibly becoming the God of Deception, Thieves, and Horses, then?"

"Why should I?" said Zaos. "Sure, I'm no big fan of lying or thieves or lying thieves, but I love horses and would love to be their god. Though truth be told, I'm not sure how good a god I could be to them, because I don't look much like a horse, which I think would make it harder for the horses to worship me."

Why does it seem like everyone else here loves horses but me? Raya thought, but aloud she said, "Well, if you win, then I'm sure the horses will respect your authority. Not like they're smart enough to rebel, right?"

"I don't know about that," said Zaos. "Horses are pretty smart. Not as smart as us humans, but smarter than we give them credit for. I used to own a horse that understood every word I said. Sometimes he tried to play dumb when I was telling him to do something he didn't like or didn't want to do, but that just goes to show how smart he was."

"I never thought of horses as being particularly intelligent creatures," said Raya.

"Well, you should, if you are going to respect them," said Zaos. Then he looked down at the purple card in his hand and looked back up at her. "But it looks like you and I are going to compete against each other, which means only one of us is going to get a shot at the title of God of Deception, Horses, and Thieves. Wish we could both win, but I guess there's only enough room in this world for one god or goddess like that, eh?"

"Yes, it would be nice if the two of us could win, but unfortunately we can't," said Raya. She held out her hand. "Let the best man or woman win, eh?"

Zaos took her hand and shook it again, but this time, he shook it a little harder than before, almost as if he was trying to harm her. When Raya looked into his eyes, she briefly saw a distaste in them that contrasted sharply with his friendly tone from before.

"Yes, Princess, sounds good to me," said Zaos, letting go of her hand and letting his own hand fall to his side. He then looked around at the other godlings, who were still trying to find their partners. "Sure would be awful if that assassin that tried to kill you last night showed up again, huh?"

Raya froze. She almost asked how he knew about that, but then realized that it wasn't exactly a secret. Still, just his mentioning of the assassin caused fear and panic to return full force to Raya's mind. She wanted to run away, but she kept her position, because she didn't want to look weak in front of him.

"Ah, yes, well, that would indeed be a bad thing," said Raya, brushing strands of her hair out of her eyes with a nervous laugh. "But you know, I don't think that that assassin will try to get me or anyone else today. If he tries, he'll be captured and stopped by the Soldiers."

"Mmm hmmm," said Zaos, though she didn't like the tone in which he said that. "Yep, the Soldiers are supposed to be real good at that. Still, if I had been attacked by an assassin like that just the night before, why, I'd never be able to concentrate on the challenge. Nope, I'd be watching every shadow, jumping at every sound I couldn't identify the source of, and not think clearly. I might even hide under my blankets and never come out again."

Raya's hands shook, but she quickly stopped that before Zaos could notice. "Yes, well, I think I will be just fine. That assassin was scary, yes, but I have nothing to worry about."

"And that is why your hands were just shaking a second ago, yes?" said Zaos. He leaned closer to her, his smile no longer

199

looking quite as friendly. "Just a tip, princess: If you want to win a competition—*any* competition—then you don't show genuine fear to your competitors that they can exploit."

Raya gulped, but wasn't sure what to say to that. All she knew was that Zaos was not nearly as friendly as he appeared. In fact, she had a feeling that he had put on that friendly face as an act, and nothing more.

Zaos stood up to his full height again, while at the same time, Alira said, "The last of the challengers have been paired up. Now go down the tunnels until you find a set of doors for each of you to enter. After everyone is set, I will then tell you when to enter the field."

Zaos, nodding at Raya, walked over to the two doors in front of the group. He took the right door, while Raya took the left, but Raya no longer looked at him. She kept her eyes resolutely on the door, now wondering just how much of Zaos's story had been true and how much of it had been false.

And he is probably wondering the same about me, Raya thought. *Unless he thinks I'm too naïve to lie about my past.*

In any case, Raya was quite glad when, about five minutes later, she heard Alira say, "Challengers, prepare to enter the field and begin the challenge. The first to succeed in taming their Steed will become one of the chosen ten that will go onto the Hollech Bracket Challenge. All of the Tournament rules apply and any cheaters will be punished accordingly."

Raya prepared herself mentally for whatever she was about to face. She still didn't look at Zaos, but she could sense that he wasn't looking at her, either, probably preparing for the challenge just like she was. She almost prayed to Grinf for aid before catching herself, as she was not certain that praying to the gods for guidance counted as cheating or not.

Finally, the doors opened before them and Alira said, "Let the first challenge of the Tournament begin!"

Chapter Fifteen

ON THE TWENTY viewer bubbles that showed the field of the Stadium, Carmaz saw all of the Hollech Bracket challengers emerge from doors with a stylized horseman on them. The bubbles displayed the competitors as clearly as if they were right there in front of him, even though they were probably several hundred feet below the box.

It didn't take long for Carmaz to spot Raya. She stepped out of the door, looking around somewhat uncertainly at her surroundings. She then went rigid when she spotted something off-screen, causing the bubble to blink and then show what looked like the biggest horse that Carmaz had ever seen in his life standing at the other end of the small enclosure in which Raya stood.

The horse was not merely big, but it also had a red mane that looked like flame and had sharp, angry-looking eyes that made even Carmaz feel unsafe around it, despite being nowhere near it. The horse—one of Hollech's Steeds—pawed the ground and sniffed the air, but it wasn't that it had not noticed Raya. Rather, Carmaz was under the impression that the horse simply did not think Raya worth its attention at the moment.

Wonder how she's dealing with that, Carmaz thought, trying not to smirk.

As if in answer to his thoughts, Raya seemed to have come to the same conclusion as him about the Steed's nature. As Carmaz predicted, she looked rather offended, but she still didn't approach it. She seemed deathly afraid of the horse, though whether it was because of its large size and its unfriendly appearance or because she was actually afraid of horses, he didn't know.

If she doesn't get over her paralysis soon, she'll end up losing before anyone else, Carmaz thought.

Then he noticed Yoji, whose bubble was directly above Raya's. Yoji had confidently approached his Steed, which had a silver mane and metallic eyes. He seemed to be having slightly more luck with his Steed than Raya was having with hers, although the Steed kept prancing just outside of his reach, eying him with distrust.

The rest of the participants weren't having much better luck, from what Carmaz could tell. The Steeds seemed to distrust the participants greatly, which was somewhat amusing to watch at first, but then it became boring after a while and Carmaz started to worry that this challenge would take all day.

Just as he thought that, however, he heard a clanging bell that caused him to look to the front of the seats. Alira was holding a bell in her hands and pointing at one of the bubbles, saying, "We have our first winner, Yoji Nama! He has successfully tamed Beluchi the Third Steed!"

Skeptical, Carmaz looked at Yoji's bubble and saw that Alira was correct. The Steed—Beluchi—was standing still by Yoji, who was stroking its mane and saying something to it in a low voice. He was even feeding it some kind of treats, though they were too small for Carmaz to see even on the viewer bubble.

203

"Yoji will move onto the Hollech Bracket Challenge," said Alira, who sounded very excited about it. "His opponent will be shipped back to his home island after the rest of the participants have finished taming their Steeds."

Yoji's bubble then vanished, as did the bubble to its right, which had featured Yoji's rival, although Carmaz didn't remember who that was. He just sat there, stunned at how quickly Yoji had won, while most of the other godlings began muttering among themselves, most of them marveling at how quickly Yoji managed to tame his Steed.

"Damn," said Braim, who sounded genuinely impressed. "That kid really knows his stuff, huh?"

"That he does," said Tashir, nodding. "I suppose all of his early bragging wasn't just empty air. He's a force to be reckoned with, all right. I'm just glad that I am not going in the Hollech Bracket. I don't think I'd stand a chance against him in a straight competition."

"Think Raya will win?" said Saia, who was leaning forward in his seat, his eyes locked on Raya's bubble. "Because she seems to be having a lot of trouble with her Steed."

"I guess it's possible," said Carmaz with a shrug. "But truthfully, I don't see her winning. I think she'll probably lose. And if she *does* win, then it will be by some kind of divine miracle."

"Can't say I'm enthusiastic about her chances of success, either," said Braim. "Not that she's not trying, but she clearly doesn't know the first thing about horses at all."

"She needs the luck of Goda if she is going to win," said Tashir flatly. "But to be fair, the others are also having trouble their Steeds. I doubt that she's the only one who doesn't know much about horses. Although if she can't get over her apparent fear of horses, then it seems to me that she is destined to fail."

As usual, there was a lot of truth in Tashir's words. Raya did manage to take one step toward the Steed, but she didn't move any further than that. She looked more like she wanted to be anywhere else but here, even though she had nowhere to run to.

I wonder if she's going to throw the match so she doesn't have to compete, Carmaz thought. *She wasn't very happy about being put in the Hollech Bracket, after all. It might be less that she is afraid and more that she just doesn't want to compete at all.*

Then—quite without warning—the bubbles flickered and vanished, showing the same blank stone wall from before.

Immediately, the rest of the godlings went into an uproar, shouting and asking what was going on and why had Alira turned off the bubbles. Alira silenced them, however, by ringing her bell loudly, so loudly that it drowned out their collective shouts of anger and confusion, forcing them all to become quiet and listen to her.

"I do not know why this happened or what caused this," said Alira in her most authoritative voice, although Braim caught a hint of fear under her authoritative tone. "I did not turn off the bubbles, but I do not know who did."

"Can you turn them back on?" asked one of the godlings sitting in the front. "I want to see how the others are doing."

"We will get to see them all again very shortly," said Alira. "But please remain seated. I will have this figured out soon enough."

The godlings did remain seated, but there was a lot of

grumbling and murmuring among them, like some of them didn't believe Alira when she said that she wasn't responsible for this sudden turn of events.

Braim looked at the others sitting on either side of him and said, "What do you guys think happened?"

"I have no idea," said Tashir. "Perhaps someone wrest control of the bubbles from Alira and forced them off?"

"But why would someone do that?" asked Saia, rubbing his hands together anxiously. "Is this some sort of dumb prank?"

"Probably not," said Carmaz. "This seems too well-planned to be a mere prank. I think that someone is trying to disrupt the Tournament."

Saia gulped. "You don't think that that 'someone' is the assassin from earlier, do you?"

"Maybe," said Carmaz. "Or maybe it's a friend or ally of that assassin. Of course, it could also just as easily be something less sinister."

"I don't know about that," said Braim, rubbing the back of his neck. "Alira is acting like it's something bad, so I figure it has to be something *really* bad if it's freaking her out like this."

Alira was facing the wall that the viewer bubbles had been in front of mere moments ago, frantically waving her arms at it like she was trying to cast a spell without really knowing how. Yet the viewer bubbles did not reappear, despite her best efforts to make them appear again.

Carmaz wished there was something he could to help, but unfortunately, he was not a mage and knew about as much about magic as a newt. He wondered if Raya and the other participants in the Hollech Bracket were still all right or if they were now at risk due to the fact that Alira couldn't see them anymore.

If I was an assassin, I'd take this opportunity to kill as many godlings as I could, Carmaz thought. *They're all alone, all separated, with nothing to help them except the Steeds, which are hardly a threat when you consider how untamed they are.*

While Carmaz still didn't like Raya all that much, he disliked the idea of her getting murdered even more. He had to figure out a way to ensure that she and the others were all right, but he wasn't sure how. He considered leaving the box and entering the Stadium's field through the door that the Hollech Bracket godlings had, but then he doubted that Alira would let him leave.

If that assassin really is *somewhere nearby, then it makes sense for us all to stay in one place where Alira can keep an eye on us,* Carmaz thought. *But that still leaves Raya and the others at risk. What if the assassin is killing them off one by one even as we sit here worrying?*

Carmaz couldn't take it. He hated leaving innocent lives at risk like this.

He stood up and looked down at Saia. "Coming with me?"

"Where?" said Saia, who looked bewildered by Carmaz's sudden movement.

"To the Stadium field, of course," said Carmaz. "We have to head down there to make sure that Raya and the others are all right."

"Hold on, Carmaz," said Braim. He grabbed Carmaz by the arm and, with surprising strength, pulled him back down into his seat. "You can't go down there. Alira told us to remain seated. She'll handle this on her own. She's the Judge. This is part of her job."

"I know, but the fact is, while Alira tries to figure out what happened here, Raya and the others are all at risk of being killed by that assassin," Carmaz argued, pulling his arm out of Braim's hand. "If I were an assassin trying to kill some godlings, I'd pick this opportunity to do so, when no one can see or stop me."

"And you think you can stop the assassin on your own, after it almost killed you?" said Braim. "I'm not convinced that there's much you can do to stop it even if it's here, frankly."

"I agree with Braim," said Tashir. "While it is possible that this sudden turn of events is due to the actions of that assassin from yesterday, it would be wiser to stay here until Alira is able to get the viewer bubbles working again."

Carmaz listened to Braim and Tashir, but he didn't agree with a single word that they said. He stood up again and said, "I'm going down there, whether you want me to or not."

With that, Carmaz climbed over the back of his seat and then ran down the steps leading to the door below. Saia followed, much to Carmaz's surprise, but he was glad that he had his best friend at his side anyway.

The two of them reached the exit quickly enough, but when Carmaz laid one hand on the doorknob to grab it, he had to yank his hand back. The knob had felt like it was on fire, even though there was no visible clues to hint at its heat.

"Carmaz, Saia," said Alira behind them, causing Carmaz and Saia to turn to see her glaring at them from behind her glasses. "Where do you two think you're going? I did not give either of you permission to leave."

"We know, Judge, but we think that the sudden and unexplained disappearance of the viewer bubbles is the responsibility of the assassin who tried to kill us yesterday," Carmaz said. "So we were going to go down to the Stadium floor to check on Raya and the others to confirm that the assassin isn't down there."

Alira rolled her eyes. "What a silly excuse. Of course they are fine. I would know if they weren't."

"But how?" said Carmaz. "If no one can see them right now, then how could you possibly know that they are fine?"

"Because I am the Judge and I know all that goes on within the Stadium," said Alira. She pointed at their now-vacant seats next to Braim at the back row. "Now return to your seats. I am perfectly capable of figuring out this issue on my own, without your unasked for help."

Carmaz wanted to continue arguing, but it now seemed utterly pointless, as Alira was clearly not going to let him or Saia go, no matter how persuasive their arguments might be. Still, he couldn't help but worry about Raya and the others anyway, so he wracked his brain for any possible argument he could use to convince Alira to let him and Saia go.

"I just want to help them, that's all," said Carmaz, even though he was aware that this wasn't much of an argument at all.

"I know, Carmaz, but the fact of the matter is, you are in no position to help anyone at the moment, especially if that mysterious assassin from yesterday is here," said Alira. "Now return to your seats or I will send you back to your apartment where you cannot view the events of the Tournament."

Carmaz's shoulders slumped. He wished that he was a mage, because then he might have been able to use magic to get out of here, but now it was pretty clear that he would just have to wait here and hope for the best.

So Carmaz nodded, albeit grudgingly, and was about to go climbing up the stairs back to his seat when the floor subtly shook under his feet.

The tremor was so subtle that Carmaz at first thought that it might have been his imagination at work, making him feel things that weren't there. Then the floor shook again. Still not hard enough to scare him, but enough that he was now certain that it was as real as anything and that he was not imagining it.

The other godlings must have felt it as well, because they were all looking around in fear, while Alira said, "Remain calm, everyone. I do not know what may be causing these tremors, but —"

She did not get to finish her sentence, because without warning, a portal popped into existence behind Braim. Braim looked over his shoulder just in time to see two large hands appear out of nowhere, grab his shoulders, and drag him directly into the portal before anyone else could react.

A second later, the portal closed, but the tremors didn't stop. If anything, they grew even worse, making Carmaz wonder if the entire Stadium was going to fall apart on top of them.

But Carmaz had little time to think about it, because soon a loud, shrieking noise assaulted his hearing, forcing him to his knees as he fell to the floor. Saia fell as well, while the other godlings slammed their hands over their ears to protect their hearing. Alira was shouting something, but it was impossible to tell what she was shouting because of the loud shrieking that seemed to come from everywhere at once.

Then Carmaz saw a crack in the floor, one that he hadn't

noticed before. And it was grower wider.

Chapter Sixteen

ONE MOMENT, BRAIM was just sitting in his seat in the Stadium's box, watching Carmaz arguing with Alira to let him and Saia go down to check on Raya and the other Hollech Bracket challengers. The next, he found himself sprawled on the ground in a place he was too disoriented at first to understand.

Scrambling to his feet, his head aching from the disorientation, Braim looked around at his surroundings. He was standing in what appeared to be the ancient stone hallways of a castle, but having never visited a castle of any sort before, Braim had no idea which castle this might have been. The air smelled ancient, but it also smelled of blood, which made him shudder. That, and it was cold. Not as cold as the Great Berg, but a lot colder than the Stadium had been.

Where the heck am I? Braim thought, looking around, hoping that he would see something that might jog his memory or clue him in to where he had ended up. *How did I get here? Who took me here?*

That was another issue. Braim did not see anyone else in here with him. The hallway was as silent as midnight. In fact, the hallway looked as though it had not been visited in years. There was a fine layer of dust on the floor and walls. Even so, Braim thought he felt someone watching him, even though there was nowhere that anyone could watch him from in the hallway without his knowledge.

It didn't help that the darkness in the back of Braim's mind was creeping up on him again. It almost overwhelmed him this time, but he forced it back in order to focus on his current situation. He had to, because he had a feeling that whoever had taken him here was not going to treat him kindly.

"Alira?" Braim said, though he didn't raise his voice very loudly because he didn't want to attract the attention of anyone he didn't want seeing him. "Carmaz? Saia? Raya? Tashir? Yoji? Malya?"

No answer from anyone. Braim looked over his shoulder, but didn't see anyone or anything down that way, either.

Looks like I really am all on my own here, Braim thought. He shivered at the thought. *Not good.*

Braim considered trying to teleport back, but then rejected the idea. For one, he wasn't a good teleporter. Sure, he could teleport short distances with no problem, but long distances (and he had a feeling that he was a *very* long distance from World's End) required more skill and magic than he was able to use.

For another, Braim had no idea exactly where he was in relation to World's End or how far he had teleported. And even if he did, that would require teleporting through solid rock, a feat that was technically possible, but only if you were a powerful mage with a lot of practice and experience in teleporting.

The truth of the matter was, Braim was neither (and based on what Jenur had told him, he had never been a very good teleporter even before his death). That meant he had to find out where he

213

was and how he got here on his own, as well as find out how to get back to World's End without help from the others.

Unfortunately, Braim wasn't sure whether to walk forward or backwards. There were no doors along the walls of the hallway in which he found himself, but he did see that both ends of the hall curved to the right. What lay beyond those curves, Braim didn't know.

Nor did he *want* to know, but the fact was that Braim had to go *some*where and he couldn't figure out how to get home just by standing around doing nothing. He would have to venture forth and deal with whatever lay ahead.

Holding his wand tightly in his hand, Braim decided to go forward, mostly on a whim more than anything. He took a deep breath and began walking, keeping his eyes and ears open for any possible traps, even though all of the evidence so far suggested that Braim was quite alone in this place.

As Braim walked, his footsteps loud due to the silence in the hall, he found that this place reminded him of North Academy's graveyard for some reason. He wasn't sure why. All he knew was that he felt a great sense of dread here, not helped by the darkness tugging at the back of his mind, the darkness that was trying to overwhelm him. It almost made him sick, but he ignored it because he could not afford to get sick at the moment.

Turning the corner, Braim saw a large, open doorway standing not far from him. Beyond it was a room, but it was hard to tell what was in that room because it was rather dark. Braim didn't want to enter that room at all, but he had nowhere else to go, so he steeled himself for whatever lay beyond the open doorway and entered the room.

As soon as Braim stepped beyond the doorway, the room's door slammed shut behind him. The sudden closing of the door made him jump and look over his shoulder, but now the door looked like it had fused with the wall, because he didn't see any hinges or doorknobs or knockers or anything else to indicate that a door had been there at all.

That's not a good sign, Braim thought.

Without warning, lights running along the top of the room glowed, dim white lights that offered Braim enough light by which to see the room itself.

In the center of the room was a depressed stone pit, in which lay what appeared to be a coffin, oddly enough, though it was currently closed, so Braim couldn't see what was in it. At the back of the room were five thrones of varying heights, though they were currently vacant of whoever might have normally occupied them. But Braim did see carvings on the backs of each throne that resembled the gods that had already passed: One for Skimif, one for Hollech, one for the Spider Goddess, and so on.

And when Braim looked at the coffin in the center more closely, he realized that it had an engraving of himself on it.

That's not a good sign, either, Braim thought.

That was when Braim heard something moving behind him. Without thinking, he leaped forward. And just in the nick of time, because four swords flew through the spot where he had been standing, swords that would have completely cut him up if he hadn't moved.

Landing on the floor, Braim turned around to see his worst nightmare: The assassin, who seemed to have recovered from its wounds from the night before, because it was no longer bleeding.

It raised all four of its arms, glaring at him from behind its mask, its swords glowing in its hands.

"Hey, what are *you* doing here?" said Braim, holding up his wand. "I thought you got tired of losing and quit. Guess you're a persistent little sucker, aren't you?"

"She's persistent only because I do not allow her to give up," came a voice behind Braim that he had never heard before, but which sounded like the creaking of an old coffin lid as it was opened.

Braim didn't like taking his eyes off the assassin, but he looked over his shoulder at who had spoken. He was surprised to see an elderly-looking man standing on the other side of the depression, but he wasn't just elderly-looking. He looked like a reanimated corpse. Thin, practically nonexistent hair; gray skin that was eaten away in some places; and no eyeballs at all. The man leaned on a dirt-covered shovel while wearing the pure white robes of a priest.

But it was the power radiating from the man that caught Braim's attention. The man was no simple human. In fact, Braim was pretty sure that this man wasn't even human at all. He gave off an aura of power far stronger than any mage could even hope to aspire to, so powerful that Braim felt like an ant under his gaze.

"And you are?" said Braim.

"I am surprised that you don't recognize me," said the man. He gestured at his face. "I would think, seeing that you came back from the dead, that you would know who I am, especially considering how you were once one of my followers. But I see that death and resurrection must have robbed you of your memories of me."

Braim looked back at the assassin, but to his surprise, the assassin was nowhere to be seen. Braim looked around the room, rotating on the spot, but the assassin seemed to have vanished into thin air.

Braim then looked back at the old man. "Are you a god?"

"Yes," said the old man, nodding. "One of the oldest, in fact. And one of the least popular among mortals, chiefly for the domain which I rule over. Can you guess which one that is?"

Braim considered the god's appearance, then nodded and said, "Let me guess: You're Diog, the God of the Grave, right?"

Diog smiled, showing that he was missing a good portion of his teeth and what few teeth remained were rotting and cracked. "Correct. I am the god that necromancers pledge their lives to when they choose to take up that discipline. It is I who rule over the dead and their graves, who decides upon the rules for burying the dead. And it is a job I hold with great distinction."

"I thought that the Ghostly God dealt with the dead," said Braim.

"My brother deals with what happens *after* a mortal dies. More specifically, with their spirit," said Diog. He sounded like Braim's confusing his duties with the Ghostly God's to be very offensive. "I deal with the body itself and how it must be treated. What happens to the spirit is none of my business or interest."

"I see," said Braim. He looked around again, but still didn't see the assassin anywhere. "So what are you going to do to me? Why am I here? Does that assassin work for you?"

Diog leaned on his shovel. "That assassin does indeed work for me, following my every order to the letter."

"So you're the one who has been trying to kill me ever since I got to World's End," said Braim. He pointed at Diog. "Why? What are you trying to accomplish?"

"Nothing terrible," said Diog. "As the God of the Grave, I am simply trying to fulfill my duty, part of which is ensuring that the dead *stay* dead."

Braim gulped. "Hold on. Are you saying that you have been trying to kill me because I'm not supposed to be alive?"

"Of course," said Diog. "I see that you have finally figured it out. I was wondering when you would."

"Can't say I saw this coming, to be honest," said Braim. He stepped back, but looked over his shoulder again just to make sure that that assassin actually wasn't there. "I thought that the gods in general were just interested in me. Not, you know, trying to kill me."

"My fellow gods don't want to kill you, but we gods are hardly homogenous, as you most likely know," said Diog. "The Godly War that split us apart the first time is proof enough of that. Besides, the other gods don't really understand why I want you dead. I would have recruited them, but the other gods bare no ill will toward you, so I have had to work entirely in secret to accomplish my goals so they would not find out and object."

"Right," said Braim. He smiled, hoping that he might be able to reason with the obviously mad god. "But why do you want to kill me? I'm not doing anything wrong. I just want to figure out who I am and what my purpose is in this world. Is that such a bad thing?"

"The laws laid down by the Powers at the very beginning of Martir state that everyone who dies *stays* dead," said Diog, his tone as firm as a mountain. "Humans, katabans, aquarians, and,

218

yes, even we gods, cannot break this law. It is the governing law that regulates all living creatures on this world, and I was made responsible for ensuring that it was never broken."

Diog pointed at Braim with one rotting, shaking finger. "You are unnatural, Braim Kotogs. You should not be. You died thirty years ago. You should still be lying in your grave in North Academy's graveyard, not standing before me like this. And all unnatural abominations such as yourself must die."

"Hold on, Diog," said Braim, holding up his wand defensively. "Can't we talk this over a little, like rational beings? I mean, even if what you say is true, that my resurrection was unnatural or went against some law created by the Powers or whatever, that doesn't necessarily have any negative consequences, does it? Martir sure seems fine to me."

Diog made a strange breathing noise that might have been an annoyed grunt. "You don't understand. You are mortal. You don't see—or feel—what I see and feel. Your resurrection has completely smashed the natural laws laid down by the Powers centuries ago, before you were even a thought in the mind of destiny. Have you never wondered why you feel so depressed and heavy all the time?"

Braim scratched the back of his head, where that darkness from before was still creeping up his spine. "Well, yeah, I have wondered about that. But the Ghostly God told me he thought that it was just Uron's remnants that were affecting me."

"My brother knows nothing about the natural laws that rule this world," said Diog dismissively. "Especially the ones that govern the dead. The truth is, even your very body knows that you should not be. It is demanding that you take your own life so that your unnatural abomination of a life ends for good."

"You mean it's trying to make me suicidal?" said Braim with a gulp. "I've never been suicidal before."

"Because you have a strong will to live," said Diog, tapping his chest where his heart should be, though Braim wasn't sure that Diog had one, considering how much like a rotting corpse the god resembled. "Your will to live is stronger than the natural reaction of your corpse to your unnatural state. And I believe that you will continue to fight it, which is why I had my servant try to kill you."

"Your servant?" said Braim. "Are you referring to Four Arms the assassin?"

"Yes," said Diog, nodding. "But please do not use such a childish name with which to refer to her. She is properly known as Ragao, the Half-Goddess of Darkness."

"Half-god?" said Braim. "Sounds familiar."

"It should," said Diog. "When Uron attacked World's End some months ago, he led an army of the Powers' unfinished and abandoned creations from the Void. My siblings and I slew the whole lot of them after Uron's banishment to the ethereal, but I kept this one hidden from the others in case I should ever need her. A wise move on my part, if I do say so myself."

Braim remembered where he had heard the term 'half-god' before. Aorja Kitano had had a pet half-god named Zeeree, but Braim forgot about that quickly enough in order to focus on the current situation.

"Half-god, eh?" said Braim. "Is that why she's not much of a talker? Can't say anything?"

"Her speech capabilities are very limited, but she can still understand my commands," said Diog. "Not only that, but she is an even more obedient servant than the katabans."

"Is that why you didn't use a katabans, then?" said Braim. "Let me guess, you were afraid that any katabans you hired would be interrogated by the other gods and forced to spill the beans about your plan because the katabans cannot deny the orders or requests of any god, right?"

"Correct," said Diog. "It is a shame I will have to kill you, because you truly are a smart mage. Nonetheless, the natural laws must be followed, no matter how I may feel about them."

"Then why didn't you just have Ragao kill me here?" said Braim. He looked around for the half-goddess again, but still didn't see any evidence of the assassin anywhere. "I mean, this seems like a pretty isolated place, and if Ragao could kidnap me right from under Alira's nose like that, then I don't think it would be hard for her to just kill me outright."

"Because Ragao has already failed to kill you twice," said Diog. He sounded supremely disappointed by that. "Instead, I ordered her to bring you directly to me so I could kill you personally."

"Oh," said Braim. "Is that why she vanished after she took me here? I thought for sure that she had gotten scared and run away so she wouldn't get beaten up by me again."

Though Braim spoke confidently, in truth he was terrified out of his mind. He knew exactly how powerful the gods were and how outmatched he was against Diog. There was no way that he could beat Diog in a straight fight, even if he had intended to try. He just hoped that the other gods or Alira might be able to track him down and find him before Diog killed him.

"Ragao isn't afraid of anything," said Diog. "That's actually why she's so incompetent, however. She doesn't understand that some things should be feared. She just attacks and attacks until she is too wounded or tired to keep fighting. Even then, the only reason she fled yesterday was because I ordered her to. Otherwise, she likely would have kept going until you and your fellow godlings killed her outright."

"We almost killed her?" said Braim. "I thought mortals couldn't kill gods."

"Half-gods do not have all of the same strengths and immunities that we full gods do," said Diog. "I suspect that Ragao, like her fellow half-gods, were from an earlier stage of our development when gods *could* be killed by mortals. In any case, the nature of half-gods is irrelevant. What is relevant is this."

Diog gestured at coffin lying in the depression in the floor. That was when Braim realized that it was the perfect size for his body, which didn't make him feel any easier about his current situation.

"This is the coffin I made for you, the one in which you will die," said Diog. "Based on your shocked expression, I can tell that you didn't see that coming. Odd, seeing as you are a necromancer, but perhaps your resurrection amnesia has made you forget important things like that."

"So you made a coffin, just for me?" said Braim. "How thoughtful of you."

"Do not mock me," said Diog. He slammed his shovel into the floor, creating a crack where he struck. "You have already mocked the laws that the Powers created by returning to life. Must you also mock the one whose job is to enforce those laws?"

"You get offended way too easily," said Braim. Then he looked over Diog's shoulders at the five thrones behind him. "Say, what are those thrones? They look kind of like the thrones from the Temple, except smaller."

Diog glanced over his shoulder before returning his gaze to Braim. "Those thrones are the headstones of the gods that died at Uron's hand. I crafted them myself after Uron's demise, in order to honor them all. Including Skimif, even though, like many of the gods, I never respected his authority very much."

"Why are they here and not in a graveyard?" said Braim. He looked around the room uncertainly. "By the way, where are we, exactly?"

"In my castle," said Diog. "Located on the once-inhabited island of Ysa in the Northern Isles. As for why the thrones are here, that is because there is no graveyard of the gods. Until Uron's attack, there was never a need for one, seeing as we gods cannot grow old and die."

Diog then struck the floor again and cursed. "Yet another being who broke the natural laws. The only good thing about your resurrection was that your resurrection brought Uron's death, who was a far worse threat to Martir than you ever were."

"Great to hear," said Braim, taking another step back. "Because we agree that I am not as big a threat as Uron, I think we can also agree that kidnapping me and killing me is a really bad idea. Just send me back to the Stadium and I promise not to tell the other gods that you are crazy."

"They already think I'm crazy anyway," said Diog. "But the truth is, none of them would understand this. You coming back to life is like Grinf getting burned by a fire. It should not happen.

Your very presence has changed Martir in ways even I do not yet understand. That is why I must kill you. It is the only way I know of that can reverse the damages you have wrought to this world."

"Listen, Diog, I don't know what kind of 'damages' I may have 'wrought' to Martir, but I bet I can fix them if I win the Tournament," said Braim. "You might not know this—okay, you probably do—but I'm a godling and I am in the Skimif Bracket. Assuming I win the Tournament, I will become the God of Martir, which means that I can use my power to help Martir."

Diog shuddered. "Why do you think I have been working hard to kill you? If your mere presence on Martir has been enough to wreck with the natural order of things, then what might happen if you become the God of Martir? Such an unnatural act might end up destroying everything or breaking it irrevocably, which is really the same thing no matter how you look at it."

"If my mere existence is such a terrible thing, why'd you wait so long to try to kill me?" said Braim. "I've been alive for a couple of months now, you know. Could have killed me anytime during then."

"Because I wanted to wait and see if your resurrection would actually cause any problems," said Diog. "Unlike some of my siblings, I do not like to rush in before gathering the facts first. And I have enough facts to prove that your resurrection has had nothing but the most negative of effects on Martir."

"Such as what?" said Braim. "I haven't seen the sky turn red or the sun fall into the sea or anything, so I'm not sure what I've done that's so wrong."

"You broke the law," said Diog. He gripped the side of his head, as though a terrible headache had just come upon him without warning. "You have not done much more than that yet. However, that doesn't mean that your existence will not cause more trouble. The world does not know what to make of a being like you. And if natural laws such as that can be broken, who is to say that other natural laws cannot be broken as well?"

Diog sounded paranoid to Braim, which combined with his godly power was probably not a winning combination. In any case, Braim knew he needed to figure out a way out of here quickly before Diog got bored of talking to him and decided to kill him outright.

So Braim said, "All right. Well, if you wanted to kill me, why'd Ragao try to kill Raya and the others yesterday? I wasn't even anywhere near her at the time."

"Because Ragao was trying to lure you out," said Diog. "I am aware of your friendship with Princess Raya, so I believed that putting her life in danger would bring you out."

"We're not exactly 'friends,' per se," said Braim, "but whatever. I guess it didn't really work, seeing as I'm still alive."

"But soon, you won't be," said Diog. He held out one hand toward Braim, a hand that no longer shook. "Soon, you will return to the afterlife, where you deserve to be, and the laws will be intact once more."

"Sure, you keep telling yourself that," said Braim. "But you know that Alira and the gods are probably looking for me. They'll probably find me very soon, and once they do, they won't be happy to find out that you're trying to kill me."

"They can't and won't find you," said Diog. "As a god, I have placed my protection upon you, which makes you impossible for the other gods to locate you with their powers. They cannot kill you, either, although I, of course, still can."

Braim, without waiting for Diog to speak further, fired a blast of light at the god. Diog deflected the blast with his outstretched hand, however, causing it to fly into one of the walls and leaving a black smoking mess where it hit.

"We gods cannot be harmed by magic, seeing as we generate magical energy all the time," said Diog. "Now cease your resistance. Accept the fate that all beings are born under. Obey the natural laws, which govern our world and ensure that chaos does not destroy it."

Diog curled the fingers of his outstretched hand into a fist.

That was when Braim felt a terrible, extreme pain in his heart. It was like having a thousand heart attacks at once. It was so painful that he could barely think. He dropped his wand and fell to his hands and knees on the stone floor, his lungs burning, making even the simple act of breathing into a terrible action that required great effort on his part.

But even through the intense pain overcoming him, Braim understood why he felt this pain:

He was dying.

Chapter Seventeen

RAYA WOULD NEVER admit it, but the reason she didn't like horses and knew so very little about them was because she was terrified of horses. She was terrified of how big and strong they were, how they could kill someone even with a light clip of their hooves. She hated the smell of horses and didn't want anything to do with them.

She wasn't exactly sure from where where this fear of horses came. As far back as Raya could remember, she'd always been afraid of the equines, even though most of the horses on Carnag that she had ever interacted with were generally pretty well-behaved. Even just riding in a horse-drawn carriage was a nerve-wracking experience for her. And the idea of actually *riding* a horse? For fun? To her, that was like jumping off mile-high cliffs into pointed rocks sticking out of the raging ocean for fun.

And the large Steed that stood before her—with its fiery red mane and its striking dark eyes—was the most terrifying horse that she had ever seen in her life. It towered over her easily, with bulking muscles all over its body. The Steed, which a plaque on the back side of the door had told her was called Abacos, barely seemed to acknowledge her existence. Even so, Raya preferred that, because if Abacos decided to actually pay attention to her, she had a feeling that it would run her down and squash her into oblivion with its large, shiny hooves.

How am I supposed to tame that thing? Raya thought, doing her best not to tremble or make any unnecessary noises. *How is* anyone *supposed to tame it? I only go up to its shoulder, if even that. And I know almost nothing about actual horses, much less horses that have existed longer than I have even been alive.*

Of course, Raya couldn't just leave, even though she wanted to turn and run away. She needed to gather enough courage to approach the massive Steed and then tame it. That seemed like a simple task on paper, but in reality, she had no idea at all how to do it.

How do you approach a Steed that has probably seen—and killed—countless number of humans like me? Raya thought. *Do horses even acknowledge royalty? Or do they treat us the same as other humans?*

Raya decided that she would just start by introducing herself. Perhaps Abacos wasn't as rude or mean as he seemed. He might have even been an even-tempered horse, a gentle one. Raya had heard of those, even though she never really believed that any horse could actually be gentle. She told herself that Abacos was probably not going to kill her, because she was a godling participating in the Tournament of the Gods and so Abacos was probably not allowed to kill her.

Besides, Raya, if you stand here afraid like this, you might end up losing to Zaos, Raya thought. *Do you* really *want to lose to Zaos? Of course not. You want to win, because it is what you, the Princess of Carnag, deserve.*

That thought gave her enough courage to walk forward toward Abacos, who still didn't seem to have noticed her (or pay any attention to her if he had). She walked with as much authority as she could, remembering all of the lessons that she had received from her parents about the ways in which royalty were expected to carry themselves. One thing Raya did know about animals was that you had to act like you were the one in charge if you wanted them to listen to you. That meant she could show no fear in the face of even a creature as mighty and old as Abacos.

Not certain how to address Abacos exactly, Raya stopped a few feet from him and said, "Steed, I desire that you pay attention to me, for I am Princess Raya Mana, daughter of King Tojas Malock and Queen Hana Malock of the House of Carnag. I am here to tame you in order to win the Tournament of the Gods and claim my rightful place as the Goddess of Deception, Thieves, and Horses."

Abacos actually looked at her briefly, but then turned his attention back to the grass underfoot, which he was now eating with obvious enjoyment. Now Raya knew little about equine facial expressions, but the way Abacos had looked at her seemed to say, *And? Why should I care?*

Raya almost lost her temper and was about ready to shout at the Steed before she caught herself. *No, Raya, shouting won't do anything. That will just convince Abacos that you aren't worthy of listening to. It might even cost you the Tournament. You need to approach this more calmly.*

So Raya, taking a deep breath to compose herself, said, "Great Abacos, what must I do to show you that I am destined to be your goddess? Is there anything I can do to prove that?"

Abacos looked up at her again, chewing the grass in its mouth and snorting. Its look said, quite plainly, *How am I supposed to know?* before returning to the grass at its hooves.

That was almost enough to make Raya lose her temper. She wanted to scream, *You stupid horse! You're supposed to be an ageless, wise entity, not a stupid animal! If you're this stupid, how in the name of Grinf have you avoided breaking your legs? You are the dumbest animal I've ever met.*

But again, Raya caught herself just as the first word leaped to her tongue. She had to take it easy. Maybe this was part of the test. Abacos was probably acting stupid in order to test her patience. If she lost her temper now, then she might never be able to tame Abacos.

So Raya, speaking as calmly as she could, said, "Great Abacos, if you let me tame you, then I promise to give you a lifetime of … er … uh … whatever it is that horses like to eat."

Abacos didn't even look up at her this time. It was almost like it was saying, *Stop bothering me. I'm busy having lunch at the moment*, which angered Raya even more. She was tempted to just kick the damn horse in the head, but she had a feeling that Abacos wouldn't appreciate that, so she once again beat down her anger and tried to think of some other way to tame him.

Not easy, Raya thought. *I don't know very much about horses at all. I don't have any treats to feed it. I am not even sure how to touch it without causing it to kick me.*

Raya tried to remember what she had learned about horses. She had never actually had any formal equestrian lessons—that just wasn't part of her royal education, seeing as horse-riding was not a very popular past-time on Carnag—but she tried to remember how the stable boys took care of the Royal Family's carriage horses. Unfortunately, she kept drawing a blank, because she never paid much attention to how the stable boys took care of the horses. That was probably because the stable boys weren't all that great to look at.

Have to stop drawing a blank here, Raya thought. *Gotta remember something, anything. If I can't ...*

Raya didn't even want to think about the consequences of her inability to tame Abacos. She did not want to return to Carnag in shame, having lost in the very first challenge of the Tournament. That was unacceptable. She knew that her parents—and the rest of Carnag, most likely—would still love her, but she still didn't think that losing was acceptable.

Think, Raya, think, Raya thought. *What did Yoji say about the Steeds? Did he possibly tell you anything that could possibly help you tame Abacos?*

The only thing she remembered was Yoji telling her about how Abacos kicked the head off of a human who once disrespected him. That hardly made her feel safer, much less gave her any ideas for how to tame Abacos. It just made her even more afraid of Abacos, even though the Steed was currently not behaving very threateningly toward her.

Raya looked around the area she had stepped in, hoping that her environment might give her some ideas. It was an enclosed area, shaped like a wedge. The back, where Raya had come from, was wide, while the corner that Abacos stood in was narrow and pointed. She imagined that the areas that the other challengers were in must have looked similar.

But unfortunately, aside from the grass on the ground that Abacos was happily munching on, Raya didn't see anything that she could use to tame the Steed with. She was so frustrated that she stomped her foot on the ground, but Abacos didn't even look up at her when she did that.

Stupid horse doesn't even acknowledge my existence anymore, Raya thought. *Why didn't Alira give us some tools or knowledge that could have helped me win? I bet she thought we all knew everything there is to know about horses before we entered the Tournament. Probably thinks that 'destiny' will decide who will win and who will lose.*

Not that any of those negative thoughts actually helped her in this situation. All they did was make her feel a lot worse about herself and her situation, but mostly it made her feel negative toward Alira. She looked up at the ceiling, wondering if Alira was watching her right now.

Bet she is, Raya thought with a scowl. *Probably even mocking me. Or laughing at my pathetic attempts to tame Abacos. Well, I'm just going to shut her up by taming Abacos myself.*

So Raya, steeling herself, carefully approached the Steed. Abacos still didn't look up at her as she approached, but she had a feeling that this horse was completely aware of its surroundings at all times. She tried not to feel freaked out about that, because she didn't want to make it think that she was more afraid than she actually was.

Step by step, Raya approached Abacos until she was within reach of its fiery mane. And again, the Steed did not look up at her. Part of Raya was offended, because she considered herself too important to simply ignore, but another part of her was thankful, because she didn't like it when horses looked at her, even if they were tamed and well-behaved.

Just go and stroke his mane, Raya, Raya told herself. *I doubt he'll mind. He already considers you a non-entity, more or less. If you stroke his mane and tell him what a handsome stallion he is —assuming Abacos is male, though not sure, since I don't know how to identify a horse's gender, but I suppose it doesn't matter— then that will probably count as taming him and you will then go onto the main challenge.*

That, of course, was easier said than done, but that was why Raya was preparing herself mentally for this task. She reached out with her right hand, slowly and carefully, trying not to look threatening. Not that she thought she appeared that way, but horses could be unpredictable and there was no telling how this one would react if it felt threatened by her presence.

The tips of her fingers brushed against Abacos's mane. As soon as they did, Abacos let out a great big snort that caused Raya to jerk her hand back. She also walked—more like stumbled— backwards as fast as she could, going so fast that she tripped over own her feet and fell on her behind. The fall wasn't painful, but it was embarrassing, especially with Abacos looking at her with his puzzled eyes.

But Raya forgot all about her fear of horses now, because her fear was replaced by the anger she felt at being embarrassed the way she was. She stood back up and, pointing at Abacos, said, "You stupid horse! Here I was just trying to stroke your mane, but then you went and spooked me! Do you feel good about yourself, spooking a delicate princess like me? Do you get some sick pleasure from doing that? Do you?"

Surprisingly, Abacos actually seemed to be paying attention to her ranting. This took her by surprise, making her temporarily stop speaking. As soon as she did, Abacos immediately returned his attention to the grass, which he apparently found far more interesting than she.

Why did Abacos pay attention to me when I was shouting at it? Raya thought. *I thought most animals hate being yelled at. Was it something in my voice?*

Unfortunately, Abacos did not seem to be in any hurry to tell her about what it was that she said that had caught his attention. That annoyed her again.

"You dumb horse," Raya said again, this time channeling her anger more consciously. "Ignoring me … how rude! I have never met a more inconsiderate horse in my life. And yet you are supposed to be the First Steed, which I take it to mean that you are the first ever horse. I see that wisdom didn't exactly come along with your age, now did it?"

Abacos looked up at her again. And unless Raya's eyes were playing tricks on her, the Steed seemed to be listening to her every word. It was like she was reminding him of someone that he had once known, someone who he was supposed to listen to whenever that person was yelling at him.

Could he be reminded of Hollech? Raya thought. *Perhaps Hollech yelled at Abacos for being such a dull horse in the past. That would certainly explain why he is paying attention to me. He must be reminded of Hollech. Perhaps the dullard even* thinks *I am Hollech reborn as a young, beautiful mortal princess.*

In any case, Raya was not going to give up this opportunity just because she didn't entirely understand it. She pointed at Abacos as sharply as ever, saying, "Oh, so *now* you're paying attention to me? I guess you think that will make me feel better. Of course it won't. And I won't feel better until you act like the

First Steed and not like a young foal."

Abacos actually looked a little ashamed of himself now. He pawed at the earth, no longer eating the grass. Raya wasn't sure if that meant that he was becoming tamer or not. She decided that it was, so she kept pushing the point.

"What do you have to say for yourself?" said Raya. "No, wait, don't talk, because I know you can't. Even if you could, I wouldn't want to hear any excuses from you. Your own terrible behavior condemns you."

Abacos now looked so ashamed of himself that Raya found it hard to remain angry with him any longer. She even felt a little bad for him. Abacos was clearly a sensitive soul, so maybe she was not right in berating him for making a mistake that he had obviously never intended to make.

So Raya lowered her pointing finger and said, "Well, Abacos, I can now see that you are ashamed of what you just did. Since you can't talk, I will accept your humble behavior as an apology."

Abacos looked at her with hopeful eyes, which made Raya wonder if she had succeeded in taming him yet. She wasn't sure exactly what would happen when she succeeded, but she expected Alira to appear out of nowhere, declare her a winner, and then whisk her away from the Stadium, hopefully to a nice party where her major accomplishment would be recognized for its greatness.

But nothing happened at all, even though Raya was now certain that she had accomplished the task. She looked up at the ceiling, hoping that maybe Alira would float down on her platform again, but there was no sign of the Judge anywhere.

Raya waited as patiently as she could—only about five minutes, though it seemed longer than that—before she said to the ceiling, "Hello? Alira? Are you there? I won the challenge. What do I have to do next?"

Still no response. She looked at Abacos, who had returned to munching the grass underfoot, as if happy that all was now forgiven. Raya walked back over to the room's entrance, wondering if for some reason she would have to go back through it herself to let Alira know that she beat the challenge, but when she grabbed the knob and turned it, the door refused to budge. She put all of her strength into forcing the door open (which really wasn't much, though she'd never admit that to anyone), but it held firmly under her strength, so she gave up eventually.

Why hasn't Alira contacted me? Raya thought, folding her arms over her chest and pouting. *I tamed Abacos. What could possibly be taking up her time? Is she taking a nap or something? Or is she ignoring me?*

That last one seemed likely to Raya. So likely, in fact, that she was quite content to think of it as fact. Alira had been quite annoyed with her yesterday, after all, when Raya had complained about getting assigned to the Hollech Bracket. This was probably just Alira's way of 'punishing' Raya, by ignoring her even though she won the challenge fair and square.

Of course she would, Raya thought, scowling at the thought of the Judge. *That's just the kind of petty person she is. But she can't ignore me forever. At some point she'll have to let me out. Then I can rub my victory in her face.*

That thought made Raya smile, but her smile vanished when she noticed Abacos raise his head suddenly. His equine eyes were looking directly at her. No, not *at* her, but just behind her, as if he saw something terrible sneaking up on her.

236

Puzzled, Raya looked over her shoulder. She didn't see anything except the currently locked entrance to the room. She did a quick look around the room, but saw no one else besides herself and Abacos present.

Still, Abacos continued to stare. It took Raya a moment to realize that Abacos wasn't actually staring at anything. His pointed ears were point forward. While Raya was no expert on equine behavior, even she understood that Abacos was listening for something, though what, she didn't know.

But Raya couldn't hear anything except her own breathing and the whipping sound Abacos's tail made as it darted through the air, so she said in annoyance, "What did you hear? A mouse or something?"

Abacos let out a sudden, deadly-sounding snort that brought all of Raya's fears of horses rushing back to her body. Her heart beat increased rapidly and she stood there stock still, like every bone in her body had completely frozen.

That was when she heard it. Something creeping behind her. It was a light sound, barely audible, but now that Raya heard it, she could not ignore it. Abacos was backing up, but there wasn't much room for the Steed to back up to, due to the tiny quarters in which they stood. He stomped his hooves, like he was trying to scare something away, but Raya could tell that it was a futile gesture.

Then Raya felt something crawling up the back of her legs. It felt like some kind of insect, maybe even a snake, but Raya was certain that it was neither. She opened her mouth to scream, but nothing came out of it. Her entire body shivered and shuddered, but she was unable to move even an inch from her current position.

    And then she heard a voice whisper in her ear: **I've got you.**

Chapter Eighteen

CARMAZ WASN'T THE only one who noticed the ever-widening crack. Saia did, too, and he pointed at it, saying, "Uh, what's that crack in the floor?"

Alira's gray eyes fell on the crack. "What in the world—"

Then, without warning, the crack became a chasm, tearing the floor apart underneath Carmaz's feet. He immediately fell and would have fallen into the darkness below if Saia had not grabbed his arm, jerking his fall to a stop. The stress on Carmaz's arm was painful, especially since it felt like the darkness below was sucking him in.

The chasm widened close to the seats where the rest of the godlings sat, forcing them to jump off their seats and run to the other side of the room as the chairs toppled over into the darkness below. Tashir and Malya, on the other hand, jumped over to join Saia. They helped him haul Carmaz back onto the solid ground, but that didn't make Carmaz feel any safer. He turned to look down at the swirling shadows below, uncertain what he was looking at or what was happening.

"Um, Judge?" said Saia, looking at Alira, who was now staring at the chasm in shock. "Is this also part of the Tournament or did Ooka get angry about something?"

"I have no idea what this is," said Alira. She reached out

toward the chasm with one hand. "But whatever it is, it is not in the Rulebook, so I must eliminate it. Stand back."

Carmaz, Saia, Tashir, and Malya stepped back as far as they could, which admittedly wasn't very far, as two beams of light shot out of Alira's hand and latched onto either side of the chasm. The two beams began to pull the sides of the chasm back together, but then a shadow tendril rose from the darkness and cut both beams in half. It must have somehow hurt Alira as well, because she let out a cry of pain and staggered backward as if punched in the face.

The shadow tendril then flew toward Carmaz and the others, but Tashir drew his glowing sword and cut the tendril in half before it could harm anyone. Half of the tendril fell to the stone floor and dissipated in an instant, while the other half slithered back into the shadows below.

"Where are the gods?" said Saia, his voice higher than usual as he looked around. "Why aren't they here helping us?"

"Something must be preventing the gods from saving us," said Tashir, never lowering his sword or taking his eyes off the darkness below. "I only wish I knew what, though I can guess that it must be related to this shadow."

"If the gods can't beat it—" Malya said, before Carmaz cut her off.

"Then they're even more useless than I first thought," said Carmaz. He looked at Alira. "Judge, we need to get the godlings out of the Stadium before this thing kills us all."

"But the Tournament is not yet finished," Alira protested. "The Rulebook says—"

"Do you think that what the Rulebook 'says' matters right

240

now?" said Carmaz. He pointed at the other godlings, who were crowded on the other side of the room together. "Just get them out of here. And get the ones in the field as well, even if they haven't won or lost the challenge yet."

Alira looked rather offended that Carmaz was bossing her around, but thankfully she was more reasonable than she appeared, because she gestured at the godlings and they all vanished. "There. I have teleported them outside of the Stadium, so they should be fine."

"Hey, what about us?" asked Saia, looking at the shadows in the chasm. "Shouldn't we be teleported as well?"

"I was just about to do that," said Alira.

She raised her arm to point it at them, but without warning another shadow tendril launched out of the shadows and slapped Alira in the face. The blow must have been powerful, because it knocked Alira flat off her feet and sent her glasses flying off her face. Her giant Rulebook fell with a loud *thump* by her side and Alira herself did not move or rise again.

"Oh gods," said Saia. "It knocked her out."

The shadow tendril then turned in the air, focusing on Carmaz and the others. Both Tashir and Malya held up their glowing swords defensively, while Carmaz and Saia stood there defenseless. It made Carmaz wish that he had some kind of magical weapon of his own, or even just a regular weapon, but unfortunately he had nothing he could use to defend himself or Saia. He would just have to use his wit and brains. Unfortunately, he wasn't sure how useful either of those things would be against a shadow tendril that could knock out a pseudo-god like Alira in one hit.

Saia, meanwhile, slammed his fists against the exit and kicked it with his feet, but the door unfortunately still didn't budge. Yet Carmaz wondered if maybe it would eventually give now that Alira was out, seeing as she was probably unable to maintain the spell she cast on it while she was unconscious. It just might need some team effort, however.

"Tashir, Malya, you keep that thing busy," said Carmaz. He jerked a thumb over his shoulder at the door. "Saia and I will try to open the exit so we can all get out of here alive."

"Sounds good," said Tashir. "But you must hurry. Without Alira to protect us, I doubt we will be able to hold this thing off for long."

"Agreed," said Malya. "But that doesn't mean that we can't try our best anyway."

"Just do what you can to hold if off until Saia and I knock the door down," said Carmaz.

The two makhimancers nodded and turned to face the shadows again, while Carmaz ran up to the door with Saia. Saia looked rather defeated now, leaning against the door rather than trying to knock it down.

"It's no use, Carmaz," said Saia, shaking his head. "The door won't budge."

"We need to work together to do it," said Carmaz. He patted the door. "On the count of three, we'll slam into the door as hard as we can with our shoulders. All right?"

"Okay," said Saia, though he didn't sound terribly enthusiastic about the plan. "But what if it doesn't work?"

"We worry about that when or if that happens," said Carmaz. "Now come on. We don't have time to waste doubting."

Carmaz and Saia stepped back a few feet from the door, while Tashir and Malya slashed at some shadow tendrils that had gotten too close. Carmaz ignored the shadows, however, in order to focus on the task at hand.

"One ... two ... three!"

Carmaz and Saia slammed their shoulders into the door with all of their strength. The door was solid under their combined blows. It did, however, groan, an encouraging sign that promoted Carmaz to shout, "Again!"

The two kept ramming the door with their shoulders again and again, each blow weakening the door further until it finally gave out and swung open. Carmaz and Saia staggered through the doorway, almost tripping down the staircase, but Carmaz caught himself and Saia as well before they could go stumbling head first into the dark staircase.

He looked over his shoulder at Tashir and Malya. "Guys, we opened the door! Come on!"

Tashir nodded, but said, "Just one moment."

The makhimancer, showing more athleticism that Carmaz thought someone of his age should have had, leaped over to where the unconscious Alira lay and hauled her over his shoulder. Another shadow tendril came at Tashir, but he slashed it away with his sword. Malya jumped over to join him as well and hauled the heavy Rulebook under one arm, which again surprised Carmaz, as Malya did not look strong enough to carry something that looked so heavy.

The two of them quickly rejoined Carmaz and Saia, the latter of whom led the way down into the staircase. Carmaz made sure to shut the door behind them as they left to ensure that the shadow tendrils would not be able to follow them, although he wasn't sure how effective that was going to be. He could already hear the tendrils beating against the door, which prompted him to walk down the staircase after the others as fast as he was able.

But then, when they were several feet down the staircase, Carmaz heard the sound of the door breaking above him, probably the tendrils breaking through. He thought, however, that they could possibly outrun the tendrils before Tashir, who was in the lead and still carrying the unconscious Alira over his shoulder, came to a dead stop, forcing the others to stop behind him as well.

"Tashir, what are you doing?" Saia asked, his voice higher-pitched than ever. "The shadows—"

"Have us surrounded," Tashir said, without looking back at any of them. "Look."

Carmaz looked ahead of Tashir and saw that he was correct. More shadow tendrils were making their way up the staircase toward them, albeit at a somewhat slower pace than the others. Still, the tendrils ahead had the staircase effectively blocked, as did the ones behind them.

Saia then looked at Carmaz with fear in his eyes. "Are we going to die, Carmaz?"

Carmaz didn't know what to say to that, mostly because he had the sinking feeling that the answer to that question was yes.

Chapter Nineteen

BECAUSE OF THE amnesia that he had experienced upon his resurrection, Braim hadn't known what dying felt like. It was actually one of the most common questions that others had asked of him when he came back the first time: "What did dying feel like?"

That was an unusual, even morbid, question, but Braim never felt offended by it, probably because his answer was always, "I don't remember."

It was the honest truth. Braim had always supposed that he should have felt grateful that he didn't remember it, because according to Jenur, Braim had died after getting thick smoke in his lungs courtesy of his father who had killed him (probably because his father had been a bad dad). It certainly explained why Braim had an aversion to smoke in general, even if it was only a tiny wisp from a warm fire.

But now, the pain that had taken over his whole body was starting to jog Braim's memory. He recalled feeling his body dying now, how he had felt his consciousness slip through his fingers inch by inch. His current method of dying—having his life force drained from him by a god who hated him—was different from how he had died the first time, but he supposed that in the end there wasn't much difference in how you died, only that you died, period.

Braim looked up at Diog. The god showed no mercy or forgiveness on his face at all as he looked down upon Braim. He clearly thought that Braim didn't deserve any mercy or forgiveness, probably because Braim had committed an unforgivable offense in this god's eyes.

This idiot's more like the God of Justice than the God of the Grave, Braim thought.

But that didn't matter to him. Right now, Braim needed to figure out a way to survive, but he unfortunately was not sure how. The pain of dying was making it hard, if not impossible, to think through a plan that would help him survive. He could feel his life draining from his body rapidly, which prompted him to briefly wonder what would happen if he died again.

Maybe the Mysterious One would just send me back to the physical realm, Braim thought. *Regardless, I need a survival plan, and fast.*

Braim reached for his wand, but it was too far out of his reach for him to grab. Besides, he was so weak now that he doubted he could actually lift the wand, much less channel magic through it.

Must keep trying, Braim thought, still reaching for the wand. *My ... only ...*

Diog pointed with his other hand at Braim's wand, causing it to snap in half instantly. Braim looked up at the God of the Grave, his eyes wide.

"I saw what you were trying to do," said Diog. "And, while you may not be able to hurt me, I know how tricky you humans can be. You have no hope now. So why don't you just die and stay dead, as you did for three decades?"

"Because … I still haven't found … my purpose," said Braim, forcing every word from his mouth with all of his strength.

"Your purpose?" said Diog. "Your purpose in life is to die and stay dead. That is the end of all mortals such as yourself. You should know that, seeing as you are a necromancer yourself."

That may have been true, but Braim hardly remembered much about necromancy, even after he had gotten some training in the subject at North Academy after his resurrection. Not that it mattered either way. At this point, Braim was pretty much convinced that he was going to die.

For the 'greater good,' of course, Braim thought, scowling.

One thing that did reassure Braim somewhat was the knowledge that he was not entirely defenseless. While mages required wands in order to use their magic without damaging their bodies, it was still possible for a mage like Braim to use magic without a wand. Diog no doubt knew that, but he probably also didn't think Braim would risk using magic without a wand, as that sometimes had very negative effects on the mage who did that.

I really don't feel strong enough to do anything except grovel, Braim thought. *But I gotta try. Even if I fail, I can at least say I tried.*

The problem was obvious: Diog was draining Braim's life force. How much Braim had left, he didn't know, as life energy was not a substance that could be measured in the same way as water or air.

Nonetheless, Braim figured that if Diog could remove his energy, then it was possible for Braim to restore it. He recalled Jenur explaining the concept to him once, when she was reminding him about his first life and he had inquired about the exact powers of necromancers. Jenur had explained that, based on her own research into the subject, she had discovered that necromancers could not only drain the life force of individuals, but also draw it back into themselves. It was supposed to be an extremely difficult move, however, so difficult that only necromancers who had achieved Limitlessness—a state in which a mage could use magic without running out of magical energy—could do it.

Braim was not that kind of mage. At one point in the past, Braim had been so good that he had been the Magical Superior's personal pupil, but ever since returning to life, Braim had had to start over from square one. Granted, he had found magic easier to learn than most people did, but the fact was that Braim was nowhere near as skilled as Darek or Jenur or most of the other faculty at North Academy.

But I have to try, Braim thought, punching the floor to avoid crying out from the pain that was crippling him. *Otherwise, I'll have lived an even shorter life than I lived before.*

So Braim closed his eyes, focusing on Diog. In his mind's eye, he could see his life force like a great big cloud that was being sucked into a vacuum that was Diog. Diog was vacuuming his life force without any resistance from Braim, which was why his life force was depleting so rapidly at the moment.

Now Braim had to focus very, very hard on asserting his rights over his life force. He focused hard on grabbing hold of his life force and holding it firmly in his hands so that Diog couldn't take any more of it. That was hard, because visualizing it as a cloud made it almost impossible to visualize grabbing and taking it away from Diog.

248

Nonetheless, Braim pulled as hard as he could until finally he felt his life force break off from Diog's sucking force. The pain that had tormented Braim suddenly vanished, replaced instead by a high that Braim had not expected to feel. It was like all of his life energy had returned to his body at once, making him feel giddier than ever.

Diog, on the other hand, actually staggered backwards from Braim's actions, almost like Braim had hit him hard. The god even fell on his behind, dropping his shovel, which fell to the stone floor with a clatter by his side.

"What ..." Diog sounded and looked bewildered by this sudden turn of events. "How did you do that?"

Braim got to his feet. He felt better than ever, like he could run laps around Diog without even trying. He felt so good that he clapped his hands twice and said, "I just got my life force back, Diog. Do you really need to know *how*?"

Diog scowled and grabbed his shovel. He then stood back up, still leaning on his shovel for support, and said, "It doesn't matter how, I suppose, because there is more than one way to skin a cat."

Diog waved his hand and Ragao appeared as if by teleportation, wielding her four swords as usual. Diog then barked at the half-god, "Kill him! Tear him apart with your bare hands if you must!"

Ragao nodded to show that she understood. Then she launched herself at Braim, swords flying through the air before her.

But Braim wasn't afraid of her. He raised his hands and unleashed a powerful burst of light from them that struck Ragao directly in the chest. The blow sent Ragao flying backwards into the far wall, which she struck hard. She then slid to the wall's base, dropping her swords. She did not get up again.

"Ragao?" Diog repeated in a horrified tone. "Ragao, please answer me."

Through the eye holes of Ragao's mask, Braim saw that she wasn't conscious. She wasn't dead, because her chest was still rising and falling with each breath, but it was pretty clear that Ragao was not going to be getting back up for another round anytime soon.

So Braim lowered his hands—which hurt from the light blast he had fired, although his high allowed him to ignore the pain for now—looked at Diog, and said, "Looks like your little servant is out for the count."

"Impossible," said Diog. He was now shaking. "Strictly impossible. The half-gods may not be on the same level as us gods, but they should be much stronger than you humans. How, then, did you knock her out in one hit?"

"Not sure," said Braim with a shrug. "Guess I just got lucky."

"Only fools and thieves believe in luck," said Diog. "You are even worse than I thought. There must be something about your nature that has made you stronger than you should be. It is unnatural. It is time I stopped holding back."

Diog pointed at the coffin with Braim's picture on it. The lid lifted open and then the coffin itself flew through the air toward Braim.

Taken by surprise, Braim did not move in time to dodge the coffin, which closed around him immediately. Braim found himself in a tight, narrow, and completely black space, which would have been easier to break out of if he hadn't felt the air being rapidly depleted from the coffin's interior.

He's trying to suffocate me, Braim thought. *No, you don't!*

Braim punched the coffin lid as hard as he could. His hand broke through the stone lid as though it were paper, allowing air to flow in. He then punched another hole in it with his other hand and tore open a gap large enough for him to dive through, which he did.

Rolling to his feet, Braim looked to see the coffin fall to the floor where he stood mere moments before. Diog looked absolutely enraged now. He was panting hard and gripping the handle of his shovel so tightly that it looked like he was about to break it.

Before Braim could say anything, Diog roared in anger and jumped through the air toward Braim, landing before Braim with a hideous scowl on his face. He swung his shovel, aiming directly for Braim's head, but Braim managed to duck and avoid it. Braim then began walking backwards outside of Diog's reach as quickly as he could as the god advanced on him with an angry scowl on his foul features.

"Hey, we don't have to fight, you know," said Braim, holding up his hands to pacify the angry god. "If you would just take me back to World's End, I promise I won't bring this up if I win the Tournament and become the God of Martir."

"Idiotic mortal," said Diog. "Did your brain come back faulty? I will only be happy when you are dead and not a moment before that."

"Then I guess you're never going to be happy, because I intend to live a long time," Braim said.

Diog stabbed at Braim with his shovel. Braim grabbed the

shovel's head, however, and ripped it out of the god's hands. With a grunt, Braim then threw the shovel away out of both of their reach.

"There," said Braim, looking at Diog again. "Now we're both unarmed. If I were you, I'd—"

Braim was interrupted when Diog appeared right in front of him, the stink of death radiating from the god's body, and grabbed Braim by the neck. Shocked, Braim grabbed Diog's arm and tried to remove it from his neck, but the god's grip was like iron and there was nothing Braim could do but flail his limbs about uselessly as Diog choked him to death.

"I dislike getting my hands dirty, but if this is what I must do to ensure the continued survival of Martir and the gods, then so be it," said Diog. "But do not worry, Braim Kotogs. I will take your body back to World's End as proof of my deed and then return it to your friends in North Academy, where they can bury it again in the grave that you are destined to rest in for eternity."

Panicking, Braim did the only thing he figured had any chance of working: He grabbed Diog's arm and tried to suck out the god's life force.

This was another necromancer technique that he had never done before, but Braim was so desperate to live that he would have tried literally anything at this point if it offered him even the slightest chance of survival. He quickly visualized Diog's life force as a large cup of water from which he drank with a straw. He drank and drank as much as he could, feeling his body fill with the stuff to the point where he could barely contain it all.

And much to Braim's surprise, he could already see and feel the effect that it was having on Diog. The god looked weaker and weaker, his grip became limper and limper, and he seemed to be having trouble standing. Still, Diog was a god and therefore had a ton of life force, perhaps an infinite amount, considering how it was impossible for a mortal to kill a god.

Even so, Braim must have been draining a ton of it at a rate faster than he thought, because he now felt stronger than ever. He kicked at Diog's chest, which caused the god to drop Braim, who fell on his feet. Braim's throat still hurt from where Diog had tried to choke him, but he didn't focus on that. Instead, he focused on absorbing more of Diog's life force, because he still held the god's arm and did not intend on letting go until he was sure that Diog was down for good.

The god tried to pull his arm out of Braim's grasp, but he could not succeed because Braim was holding on as tightly as he could. Under ordinary circumstances, Braim would have been absolutely shocked by this turn of events, but he was so focused on taking down Diog that he didn't let himself be shocked.

"Let go," Diog said, his voice weaker than ever. "Let me go, you unnatural abomination, or I'll—"

"Or you'll what, kill me?" said Braim. He felt stronger than ever, so strong that even Diog didn't scare him anymore. "That's not exactly the most compelling reason for me to let you go, you know."

Diog lashed out with his other arm, striking Braim in the stomach. The blow—while not as strong as it could have been, perhaps, because Diog was weaker than he normally was—still hit like a boulder rolling down a steep hill and the impact sent Braim flying. A ripping sound followed as well, but Braim paid no attention to it due to the fact that he was currently flying uncontrollably through the air.

But Braim managed to recover in midair and land on his feet, albeit unsteadily. The impact jolted him, but a quick shake of his head reoriented his senses and made him realize that he was holding something.

Looking at his right hand, Braim saw that he was holding Diog's arm, which was little more than a dry, weathered husk now. The sight of it made him look up at Diog, who was indeed missing the lower half of his left arm. The God of the Grave, however, didn't look like he was in pain at all, though he rubbed his left elbow just the same.

"Clever ... clever move, Braim Kotogs," said Diog, whose voice sounded a little stronger now than it had before. "Very clever. Very few human mages would have dared to even attempt to absorb the life force of a god. I am surprised that the effort didn't outright kill you."

Braim threw Diog's severed arm onto the floor. It immediately turned into dust. A second later, Diog's arm regrew out of the stump of his left arm. The God of the Grave glanced at his newly-regrown arm before looking at Braim again.

"Yeah, well, I'm pretty creative that way, I guess," said Braim with a shrug. "Maybe I survived because I'm special."

"Or unnatural," said Diog. He flexed the fingers of his newly-regrown arm. "But it doesn't matter how you were able to handle that, because I will kill you just the same and restore the power that the natural laws of Martir once held in this world."

Braim sighed heavily. "Come on. You've already tried—and failed—to kill me several times. I know you gods tend to be stubborn, but don't you think your time might be better spent doing something else? Like, I dunno, attending a funeral or something?"

Diog didn't answer. He just ran at Braim again, his hands balled into fists.

Braim didn't run, however, because he was tired of fighting and he wanted to end this now. He punched his fist into his other hand and drew upon all of the godly power that he had absorbed from Diog. He was going to wait until the god was just within his reach, which would be soon, based on how fast Diog was running toward him.

Just a few more feet now ... Braim thought, staying as still as possible so Diog could not anticipate his next move. *Just a few more feet and ...*

In a second, Diog was in Braim's reach. And Braim struck, punching the god in the face with as much strength as he possibly could. It wasn't just his own mortal strength he called upon, but also Diog's own strength which he had absorbed earlier. It made his fist feel strong enough to smash boulders into pieces.

And when his fist struck, the blow sent Diog flying. The god didn't even let out a shout of surprise as he flew through the air and struck the back wall of the room, the impact causing the entire building to shake. Then Diog fell to the floor face-first, revealing a huge, ugly crack in the wall from where he had crashed into it.

Braim waited ten seconds, waiting for Diog to get back up and go at him again. The longer he waited, however, the more unlikely it seemed that Diog would get up again.

Damn, Braim thought, looking down at his fist, which didn't hurt at all despite the fact that he had just punched a god hard enough to send him flying. *I must have hit him pretty hard. I don't think I killed him, but maybe he'll have a really bad headache for the rest of the day.*

In any case, Braim was happy that the fight was over and that he had, somehow, won. He was pretty sure that he shouldn't have won—gods were so far above mortals that it was like comparing the strength of an ant to that of a human—but he didn't like questioning strokes of luck like this, so he decided to find his way out of here and get back to World's End.

So Braim ran over to the closed door and pulled it open. He was just about to dash through it when he caught a glimpse of shining metal from within the darkness of the hallway, a sight that forced him to jump back.

But then Ragao's blades came flying out of the darkness and cut across his chest. Blood shot out from his chest and ripples of pain went across Braim's entire body as the blades cut through him.

Crying out in pain, Braim staggered backwards, staying just out of Ragao's reach, but the half-god was advancing on him rapidly. She glanced at Diog briefly, let out a deeply primal and unsettling growl, and then resumed advancing on Braim, his blood glinting off her swords.

Damn beast, Braim thought, scowling. *I don't have* time *for you.*

Braim raised his hand and unleashed a burst of light from it. The light burst stuck Ragao in the face; and since it was powered by Diog's life force, it was strong enough to knock her flat on her back. Ragao's swords clattered around her when she fell, but she did not get up again.

That did not solve Braim's chest problems, but he knew enough panamancy to cast a quick healing spell to heal his chest, which he performed without delay. His clothes were still bloody and he was still worn out from the shock of the blow, but at least he wasn't bleeding anymore. He would have to have a more qualified healer look at his chest later, however, to have it healed fully, because the spell he had cast only really healed the skin and not much else.

Now time to get out of here, Braim thought as he walked around Ragao, who seemed to be out like a light now. *I wonder how the others are doing and if they're trying to find me.*

But that thought made Braim stop. He realized that he didn't know how he was going to get out of here. He knew nothing about the general layout of Diog's castle; and even if he did, that didn't mean he could get off this island and back to World's End in a reasonable amount of time. While Braim could teleport, he wasn't good enough at it to teleport great distances.

Am I stuck here until these two wake up for round two? Braim thought, his shoulders slumping at the thought. *There's no way I could go another round with these two, not again.*

Then a thought occurred to Braim. He looked down at Ragao, who was still unconscious, and wondered if he could possibly use her powers to return to Martir. She was clearly capable of traversing great distances, after all, so he would just make her take him back.

So Braim kicked the half-god in the head to wake her up. The blow worked, because as soon as he kicked her, Ragao's eyes opened underneath her mask and looked at him with anger. She reached toward her swords, but Braim aimed a hand shining with light energy at her face, causing her to stop.

"Listen, Ragao, I think the two of us got off to a rough start, what with you trying to kill me three times in a row and all," said Braim, keeping his tone friendly, but deeply serious so she wouldn't think he was someone to underestimate. "And if you keep trying to kill me, we might have to end our relationship on a grim note, if you catch my drift."

Ragao stared at Braim, but she seemed to understand his words well enough, because she didn't move any of her arms. Still, Braim could tell that she was just waiting for him to lower his guard so she could kill him as mercilessly as a baba raga.

"So I thought I'd cut a deal with you," said Braim. He nodded at Diog, who was still lying unconscious on the base of the wall on the other side of the room. "See your old master? Diog? He's down. I beat him. And I'll do far, far worse to you if you don't help me get to where I need to go."

Ragao said nothing, but he could tell that she was thinking about what he just said. Braim briefly wondered what the thought process of a half-god was like before returning his focus to the current situation.

"Now, I need to get back to World's End, and fast," Braim continued. "I, however, don't know how to get back to World's End from here. So I want you to take me back. If you do, I promise not to attack and beat you ever again. Sound like a good deal?"

Ragao let out a deep, throaty growl, but even he could tell that she was not going to try to kill him again. She then nodded her ugly head, though she hardly looked happy about it.

"Awesome," said Braim. "Just take me back to the Stadium

and I'll handle the rest from there."

Chapter Twenty

THE VOICE WAS cold and unsettling and unnatural. It was like listening to the howling wind in an empty valley, only a thousand times worse. And Raya could still feel whatever it was that was crawling up her body in a way that made her feel very violated.

Raya could hardly breathe. Abacos stepped back into the corner, but the Steed had nowhere to go. He kept snorting and pawing at the ground, but he was clearly doing that more out of fear than anything.

"Who … who are you?" said Raya, her voice so tiny that she felt more like a child than an adult now. "What … what are you doing?"

Do you not recognize my voice? said the voice in her ear. Raya thought that it sounded vaguely feminine. **I suppose not, seeing as we have never met before. But I have seen your father, the brave man who saved this world from its own creators in his youth. It has been ages since he came close to my realm, but I can see that his daughter is as arrogant as he was.**

Raya gulped. "How do you know my father? Are you some kind of goddess?"

Goddess? Of course not, said the voice. **I existed before the**

gods, who are as ants beneath me. No, I am the Void, the primordial force that once ruled the wastes of the world before this one until the Powers came and built Martir.

Raya shuddered. "I've heard of you. But I thought that you were returned to your original boundaries after Uron's defeat."

Silly girl, said the Void. **Uron did do that, true, but with Uron and Skimif's deaths, and the resurrection of the human known as Braim Kotogs, the natural laws of Martir have grown weaker. Now more than ever, I have a chance to finally consume this world, and all who dwell within it.**

Raya had no idea what these 'natural laws' were, but it didn't really matter because at this point she was pretty sure that the only reason that she was still alive was because the Void was allowing her to live. She tried to move, but it was impossible. It felt like the Void was restricting her movement and she had no idea how to break free of its grip on her.

"You can try," said Raya, "but even if Skimif is dead, there are still the rest of the gods. They will stop you, you know."

If the gods could stop me, why haven't they already? the Void said. **You do not realize how much weaker the gods have become ever since Skimif's death. They can no more stop me than you humans can stop the tide.**

Raya had no idea if the Void's words were true or not, but then she realized that the Void had a point. She didn't see or hear the gods anywhere, which made her realize that she and Abacos were on their own here, at least for now.

And don't bother hoping that Alira will come and save you, either, said the Void. **She's currently incapacitated. Truly, you are on your own, as all beings ultimately are.**

Raya found that rather pessimistic, but she didn't say that aloud because she knew that the Void could kill her instantly. In fact, she found herself wondering why the Void had yet to do so, considering how it had her in its grasp.

Maybe I can somehow convince the Void to let me go, Raya thought. *I mean, I can clearly communicate with it, so maybe if I just talk to it, it will listen.*

But finding the words to speak was much harder than it should have been. It was probably due to the way in which the Void felt against her skin. It was a shuddering, creeping feeling that made Raya want to throw off her clothes and jump into a lake. She found herself wishing that Carmaz was here. Or really, any of the other godlings. She would have even been happy to see Saia.

There's no way I can get out of this situation on my own, Raya thought. *I'm not as strong or as powerful or as smart as the others. Just like when that assassin attacked me. I only survived because the others arrived in the nick of time.*

Raya flicked her eyes toward Abacos. The Steed was looking at Raya with terrified eyes. She didn't know how she must have looked—the Void was holding her head and making it impossible for her to look down at herself—but she could guess that she was giving off a very unnatural aura that was probably scaring Abacos.

I need Abacos's help, Raya thought. *He's the only being I can depend on in here right now. But how?*

Raya tried to think about what kind of powers that the Steeds must have. Unfortunately, Teacher had never taught her much about Hollech or his Steeds. As a matter of fact, Raya recalled how violently her father reacted anytime anyone even mentioned

Hollech around him. That still puzzled her to this day, but right now Father's reaction to Hollech's name was irrelevant to her current situation.

If only Father were here, Raya thought. *He could help me.*

Then Raya felt the Void touching the back of her ears, causing her to shudder at the cold, slimy touch.

You are rather silent for a human, said the Void. **I thought you were going to speak defiantly about how humanity will continue to survive against the forces of nature or some such cliched garbage like that.**

Raya huffed. "That's because I *don't* speak to my obvious inferiors. Father always taught me that being royalty meant never lowering yourself to the levels of wretched creatures like you."

Inferiors? You truly do not understand the power that I wield, said the Void. **You must think that I am nothing more than a slight breeze, when the truth of the matter is, I am far closer to a raging tornado.**

Then Raya felt it. Along her back, she felt something that might have been long, thick claws raking her skin. She opened her mouth to scream, but then felt the Void's shadows enter her body through her open mouth, causing her to choke on them. She couldn't feel any air coming into her mouth and her eyes were starting to water heavily.

But I have no reason to continue to let you live, you pathetic mortal, said the Void. **You may be a princess, but I am the Void, a force greater than any mortal individual. I will consume you from the inside out, until soon there is nothing left of your body, not even a withered husk to act as a warning to other mortals arrogant enough to cross my path.**

This time, Raya *knew* that she was going to die. She could feel the air leaving her body, feel the Void as it tore at her back, but there was truly nothing she could do about it. She just prayed one final prayer to Grinf and the gods to save her, though it was an incoherent prayer because she couldn't think rationally or coherently due to the pain she was in.

That was when a powerful, blinding flame came out of nowhere, causing Raya to close her eyes to avoid being blinded herself. Even with her eyes closed, however, Raya could see the light from the flames and feel the heat all around her. She even heard the Void let out a shout of surprise from the attack, as if it, too, had not expected this to happen.

Then Raya heard a loud whinnying sound and opened her eyes in time to see Abacos charging at her. She at first thought that the Steed was going to kill her, but then much to her surprise, Abacos ran around Raya. She looked over her shoulder (which she realized meant that the Void had let her go) and saw that it was Abacos who was firing flames from his mouth. The light tore away at the deep darkness of the Void, which surprised Raya, as she hadn't thought that anything less than a god could come close to damaging the Void.

That was also when Raya realized that she actually was free of the Void. Air returned to her lungs, which tasted sweeter than ever, but she hardly gave herself time to focus on that. She just stepped back, watching as Abacos burned away the flames with his fire, leaving charred grass or blackened walls wherever his fire touched.

Why is Abacos saving me? Raya thought, too stunned by this unexpected turn of events to move. *I barely even know him.*

Could it be because he thinks I'll win the Tournament?

Raya shook her head. Now wasn't the time to worry about that. She could see already that Abacos was burning a path for her to reach the exit. She just had to gather the courage to do it, and quickly, because she could already see the shadows of the Void returning to smother the flames from Abacos.

When Raya saw a break in the flames, she ran toward the exit. She ran so fast that she almost slammed into the door. She caught herself in the nick of time, however, and pulled at the door's handle. Unfortunately, it wouldn't budge, even when she put all of her strength into opening it.

Come on, Raya thought, scowling as she pulled and heaved. *Open, damn it, open! Who had the bright idea of locking this door? Did they really think that we godlings might try to run away or something?*

Raya stopped pulling at the door and looked over her shoulder. She saw Abacos still breathing flame and kicking with his hind legs, which was a great way to distract the Void. Unfortunately, she could also tell that the Void was beginning to recover from Abacos's initial assault. The shadows were thicker and even absorbing the fire that Abacos breathed. It would likely be only minutes before the Void achieved enough power to put an end to Abacos's assault, at which point Raya was pretty certain that there was no way that she or Abacos would survive.

So Raya shouted, "Abacos! Get over here, you stupid horse! I need you to break down this door! It's the only way we'll survive!"

Much to her relief, Abacos understood what she said, because he let out one final burst of flame at the approaching Void tendrils and then dashed over to her faster than she could blink. When Abacos reached the door, he turned around and kicked the door in with his two powerful hind legs. The impact knocked the door inwards, but it didn't actually give out until he kicked it again, which finally sent the door flying off its hinges into the dark room on the other side.

Relieved, Raya dashed through the open doorway, but paused when she heard Abacos give off a whinny of surprise. She then looked over her shoulder to see what had happened. She wished she hadn't.

The Void had pierced Abacos through his heart with one of its tendrils, which had become as sharp and pointed as a knife. Abacos's blood dripped golden, like a god's, but despite that, the Steed tried to move forward toward her, as if the sharp shadow knife in its heart wasn't an issue.

"Abacos!" Raya shouted.

But then Raya felt a shudder in the darkness and a gigantic set of dark teeth appeared above and below Abacos. Then, before Raya could say anything else, the teeth slammed shut down on Abacos. There wasn't even a sound. The teeth simply slammed shut and Abacos was gone.

Although Raya wanted to run, she could not help but stand there and stare at where Abacos had been standing mere moments before. She thought that her eyes had to be playing tricks on her or something, even though she knew that they were working just fine.

"Abacos?" Raya repeated. "Abacos!"

Your horse is dead, said the Void, its voice coming from everywhere around her now. **I don't see why you are so**

despondent. You never even liked horses anyway. You mortals always get upset about the silliest things.

Raya's every instinct told her to run, but she couldn't. She had to avenge Abacos. She couldn't just let the Void get away with its vile actions. It wouldn't be just.

She stepped back into the room, her hands shaking at her side as she faced the Void. "You monster. How dare you kill Abacos. He was just an innocent horse."

Innocence and justice matter not to me, said the Void. **All that matters to me is that I consume everything. Gods, humans, and yes, even horses. Nothing is above my hunger. Nothing.**

The Void's words just made Raya even angrier. She pointed at the Void and said, "I will make you pay for what you did, Void. I swear by Grinf's name that I will ensure that you receive the judgment you deserve for your vile and wicked crime."

How do you intend to hurt me? said the Void. **You can't even touch me. And if it hadn't been for the horse, you would already be dead. You are nothing more than an insignificant candle fighting against the powerful hurricane that is me.**

"I …" Raya tried to figure out how to respond to that, but the words just didn't come to her no matter what. "I … I will …"

And it is hilarious, isn't it, how you act so high and mighty when I know how selfish you really are? said the Void. **I know of your 'takings,' mortal, and while I do not care about human morality, even I can see the irony in your talk about 'justice' when you are anything but.**

"My takings?" Raya repeated. She gasped. "Did *you* put that letter in my room?"

One of my followers did at my orders, said the Void. **He sneaked into your room and put the letter there in order to scare you, for mortals who are afraid are easier for me to consume than mortals who are not.**

"How dare you," said Raya as righteous indignation rose in her. "Why, I am so angry that I—"

Save the words, mortal, the Void interrupted. **You should have run when you had a chance. At least then, you would have had a chance at survival, if nothing else.**

The shadows of the Void drew closer to Raya. She stepped back instinctively, but then looked over her shoulder and saw that more of the Void's shadows were coming from behind. She was completely surrounded on all sides and, without Abacos, she was certain that she was going to die.

Raya looked around desperately, but no matter where she looked, she only saw the Void's shadows closing in on her. She was beginning to rethink her decision to stay behind and avenge Abacos. She could just imagine the shadows of the Void clamping down on her, just like poor Abacos, and killing her instantly.

At least my death won't be drawn out, Raya thought. *Not that that is much of a comfort.*

But Raya would not give up. She forced herself to think as fast as she could, considering any and all possibilities that she could use to get out of this situation alive. She would avenge Abacos later, she decided, after she made sure that she was safe here.

The Void's shadows were now mere inches away from Raya's feet. Raya kicked at them, but her feet touched nothing, and even if they could, she doubted the Void would care. The Void was so much more powerful than she that she really couldn't hurt it no matter how hard she tried.

I guess this is it, then, Raya thought, trying to fight back the tears welling up in her eyes. *This is the end.*

But then an idea occurred to her: Raya was half katabans. It was not a fact that she focused on too much—she had always received unconditional love and acceptance from her parents and everyone else on Carnag for it, after all—but it was a fact. And katabans could access the ethereal, that other plane of existence that could be used to travel great distances all across Martir without needing to use ships, airships, or land vehicles of any kind.

Can I access the ethereal? Raya thought, wiping the tears from her eyes that were now coming whether she wanted them to or not. *I've never even tried it and Mother has never tried to teach me how to do it. But I don't have any other options at the moment. I must give it my best shot.*

Raya held out a hand before her and concentrated hard on opening a portal to the ethereal, trying to ignore the Void's tendrils that were slowly coming closer to her feet. She also tried to ignore the fact that she very well might not have that power at all, because her human half might somehow negate her innate katabans abilities.

So quiet all of a sudden, mortal, said the Void in a mocking voice which Raya did her best to ignore. **That is fine. I can see you've accepted your fate. Perhaps you are wiser than you appear.**

Raya didn't respond. She just focused hard on opening a portal into the ethereal. She felt nothing except for her head starting to hurt a little from the intense concentration, but she didn't give up, and she wouldn't give up until she either succeeded or the Void killed her.

Then—quite without warning—the ethereal portal popped into existence before her. Raya hadn't sensed it coming. It merely popped open before her, without any warnings at all. That was almost enough to shatter her concentration, but she decided not to question it.

So Raya threw herself through the open portal headfirst even as the shadows of the Void touched the heels of her feet. She heard the Void let out an angry curse, but didn't get to hear much of it, because as soon as she passed through the portal, it closed behind her with a small yet audible *pop*.

As for Raya, she staggered forward across the pure white road of the ethereal, breathing hard as she did so. She hadn't realized how exhausted she was, but perhaps the combination of the Void's earlier attack on her body and opening the ethereal had drained her more than she thought.

In any case, Raya found that she could no longer retain her consciousness. She fell face-first onto the white stone road before her, but was out before she even hit it.

The last thing she saw before she fell unconscious was a glowing light before her that was walking toward her, along with the sound of mechanical joints creaking. But she soon stopped focusing on it when she completely lost consciousness.

Chapter Twenty-One

No way up. No way down. No way out. And possibly no way to survive.

That was Carmaz's opinion of their situation based on a cursory glance of the staircase in which they stood. Behind them were the shadow tendrils of whatever was coming after them, while ahead more shadow tendrils approached them at the same speed.

Carmaz looked at his friends. Saia was completely useless, because his friend didn't have any sort of weapon or magical powers at all. He was jumping from one foot to another, anxiously looking up and down the stairs as if that would somehow help them get out of this situation alive. Carmaz understood Saia's fear and worry, but all Saia's worrying did was make Carmaz's nerves worse.

Tashir and Malya were still armed, but Tashir was hauling Alira over his shoulder, while Malya carried the Judge's Rulebook in both of her arms. Had the two been free, Carmaz would have asked them to use their swords to cut them a path down below, but because they weren't, they were no more useful in this situation than he or Saia were.

As for Carmaz, he was sad to say that he wasn't much better than Saia right now, if somewhat less worried and anxious. He was weaponless and incapable of even the most basic of magical spells. Carmaz may very well have been destined to become the God of Humans someday, but that evidently did not mean that Carmaz would get any actual magic abilities until then.

"Anyone got a plan?" said Saia, looking around at them all with desperate eyes. "Any ideas at all?"

"I have an idea," said Carmaz. He looked at Tashir and Malya and held out his hands. "Give me Alira and give Saia the Rulebook. You two can then use your makhimancy to clear a path for us down to the bottom."

"Are you certain that you can carry Alira?" asked Tashir, glancing at the unconscious Judge hanging over his shoulder. "She's quite heavy."

"I'm strong," said Carmaz. "And Saia can carry the Rulebook because he's strong, too."

"Very well," said Tashir. "Here."

Tashir gave Alira to Carmaz. Though the Judge certainly did not appear to be a heavy lady, Carmaz found that she weighed more than she looked when he put her over his shoulder. She was like a bag of mud, a feeling Carmaz was familiar with, seeing as he had had to drag bags of mud from the swamps back on Ruwa whenever his village needed them.

Malya handed the Rulebook to Saia. Although the Rulebook looked a lot lighter than Alira, Saia still struggled to hold it. That made Carmaz wonder just how strong Malya was, considering how she had been holding it just moments before without showing the slightest strain.

"All right, Malya, are you ready?" said Tashir as he held up his sword, which now glowed before him in the shadows.

Malya nodded as she drew her double swords out, which glowed like Tashir's blade. "Of course."

"Then let's go," said Tashir.

The two makhimancers began slashing at the shadows with as much ferocity and speed as they could. They moved faster than Carmaz had ever seen anyone move in his life, which surprised him because Tashir and Malya had always seemed older to him. He supposed that they must somehow keep in great shape. Perhaps that was a requirement of makhimancy.

In any case, Carmaz was pleased to see that the two were making some progress. With every slash, they tore apart more shadows, allowing them to move forward a couple of steps. Carmaz and Saia followed as closely behind as they could without accidentally getting slashed by the two makhimancers.

But even with the progress that Tashir and Malya made, the shadows behind them were still creeping up on all of them due to the fact that there was no one to stop them. Carmaz prayed that Tashir and Malya would cut them a long path to the bottom quickly, but that was seeming increasingly unlikely now.

Especially when the shadows surged forward, causing Tashir and Malya to jump backwards to avoid getting consumed. This forced Carmaz and Saia to stop as well, though Carmaz didn't lose too much hope until twin shadow tendrils lashed out of the darkness at Tashir and Malya. Tashir tried to block them, but his sword was knocked out of his hands and flew into the darkness somewhere, while Malya managed to not only beat the shadows back, but also retain her swords.

"Great," said Saia, who was now huffing as if the Rulebook weighed fifty pounds. "What do we do now? Neither of you two would happen to know any other forms of magic we could use to escape, would you?"

The two makhimancers shook their heads. Tashir said, "No. Makhimancers tend to be very specialized mages, so …"

"But we'll figure a way out, dear, don't you worry," said Malya. Then she added, "I hope."

Carmaz looked over his shoulder as Tashir and Malya drew closer to them. The shadows were so close now that Carmaz suspected that it would only be minutes before he and the others were engulfed by them. Now Carmaz didn't know much about these shadows or what would happen if these shadows consumed him and the others, but he did know that he was not in the mood to find out personally.

Where are those damned gods? Carmaz thought, scowling as he looked up and down the stairs at the approaching shadows. *They sure are taking their sweet time, if they're doing anything at all about this.*

Carmaz looked at Alira on his shoulder. She was still unconscious, but he decided that they needed to awaken her. If she could teleport the other godlings out of here, then she could do the same to them if she was awake.

So Carmaz laid Alira on the steps, prompting Saia to shout, "Carmaz, what are you doing? You're supposed to carry her, not dump her!"

Carmaz ignored his friend's admonishments. He shook Alira as hard as he could, saying, "Wake up! We don't have time for this. You have to get up and you have to get up *now*."

Unfortunately, Alira didn't even stir. Carmaz hadn't realized how hard those shadows had hit her, but they must have hit her hard. In fact, he wondered if she would ever wake up again at all, considering how still and silent she was.

"Waking up Alira won't work," said Tashir, shaking his head. "She's out for good, as far as I can tell. We'd do much better to figure out another way to escape."

"How?" said Carmaz, looking up at Tashir in annoyance. "We can't use your swords, seeing as you're disarmed, and there's no way that Malya could cut through the shadows all by herself."

Tashir opened his mouth, but before he could say anything, a chilling feminine voice from within the shadows said, **Oh, how I enjoy the sound of despair in the voices of you mortals. It exhilarates me.**

"Who's there?" said Saia, looking around the shadows in alarm. "Who just said that?"

The Void did, said the voice, still as chilling as before. **Not that it matters, seeing as you will all be dead and consumed within the next few minutes anyway, but I thought you deserved to know my name so you can speak of it in despair in the last minutes of your life.**

"The Void?" said Carmaz. He stopped and looked at Saia. "Know what that is?"

Saia shrugged, while Tashir sighed and said, "The Void is the darkness that lies beyond the edge of Martir, not far from World's End, in fact. I should have recognized this darkness for what it is. The Void invaded the Undersea not long ago and my friends at the Undersea Institute told me all about it."

That I did, said the Void, sounding annoyed. **And I would have succeeded in destroying it if that god and that half-god had not gotten in my way. But it doesn't matter, because soon**

I will destroy not just the Undersea, but all of Martir once more.

Carmaz thought about asking why the gods weren't stopping her and how the Void had gotten here at all. But with the shadows on all sides drawing closer, he decided that it was more important to come up with a survival plan than ask questions the Void would probably just ignore anyway.

"Okay, so what's the plan?" said Saia, looking around at everyone again. "Run and hide?"

Tashir snorted and gestured at the Void's shadows all around them. "Run and hide where? The Void will find us no matter where we go. I am sorry to say, but I don't think there is a way we can get out of here alive."

"There must be," said Malya, a hint of fear in her voice. Her swords trembled slightly in her hands. "We can't let despair overcome us. As long as we work together, we can survive."

Carmaz didn't have anything to add because he had returned his attention to Alira. He was still shaking her, trying to get her to wake up, but it seemed like no matter how hard he shook her, Alira would not even stir. He was even starting to believe that Alira might have somehow fallen into a coma, which would explain why she wasn't waking up.

Think, Carmaz, think, Carmaz thought. *What could I do to wake her up that I haven't tried yet? Hold on, I think I've got it.*

Carmaz raised his hand and slapped Alira straight across the face as hard as he could. Slapping her face was actually quite painful. It was almost like slapping a brick wall, which made him wonder just what the Powers had made Alira out of.

But he soon forgot about the pain in his hand when he saw

Alira's eyes snap open. She then looked up at Carmaz with shocked and confused eyes, as if she did not quite know what Carmaz had done but was surprised by it anyway. Her eyes looked slightly less severe without her glasses, though they still didn't look very friendly to him.

"What … what happened?" said Alira, shaking her head as she rubbed the spot on her face where Carmaz had slapped her. "Did someone slap me?"

"Yes, I did," said Carmaz, nodding. He pointed at the darkness around them, which was so close now that he could see literally nothing else beyond their tiny little circle. "And if you don't do something fast, then the Void will kill us all."

"The Void?" said Alira. She sat up, forcing Carmaz to back away slightly to give her room. She looked around at the darkness around her and frowned. "This is against the rules."

Carmaz sighed heavily, but refrained from hitting her again. "Yes, Judge, we know. That's why we awoke you, so you could get us out of here."

Do you really think I will just let you five escape like that? said the Void. **I'm not that stupid, you know.**

Without warning, a dozen shadow tendrils shot out of the darkness toward them. But Alira raised her hand and unleashed a barrier of light that surrounded all of them. The shadow tendrils disintegrated as soon as they touched the barrier, though Carmaz noticed how tired Alira looked from that effort alone.

Clever, said the Void. **But I wonder how much longer you will be able to maintain that barrier. Not much, I should think, considering how weak you are.**

"She has a point," said Alira through gritted teeth. She was already starting to sweat, which glistened in the light of the barrier. "I'm supposed to be a Judge, not a fighter. I'm not as strong as the gods. I can barely hold on as is."

"Then why don't you just teleport us out of here?" said Carmaz. "Don't you have enough energy to do that, at least?"

"I do, but I would need to drop the barrier first," said Alira. "And the Void moves fast. She might be able to move fast enough to kill us all before I can teleport us to safety."

"Do it anyway," Carmaz said, glancing at the shadows on the other side of the barrier, which were as thick as storm clouds now. "I think we can escape if we move fast enough. Everyone, grab —"

Carmaz was interrupted by a shattering sound and Saia screaming. He looked in Saia's direction to see that one of the shadow tendrils had broken through the barrier and grabbed Saia around the neck. It was trying to drag him through the hole in the barrier, but Saia was somehow managing to stand his ground. But he was still moving closer and closer to the hole in the barrier, so Carmaz ran over to save him before he was pulled in entirely.

He wrapped his arms around Saia's body and pulled as hard as he could, but he could feel his feet slipping underneath him. They were both being dragged closer and closer to the Void, despite Carmaz's best efforts to pull him back. He didn't know what the Void would do to Saia or him exactly, but he doubted that it would be anything good.

"Carmaz!" Saia screamed, his voice sounding choked due to the tightness with which the Void held his neck. "I can't breathe!"

"Hold on, Saia!" Carmaz shouted in return. "Don't worry. I got you."

Then Carmaz felt two strong arms wrap around his waist and, looking over his shoulder, saw Tashir was helping him save Saia. Grateful for Tashir's help, Carmaz then returned his attention to saving Saia. He put even more effort into pulling Saia back and could feel Tashir doing the same.

Saia's screams seemed to get louder with every second, despite the fact that he was unable to breathe. Carmaz didn't say anything, however, because he was so focused on saving Saia that he didn't have any energy to speak.

But unfortunately, Carmaz could feel both he and Tashir being dragged closer and closer to the Void's darkness. Granted, Tashir's weight had slowed their movement slightly, but it was still obvious that Saia was going to be dragged into the shadows no matter what he or Tashir did. Carmaz banished those thoughts from his mind, however, because they did not help him do what he needed to do in order to save his friend,

Now Saia was making choking noises. They were horrible in Carmaz's ears, making him feel as sickly as if he had come down with a terrible disease.

Then, without warning, Saia dropped Alira's Rulebook. The sudden sound of the Rulebook's impact on the floor—a great, big loud *whomp*—surprised Carmaz. As a result, he relaxed his grip on Saia's body only slightly.

But it was enough. In a second, Saia's whole body slipped out of his arms and his friend vanished into the shadows of the Void without another word.

"Saia!" Carmaz shouted. "No!"

Carmaz wanted to go into the Void after Saia, but Tashir was still holding onto him and was now dragging Carmaz away from the Void as fast as he could. "Don't be an idiot, Carmaz. If you go in there after him, you'll die as well."

Carmaz didn't pay any attention to Tashir's words as he struggled to break free of Tashir's grip. All he wanted to do was delve into the Void after Saia. He didn't know how he'd save his friend or if it was even possible to do so. Still, his every instinct told him to save his friend, regardless of what harm might come to him as a result.

"Everyone!" Alira shouted behind Carmaz. "We are teleporting now!"

The light barrier immediately fell, and as soon as it did, Carmaz felt himself swept off his feet and into another world of darkness quite different from the Void. He couldn't breathe for a second. Then he felt solid ground under his feet again and he was blinded by the outside light for a moment before his eyes readjusted to the brightness.

All four of them were on the streets of World's End now. Wherever Carmaz looked, he saw the other godlings, as well as the Soldiers of the Gods, who had surrounded the godlings as if to protect them from the Void. None of them seemed hurt, but all of them seemed afraid or worried.

It took Carmaz a moment to realize that they had teleported outside of the Stadium. It took him another moment to realize that he was looking at the Stadium itself. Only now, the Stadium was completely consumed in shadow. It looked like a solid black pillar standing among the rest of the city, with shadow tendrils extending out from its top toward the other buildings like the tentacles of an octopus.

Though Carmaz noticed all of that, he didn't really focus on anything, not even when the Soldiers of the Gods ran over to them and began looking them over for wounds. A couple of them even checked on Alira, but the Judge waved them off irritably as she stood up to her full height. She squinted at the shadow-covered Stadium, looking more like her old self even without her glasses.

"Judge Alira!" one of the Soldiers said, who Carmaz recognized as Captain Garvan. "We are so glad you are safe. We thought—"

"Shut up," Alira snapped at Garvan. "Tell me, are all of the godlings safe?"

"Yes, ma'am," said Garvan, nodding. "The only ones that are unaccounted for are most of the Hollech Bracket participants, such as Princess Raya."

Raya must still be in there, Carmaz thought, looking at the Void again. *Or is dead, just like Saia.*

"That is not good," said Alira, shaking her head. "But what about Braim Kotogs?"

"We do not know where he is located at this present time," said Garvan. "We thought that he might be with you."

"He was kidnapped by the assassin that had tried to kill Princess Raya yesterday," said Alira. "That's all I know about his disappearance."

"Noted, Judge," said Garvan. "Do you want us to go and find him or—"

"No," said Alira. She pointed at the Void. "Go and find any gods you can and get them over here to help deal with this. Tell your men to relocate the godlings. Get them as far from this place as you can. Understood?"

281

"Perfectly, ma'am," said Garvan, saluting her. He nodded at Carmaz, Tashir, and Malya. "Does that include these three?"

"It does," said Alira. "We must not allow the Void to kill these godlings. Otherwise, the Tournament itself will be radically changed forever."

"Understood," said Garvan. He then gestured at Carmaz, Tashir, and Malya. "You three, come with me. I will take you away to a safer part of the city while Alira and the gods deal with the Void."

Tashir and Malya walked over to Garvan without any fuss or complaint, but Carmaz did not move from where he stood. He was too busy staring at the shadow-covered Stadium, hoping to see Saia run out of the building's entrance alive and well, for any sign that Saia was still living. He wasn't even sure that he *could* move, at least until he realized that his feet were already taking him over to Garvan without him even thinking about it.

As Carmaz walked over to Garvan, he saw a flash of light out of the corner of his eye and looked up. He saw dozens of the gods flying around the Stadium, firing energy blasts at the Void, but none of their attacks left much of a dent in the Void. The attacks simply vanished into the Void's darkness, leaving no sign at all that the Void had even been touched.

If even the gods *can't beat this thing, then how can we?* Carmaz thought, feeling his courage drain away at the thought. *What does this mean for the rest of us? And what about those who are still in the Stadium, the Hollech Bracket challengers? What about Raya?*

Carmaz looked at the others. Garvan was now leading him, Tashir, and Malya back to the rest of the godlings, who were being led away from the Stadium by Garvan's men. He knew that he should just follow Garvan and get to safety. After all, he had no real powers to speak of, which made him practically useless against the Void. Besides, he had the strongest suspicion that Raya was already dead or dying in the embrace of the Void. She was just as powerless as he was, after all, and likely had even less advanced warning of the Void's assault than they did. Going back in there to rescue her would be suicide. At best, he would only be able to recover her body so that her parents could give her the burial that she deserved.

Even so, that didn't make Carmaz feel comfortable at all. He kept thinking of Saia, how he had failed to save his best friend in the whole world. The full emotional reality had not yet hit him— that much he knew, as he was still thinking rationally—but sooner or later it would, and by then he would probably not be in any position to do anything except mourn the loss of his friend.

And if it turns out that Raya is dead as well ... Carmaz didn't finish the thought.

So, without telling anyone else what he was about to do, Carmaz turned and ran back to the Stadium, back to the Void. He heard Alira and the others yelling at him to get back, but he didn't listen to them. He just ran and ran as fast as he could, without a plan or even a thought as to how he might avoid suffering the same fate that had befallen Saia. He would just have to improvise.

As Carmaz approached the Void, a dozen or so shadow tendrils emerged from the darkness and flew toward him. This time, there was no dodging them. One of the tendrils slapped him in the face. It felt like being slapped by the cold arm of a corpse. The others, meanwhile, wrapped around his body and arms, completely immobilizing him and making it impossible for him to escape.

What foolishness, said the Void, though Carmaz thought he only heard its voice in his head. **You escaped me, but now you return to me? Though I'm hardly complaining. This just makes it all the easier to consume you.**

Then Carmaz felt the Void's slimy cold tendrils squeezing around his body. The pressure was intense enough to make him cry out in pain, but his cry was choked and barely escaped his mouth, coming out more like a pathetic squeak than anything else. Even so, he didn't give up. He fought against it as best as he could, but no matter how hard he fought, the Void's grip on his body only became tighter.

But then four swords came out of nowhere and slashed the tendrils that had grabbed Carmaz. The tendrils around his body immediately loosened and vanished, while the other half returned to the Void itself without delay.

Carmaz—whose body was now almost completely drained of his energy—fell to his hands and knees on the cold stone street, gasping for air. He was still cold, but at least now he was no longer suffocating.

He then looked up, wondering who had saved him (and thinking that it might be one of the gods), when he saw the four-armed assassin from yesterday standing above him. The shadowy giant glared down at him from behind its mask, making Carmaz wonder if he had managed to escape the muck of a swamp only to jump straight into the fire.

But then Braim appeared at the assassin's side, grabbed Carmaz by the collar of his shirt, and lifted him up to his feet.

Carmaz staggered, but managed to regain his footing quickly. He then looked at Braim in surprise.

"Braim?" said Carmaz. "How did you get here? And what are you doing with that assassin?"

"She's on our side right now," said Braim, gesturing at the assassin, who was still glaring at both of them. "I'll explain later. Anyway, what's going on? I just got here."

Carmaz pointed at the Stadium. "The Void appeared and covered the Stadium in its shadow. Almost all of the godlings got out alive, although most of the Hollech Bracket participants are still in there and we aren't sure if they are dead or not."

"Does that include Raya?" said Braim, glancing at the Void.

"Yes," said Carmaz, nodding. "I was going to go in and save her, but—"

"I got it," said Braim. "But where did the Void even come from? I thought the Powers had given it firm boundaries to make sure it didn't enter."

"I don't know," said Carmaz. "It said something about some natural laws breaking or something. I didn't understand it."

Braim, on the other hand, looked as though he understood exactly what Carmaz was talking about. And based on his expression, he looked rather guilty, even though, as far as Carmaz knew, Braim had absolutely nothing to do with this situation at all.

"All right," said Braim. He jerked a thumb in the direction of the Stadium. "I'll go in and rescue Raya and anyone else I can find. You just go back with everyone else and get the hell out of here."

"Why?" said Carmaz. He shuddered due to the cold still in his body. "You're mortal just like the rest of us. The Void will consume you just like it did to Saia."

"Saia?" said Braim in surprise. He looked around. "You mean —"

"Yes," Carmaz interrupted. "And I would have suffered the same fate as him if you hadn't saved me. So—as much as it pains me to admit this—I think we should leave this to the gods."

Braim glanced at the Void, but then shook his head. "Nah. I'm partially responsible for this mess. I think I have to fix it."

"You?" said Carmaz. "But how?"

"Again, I'll fill you in another time," said Braim. "For now, I have to deal with the Void. I can help the gods."

Carmaz wasn't sure that he believed Braim, yet the firmness in Braim's voice told him that this mage was not to be argued with. And frankly, after almost getting killed by the Void, Carmaz felt grateful that someone else was going to go in there and save the day rather than himself.

So Carmaz placed one hand on Braim's shoulder and said, "All right. But be careful. Even the gods cannot harm it."

"Yeah, I know," said Braim. "But I'll be fine."

With one final nod, Carmaz turned and ran back to join the others. Still, he looked over his shoulder one last time to see Braim and the assassin disappear into the Void.

And—perhaps for the first time in his life—Carmaz prayed to the gods to keep Braim safe.

Chapter Twenty-Two

RESCUING CARMAZ FROM the Void's grasp had been Braim's idea the minute he and Ragao appeared in the streets of World's End again. He had ordered her to do it and was surprised when she actually listened and did it, which made him wonder if Ragao was starting to see *him* as her master, rather than Diog. Braim knew that half-gods weren't exactly the most intelligent of creatures—he had known one, for a brief period of time, back in North Academy that had been little more than an overgrown and overly-violent child—but it had never occurred to him that he might get a half-god servant of his own someday.

In any case, Braim was grateful that he had Ragao by his side, because the Void was deep and dark and he wasn't sure he could beat it on his own.

Then again, Braim wasn't sure how he was supposed to beat it at all. The only reason he had told Carmaz to let him handle this was because of the whole 'natural laws' thing that Carmaz had mentioned the Void talking about. If Braim had to hazard a guess, that meant that his resurrection had somehow weakened Martir's boundaries, thus allowing the Void to enter and wreak havoc on World's End. He didn't want that to be the case, but it fit with what Diog had told him earlier about how his own resurrection had somehow broken Martir's natural laws.

Braim believed that he might somehow be able to drive the Void off with his resurrected body. He figured that he would probably react differently to the Void than the others. Indeed, he might even be immune to its dark effects or at least better able to resist them, anyway.

So when Braim and Ragao stepped into the Void, Braim didn't feel anything. It became dark, almost too dark for him to see, which was why he summoned an orb of light in his hand. Even then, the light orb barely showed anything, while Ragao had averted her eyes, likely to avoid blinding or injuring them.

Braim fully expected the Void to attack him and Ragao the instant he summoned his light orb, but the Void was silent. He looked around the darkness, wondering if the Void had some sort of body he could interact with, but it seemed like he and Ragao were the only two beings in the whole world now. He couldn't even hear his own heartbeat, which would have frightened him, but as usual, he didn't even notice it until his mind told him that he should have heard it. Besides, his heart was still beating, and that was all that mattered to him.

"All right, Void," said Braim. He kept the fear out of his voice because he didn't want the Void to think he was afraid. "I'm here. Why don't you show yourself?"

Still no answer. This puzzled Braim. The Void had obviously heard him, so why wasn't she talking to him? Was she ignoring him? If so, why?

"Afraid of me, Void?" Braim said again, this time increasing the volume of his voice for effect. "Do you consider me an abomination, just like Diog did?"

Then Braim heard steps from somewhere within the darkness ahead. They were heavy, dragging steps, like someone was limping. It was impossible to tell how far away the walker was. They might have been on the other side of the Stadium or two feet away. Sound seemed to travel strangely in the Void.

Without warning, a portion of the darkness pulled away, like a curtain, allowing Braim to see someone standing two dozen or so feet away from him and Ragao.

It was a large, muscular man, though Braim didn't recognize him. The man wore a black tunic. At least, it looked like a black tunic, until it moved and Braim realized that it was actually the shadows of the Void covering the man's body. The man had a large gray mustache and appeared to be middle-aged, but it was impossible to guess his age for sure in such dark conditions.

"Who are you?" Braim said. "One of the Hollech Bracket participants?"

A feminine chuckle escaped the lips of the man, which deeply unnerved Braim. **This is the body of the man known as Zaos. He was easily dispatched when I consumed the Stadium. Now I control his body as easily as a puppet. Not that I need a body, but sometimes I prefer to do this in order to frighten my opponents.**

"That is pretty freaky," said Braim, nodding. "But what about Raya and the others?"

Why should I tell you? Zaos—no, the Void—said. **Knowledge is power, after all, and I am not in the business of granting others power. I take away power, actually, because the Void consumes everything at some point or another.**

"Yeah, sure," said Braim. "Keep telling yourself that.

Anyway, I'm glad you actually decided to show up and face me. Guess you aren't such a frightened little shadow after all."

The Void fears nothing, said the Void. **The Void fears not the gods, nor the humans or the aquarians or the half-gods or the katabans. The Void cannot feel fear. The Void only creates fear in its enemies.**

"Uh huh," said Braim, nodding. He looked around the shadows. "But I guess the Void also likes to talk, because otherwise I wouldn't be alive right now, right?"

The Void has its reasons for not killing you, said the Void. **You are ... unique among mortals.**

"Yeah, I've been told that before," said Braim. "Just had someone try to kill me over it, in fact, less than fifteen minutes ago. What about it?"

The Void always consumes everything, the Void said. **Yet I also have a sense of ... gratefulness, I suppose you would say. Because it is your resurrection that helped to weaken the world's boundaries enough for me to try conquering Martir again. And this time, there is no one to stop me.**

"I suspected as much," said Braim. Then he paused. "Wait a minute ... are you *thanking* me?"

I never said that word, said the Void. **I am only acknowledging that I am grateful for what you did. For too long, my desire to consume everything has been denied me by the boundaries that the Powers set around Martir ages ago. I believed Uron would be the one to help me, but then he betrayed me at the last minute. But now, I am once more free to do as I wish, which is to consume the whole world and all that reside within it.**

"Not unless I stop you," said Braim.

The Void laughed, which was a strange mixture of male and female voices that made Braim feel even less comfortable than he already did. **You are perhaps the third mortal to tell me that today. Why do you think you are going to do it when all of the others have utterly failed?**

"Because you're afraid of me," said Braim.

The Void stopped laughing. Her expression was blank, but Braim could tell that he had hit a nerve. **What?**

"You're afraid of me," Braim repeated. "You heard that correctly. You, the Void, are afraid of me, Braim Kotogs. Can't put it in any plainer language than that."

I am not afraid of any mortal, said the Void. **It is you who should be afraid of me. I am older than Martir, older than the gods, even older than the Powers. My power dwarfs the combined might of the sun and the sea. There is nothing anywhere in the universe that comes close to my power. Why, then, would I _ever_ be afraid of you?**

Braim yawned a little. "Because I'm different from everyone else you've faced. I'm the kind of thing that you are afraid of."

I still do not understand, said the Void. **I am not afraid of mortals, not even cocky ones like you. Mortals fear me.**

"It's not my status as a mortal that scares you," said Braim, shaking his head. "You know, for being such an all-powerful entity, you sure seem incapable of sensing implications in a mortal's words."

Stop insulting me, said the Void. **Or I will kill you where you stand, you and your stupid half-god underling.**

Ragao actually stepped back, like she wanted to run away, but

Braim gestured for her to stay.

"I don't care much for Ragao, but leave her out of this, all right?" said Braim. He tapped his chest. "What you are afraid of is my life. I am supposed to be dead, but I'm not. I came *back* from the dead—an impossibility by all definitions of the word— and I don't intend to die again anytime soon."

So what? said the Void. **You are not immortal. I see nothing frightening about you.**

"Still don't see it," said Braim. He sighed heavily. "Okay. I'll use simple words and speak slowly so you get it, beauti— actually, you're not all that beautiful for a woman or for a man for that matter."

Get to the point, you stupid mortal, said the Void.

"Okay, okay, don't be so rude, geez," said Braim. "So anyway, you want to consume everything, right? Plunge all of reality into an endless darkness or whatever? Extinguish the spark of life from all of creation and everything?"

If you wish to put it that way, yes, said the Void.

"Essentially, you want to make it impossible for life to return," said Braim. "You want the dead to stay dead and for life to end. And, under ordinary circumstances, that's usually how life and death work. Except for me."

Except for you, said the Void.

"Exactly," said Braim. He gave her the thumbs up. "Now you're getting it. Anyway, you are afraid that if I came back from the dead, then *anyone* could, right?"

Of course not, said the Void, though she said it a little too quickly. **You are the exception, not the rule. There is no other way for mortals to come back to life except through what you**

did, and that was only under extremely unusual circumstances. The chances of even one other person coming back to life are so slim as to practically be zero.

Braim wagged a finger at her. "There's the catch, though. You *don't* know that there aren't other ways for people to come back. Until I woke up naked in that graveyard a few months back, no one in the world, not even the gods, believed it was possible for someone to come back to life. What if there are other ways— methods yet to be discovered—that could allow *anyone* to come back to life?"

The Void shifted uncomfortably where she stood, which was the first visible sign of discomfort that she had shown so far. **Maybe there are other ways to come back from the dead. But if I destroy Martir before that happens, then they will never be able to come back from the dead no matter what.**

"Can't be so sure about that," said Braim. "The other methods to return to life might exist in the Spirit Lands, which I *know* you can't touch. And that's what scares you about me: I am living proof that your consumption of the world might not be enough. Life could come back, despite your best efforts. It would mean you aren't as all-powerful as you think you are. It would mean that you can be beaten, just like anyone else."

Shut up, the Void said. **You treat me like I am a person, like you, with fears and worries. I fear nothing and worry about even less.**

"You're definitely not human or a person, but that doesn't mean you don't have any fears at all," said Braim, shaking his head. "You're just trying to hide your fears because you know I'm right. You know that I'm onto something. You can pretend all you want that I'm not, but the reason you've let me live so long is because you aren't sure that you can kill me at all."

Braim said those last words with as much finality and emphasis as he could. He looked at the Void as he said that, looking her in the eyes, even as she tried to avoid looking at him.

The Void did not answer right away. Her hands balled into fists, she was making growling noises, but otherwise seemed to have no words at all to answer his accusation. In other words, she was totally speechless.

Then, much to his astonishment, the Void's body collapsed. It fell face-first onto the stone floor of the Stadium. Braim at first thought that this was some kind of trick on the part of the Void, so he looked around wildly, expecting its tendrils to shoot out of the shadows and kill him and Ragao where they stood.

Yet that did not happen. In fact, the darkness seemed to be leaving. Braim could see more things now, such the rules written on the walls, the doors leading to the field and to the box, and even the stone platform that Alira had stood on a couple of days ago when she first assigned the godlings to their respective brackets. The temperature rose as well, back to its normal height, and the smell of death vanished from his nostrils as well.

In seconds, there was no trace of the Void anywhere in the lobby at all. Aside from Zaos's corpse, the only two beings in the Stadium lobby were Braim and Ragao. This time, however, Braim felt good about it.

Chapter Twenty-Three

RAYA AWOKE WITH a start and her head started aching like she had been slammed in the face with a mallet. She grabbed her head and moaned because of the pain, which was almost overwhelming in its intensity. It was the worst pain that she had ever felt in her whole life, which made her wish it would just all go away.

Not only that, but her chest was tight and her stomach rumbled. She wanted to throw up, but her stomach felt as empty as a dry bucket. All Raya wanted to do was go back to sleep, but now that she was awake, the pain prevented her from returning to sleep again.

Is this what happens when you open a portal into the ethereal for the first time? Raya thought. *God, this sucks. Who would ever want to open an ethereal portal again after feeling this way?*

But Raya managed to look up at her surroundings, just to see where she was. The last thing she remembered was falling unconscious earlier, but even a brief scan of the room she was in told her that she was no longer in the ethereal.

Instead, she was sitting upright on her bed in her room in her apartment on World's End. Everything was silent around her. She didn't even hear her neighbors in their apartments next door making any noise. It was as though Amare, the Goddess of

Sound, had taken away all of the sound in the world.

Then Raya heard her heartbeat and realized that it was just very quiet today for some reason. That left a powerful relief in her heart, but it still left her with many unanswered questions.

How did I get here? Where is everyone else? What happened to the Void? Raya thought, each question speeding through her mind one after the other. *More importantly, did I win the challenge? Or did I lose?*

At that moment, the door to Raya's room opened. Her heart practically leaped out of her chest when she saw Carmaz enter. He looked tired, but was carrying a tray with some kind of hot soup and bread on it. It was a simple meal that Raya normally would have turned away due to its obvious plainness, but because it was in Carmaz's hands, she was more than eager to try it.

"Oh," said Carmaz, stopping in the doorway, his hand on the doorknob, while the other one carried the tray rather expertly. "You're awake."

Carmaz sounded neither happy nor angry about that. He was just stating a fact. Nonetheless, Raya thought that she sensed something in his voice that indicated he was pleased to see that she was alive and in one piece.

"Of course I am," said Raya, ignoring the throbbing pain in her head. She knew that Carmaz didn't put up much with weakness, so she tried to appear as strong as she could. "Why wouldn't I be? We Carnagians are a hearty bunch."

"It's just that you have been out for a couple of days now," said Carmaz. "Granted, the katabans have been working their magic on you to help you recover more quickly, but I didn't think that you'd wake up for at least a week."

296

"My head still hurts and I want to throw up, but I feel fine aside from that," said Raya. "And, I know I just said I would throw up, but I can still eat that food you've got there. I'll be able to keep it down no problem. I'm hungry."

That last part was true. She was very hungry, probably due to the fact that she had been unconscious for the past couple of days without getting even one bite to eat. The food on the tray didn't look nearly as delicious or amazing as the food that she had grown up eating in Carnag Hall, but at this point she was willing to eat just about anything, especially if Carmaz fed it to her.

Carmaz looked a little skeptical at that, but he shrugged and said, "Well, that's why I brought you this food in the first place. I didn't know you were awake, but in case you were, I made sure to have some food with me."

Carmaz walked over and placed the tray on her lap. It felt warm on her legs and the soup, whatever it was, smelled really good. Raya started eating as Carmaz pulled up a chair leaning against the wall and sat down in it.

"Where do you want me to start?" asked Carmaz, resting his arms on the back of the chair, which was facing her.

"How I got here," said Raya, gesturing at her room in between gulps of soup, which she shoveled into her mouth with a spoon. "Last I remember, I fell unconscious in the ethereal. How did anyone find me?"

Carmaz frowned. "You were in the ethereal? No, we found you on the streets outside the Stadium after the Void left. No one knows how you got there. Even the gods aren't sure how you got there. But you mentioned something about the ethereal?"

Raya nodded. "Oh, yeah. I'm part katabans, as you know, but

I've never opened the ethereal before. Didn't even know I could, but I did because I had to escape the Void and that was the only way I knew how. It took a lot out of me, though, so I lost consciousness when I entered the ethereal."

"Very interesting," said Carmaz, stroking his chin. "Did you see anyone in the ethereal? Any katabans, perhaps?"

Raya shrugged. "No. I just remember seeing this light, but don't ask me about it, because I honestly don't remember a whole lot about it. It might have just been a natural phenomena in the ethereal or something."

"I'll have to let Alira know about that," said Carmaz. "So anyway, after we found you in the streets, we took you here and I was given the task of keeping an eye on you and helping the katabans doctors heal you. Looks like all of their hard work paid off."

"Of course," said Raya. She paused her eating. "Wait, did you mention that the Void left? Of her own free will?"

"Yep," said Carmaz. "Braim somehow managed to convince her to go away. Don't ask me how. He just went in there, talked to her, and then she was gone. I wouldn't have believed it myself if I hadn't seen the Void leave with my own eyes."

"Impossible," said Raya, shaking her head, though she kept eating nonetheless. "I don't know much about the Void, but when I was in its embrace, I felt that it was too powerful to reason with. You'd have to be a god to come close to getting that thing's respect, and Braim isn't even half of a god."

"Tell that to him," said Carmaz. "Anyway, the fact of the matter is that the Void is gone. But Braim thinks it will probably return at some point, as do the gods, who are now setting up security measures to ensure that it won't come back again."

Raya shuddered, causing tiny droplets of the soup to fall on her sheets (which dismayed her quite a bit). "What will happen if the Void comes back again and doesn't listen to Braim?"

"Hopefully by then the Tournament will be over and there will be a bunch of new gods around to keep the Void from returning," said Carmaz. "From what I've gathered, the reason the Void attacked is because the 'natural laws' are weakening. If we get a God of Martir, then they might be able to strengthen the natural laws and thus keep the Void out of Martir for good."

"I do hope you're correct," said Raya, "because I was right there in the midst of the Void and I know just how powerful it is. I'm afraid that we won't be able to deal with it next time it comes around, whenever that might be."

"Got to say, I have to agree," said Carmaz. "Had Braim not talked it down, we'd all be dead by now."

Carmaz stated that rather matter-of-factly, which Raya found herself admiring about him because she could never have stated such a blunt truth so calmly herself.

"Speaking of the Tournament, did I win?" said Raya. "What was Alira's verdict?"

"Alira says you won," said Carmaz. He frowned. "Well, 'won' is not exactly the most appropriate term for it. See, when the Void attacked, it killed half of the Hollechian godlings. The others are in critical condition, like you, though they will probably survive and be ready to take on the next challenge soon. That means you technically won by default."

Raya smiled. "Who cares if I won by default? I *won*, which is an amazing honor. It means I am that much closer to achieving godhood, which is what I rightfully deserve."

"I thought you'd be angry about that, considering how much of a hissy fit you threw when Alira assigned you to the Hollech Bracket," said Carmaz in surprise. "Resigned to your fate already?"

"No," said Raya, shaking her head. "I've just learned to take advantage of whatever comes my way. A far healthier way of looking at things than whining about it, in my opinion."

Carmaz was now looking at her as though she had come from some other world, but he said, "All right, then. Sounds good."

Raya nodded and said, "So what about the next Hollech Bracket Challenge? When is that supposed to be?"

"Alira said it will be after the rest of the sub-bracket challenges are done," said Carmaz. "According to her, the next one is going to be the Human God Sub-Bracket Challenge, which I will be participating in."

"That's great," said Raya. "I just know you will do wonderfully. And think about it. If you and I both win our respective brackets, then we will both become gods and get to live with each other forever."

Carmaz looked like he had not thought about that. Unfortunately, he was frowning at the thought, like it disturbed him greatly, which annoyed Raya, because she saw no downside to spending all of eternity with him.

"Anyway," Raya continued, looking around the room, "where is your friend? Saia is his name, right?"

"Was," Carmaz said. His frown became even more pronounced. He rubbed his eyes, as though he was trying to fight back against the tears trying to burst out from them.

"Was?" said Raya. "Whatever do you mean, Carmaz? Have you and Saia had a falling out recently?"

Carmaz shook his head. "No. Saia … the Void got him before Braim made her leave."

Raya stopped eating her soup. She suddenly felt rather embarrassed about asking that question due to the sheer pain in Carmaz's voice. She wasn't sure what to say.

But she had to say something, so she said, "Well … that's awful, Carmaz, and I am sorry to hear about it. Would you mind telling me the details or—"

"No," Carmaz said abruptly. He looked away from her. "You just need to know that he's dead. That's all you need to know."

"But I want to know the details," said Raya. "Is it really that hard for you to—"

Raya was interrupted by the screeching of the chair's legs against the floor as Carmaz stood up. He glared down at Raya with anger in his eyes. It almost reminded Raya of how Father sometimes looked when he got angry at her for doing or saying something that she was not supposed to, but it was much wilder and more primal, like the kind of anger she always imagined that violent criminals had.

Carmaz pointed at her soup and bread and said, "Eat up. I'm going to go tell Alira that you are awake and recovering. I'll tell the Soldiers standing guard outside the apartment to get you any food or water or anything else you need."

Carmaz turned and walked back toward the door of Raya's room. Raya held out a hand, saying, "Wait, Carmaz, when will you be—"

"I'll be back when I get back," said Carmaz without looking

over his shoulder at Raya. His tone was so harsh that Raya didn't say anything else as Carmaz wrenched open the door, stepped outside, and slammed it closed behind him in one smooth motion.

Raya leaned back against her pillows. She looked at the soup and bread on the tray on her lap. The warmth of the soup felt nice on her legs, but she didn't really feel like eating it anymore, even though she was still hungry.

What did I say? Raya thought. *I just wanted to know the details about how Saia had died. I wasn't disrespecting his memory or anything. Must be a Ruwan cultural thing or something.*

Raya tried to tell herself that she didn't particularly care if Carmaz was offended or not, because she didn't do anything wrong. Even so, she found it hard to enjoy her soup and bread afterward, mostly because she wasn't sure if Carmaz would ever speak to her again after this.

Chapter Twenty-Four

THOUGH CARMAZ HAD said that he was going to go tell Alira about Raya's awakening, he didn't intend to do that right away. He left the apartment building and walked off in a random direction, not even thinking about where he was going. He just followed the street wherever it led, keeping his head down and his hands jammed into his pockets. There was no rush. Alira had said that the next sub-bracket challenge was going to start whether Raya awoke from her coma or not. He had plenty of time to stew over the dumb question Raya had just asked him.

Raya's a class act, Carmaz thought, ignoring a katabans merchant who was hawking what looked like oddly-shaped shoes, though he didn't stop to look at them. *Just want to know the details, huh? For royalty, she sure doesn't act royal.*

Part of him should have expected that, considering how much tact Raya lacked. Still, he had no tolerance for that kind of disrespect from her. He didn't care that she was royalty. Here on World's End, in the Tournament of the Gods, she was just another godling to him, and not a particularly bright one, either.

Of course, part of the reason Carmaz was so angry was that he was trying to avoid crying. He could feel the tears trying to well up in his eyes, but he didn't want to be overcome by his sadness. He had already cried over Saia's death a couple of days ago.

Besides, he was used to tragedy. During his twenty-five years of life on this world, Carmaz had seen men get torn apart by crustaceans, watched young children die due to a lack of nutrition, often in the arms of their weeping mothers. He had thought that he had gotten used to tragedy, yet every time he thought about Saia's death ... it almost overwhelmed him.

Carmaz kicked a stone in his path, which bounced along the street before him. That was when he saw a crowd of katabans coming his way, a large crowd that made a lot of noise as the katabans in it chattered among each other. Not wanting to interact with other living beings at the moment, Carmaz stepped into a side alley and continued his wandering of the city in there.

The streets are too clean, Carmaz thought, scowling as he looked at the back alley he had ended up in. *I know that this is the Throne of the Gods and all, but it seems almost unnaturally clean. Wonder if the God of Cleanliness is behind this.*

But Carmaz didn't really care much about the gods. He cared about Saia. Saia had been his childhood friend. He had known him for as far back as he could remember. To just lose him like that ... so fast, without a chance to say good bye ... Carmaz was truly at a loss for how to deal with that.

I can't handle the grief, Carmaz thought, wiping the tears that were starting to flow from his eyes. *I should throw the upcoming challenge. Then Alira can send me back to Ruwa and I can tell everyone else there about Saia's death. There's no way I can compete in this sorrow. I'm not that strong.*

If only there was some way to bring Saia back ...

Carmaz stopped in the street and frowned. Where had *that* thought come from? He certainly didn't think it on his own. He looked around, but did not see anyone else in the alley with him.

Resurrecting Saia is silly, Carmaz thought. *He's dead. It's impossible to bring back the dead.*

"Braim would disagree, I would think," said an unfamiliar voice above him that made Carmaz look up.

Floating in the air above him was a pale-skinned, armored brute with a wispy, ghost-like tail. Carmaz's first thought was that it was another half-god, but then he recalled seeing a statue of this god near the apartment building where Raya was staying, though that didn't make him any happier to see the deity.

"The Ghostly God," said Carmaz, watching as the god floated down in front of him. "God of Ghosts and Mist."

"So you recognize me," said the Ghostly God. "Am I really that famous now?"

"No," said Carmaz, shaking his head. "I don't think we've ever met."

"But you don't need to introduce yourself, Carmaz," said the Ghostly God. He smiled and leaned forward, though Carmaz didn't move from his spot. "I know the names and faces of every single godling participating in the Tournament of the Gods. Including yours, though it's hardly one to remember. I have no idea what Raya sees in you."

"Neither do I," said Carmaz. He tensed. "I don't trust the gods, especially you southern gods. Did Alira send you to get me?"

"Neither Alira nor any of the other gods are even aware that we are alone together," said the Ghostly God. "Alira is obsessed with the Tournament, as she always is, while my brothers and sisters are debating what to do should the Void attack again. I took the opportunity to slip out and find you while they talk uselessly about the future. No one noticed, since I have a habit of leaving boring conversations like that."

"Why did you want to find me?" said Carmaz. "I'm nothing special. I think you'd want Braim, considering how he is the guy who came back to life."

"Braim has proven very … uncooperative," said the Ghostly God. He sounded frustrated about that. "He has not let me study him and the secrets of his resurrection. I know that if I got a chance to study him, it would only broaden our understanding of death and make us that much more powerful."

"I still don't see why you are talking with me about all of this," said Carmaz. He sidestepped the Ghostly God and kept walking. "I don't want to talk with you or anyone else right now. Just leave me alone."

Carmaz got perhaps ten steps away from the Ghostly God before a cold hand rested on his shoulder. He looked over his shoulder and saw the Ghostly God behind him. He didn't like the disappointed look on the deity's face.

"Get your hand off me, you—" said Carmaz.

The Ghostly God removed his hand from Carmaz's shoulder and said, "You are just as childish as Raya, you know. Storming off when you're angry, not wanting to talk to anyone … actually, I think I am starting to understand why she likes you so much."

"Unlike Raya, I have an actual reason for my moodiness," said Carmaz. He jabbed a thumb at his chest. "My best friend in the whole world just died a few days ago. Not that you'd understand. You gods don't have friends, do you?"

"We gods do in fact form friendships among each other," said the Ghostly God. He shrugged. "It's just that no one has ever formed a friendship with me. Not that I need friends, really. Friendship is overrated."

"So are you actually going to tell me why you are talking with me at all or are you just going to waste more of my time?" said Carmaz. "Because I know how much you southern gods hate talking with us mortals, so I can't imagine that this is pleasurable for you."

"You spoke of your best friend dying earlier," the Ghostly God said. "Have you ever considered the possibility that we could bring him back?"

Carmaz's hands shook, though he tried to keep his tone level. "I don't indulge in fantasies, Ghostly God. I focus on reality. And the reality is that Saia is dead and there's no way to bring him back."

The Ghostly God chuckled and then laughed. It was a mocking laugh, one that only made Carmaz's temper become even shorter. He wanted to strangle the Ghostly God with his bare hands, but because he couldn't, he just glared at the god until he stopped laughing, which took the Ghostly God a good few seconds to do.

Still chuckling, the Ghostly God said, "You mortals truly are stupid. Have you already forgotten Braim Kotogs? The man who came back from the dead?"

"He's an exception, not the rule," said Carmaz. "He doesn't even understand how he came back to life, so it's not like he can give me some pointers to help bring Saia back."

"But what if we *could* find out how to bring Saia back?" said the Ghostly God. "If we could just study Braim's body and his soul, then we might be able to understand how he defied the natural laws and returned to life."

"Are you suggesting … an alliance?" said Carmaz.

"A partnership," said the Ghostly God. He shuddered. "The thought repulses me as much as it does you, but the two of us have similar goals, I feel. You want to bring back your dead friend and I want to learn how to bring back your dead friend. And do you know who might hold the answers to both questions?"

Carmaz's hands stopped shaking as he thought over his answer. "Braim Kotogs."

"Exactly," said the Ghostly God, nodding. "The only trouble is, of course, that he would never let me study his body long enough to figure out how to replicate the process he underwent to return to life. Do you know what that means?"

Carmaz shook his head. "No, I don't."

"It means that I want to offer you a deal," said the Ghostly God. He held out one large hand to Carmaz. "You help me capture Braim. In return, I will help you resurrect your friend Saia with whatever knowledge I learn from my study of Braim's body and soul. How does that sound?"

Normally, Carmaz would have told the Ghostly God to capture Braim himself, but then he thought about the offer a little bit more. Braim had indeed proven that it was possible for a human being to defy death and return to life, even thirty years after they had passed away. Saia had been dead only a few days by now. Resurrecting him should be a piece of cake.

Besides, Carmaz didn't really like Braim that much. While Braim was more tolerable than Raya, Carmaz was still not close to the resurrected man and therefore would not feel guilty if he helped the Ghostly God to capture him.

So Carmaz grasped the Ghostly God's cold, metallic hand and shook it. "It's a deal."

The Ghostly God smiled, showing his ugly crooked green teeth. "Excellent. I will send you your first orders later, but right now, let's go over the general plan so that you and I will be on the same page. I promise that you will not regret this."

Chapter Twenty-Five

BRAIM KOTOGS LAY on his bed in his room in the inn he had been staying at for over a month now. Even though he had gotten much-needed sleep over the last couple of days, he still felt exhausted. He supposed it was due to Diog draining his life energy, but Braim was puzzled about why his body had not simply used the life energy he had stolen from Diog to replace what he had lost.

Maybe it's another one of those weird aspects of resurrection, Braim thought with a yawn. *Can't retain life energy as well as I normally do. Hopefully it won't have any long-lasting effects.*

Then Braim saw movement just outside his window. He started, sitting up and aiming his newly-repaired wand at the window, before he realized that it was just an unusually-tall katabans passing by and making the light look strange.

Guess it was nothing, Braim thought, lowering his wand. *Just glad it wasn't Ragao.*

Braim was not exactly sure what had happened to Ragao after he succeeded in talking the Void out of destroying World's End. All he knew was that the gods had taken her, but whether they were going to destroy her or not, he couldn't say. He doubted they'd let her live, considering how the gods treated other half-gods. He actually hoped that they'd kill her. After all of the trouble that she had caused him and the other godlings, Braim was pretty much convinced that Martir would be better without entities like her messing it up.

Thinking about Ragao inevitably turned Braim's thoughts to Diog. After the Void left, Braim had told Alira and the gods about Diog's plan to kill him. He had been told that they were going to bring Diog to the Hall of Justice—apparently a building on World's End where criminals on the island were tried for their crimes—where he would be tried for his crimes. Braim wasn't sure exactly what they could do to Diog, considering he was a god and all, but it now seemed unlikely that Diog was going to harm Braim again anytime soon.

But what if the gods take Diog's side? Braim thought. It was a thought that had entered his head many times over the last couple of days, not helped by the fact that he knew how much the gods generally favored each other over mortals. *If Diog manages to convince them that my mere existence is a threat to Martir in general, there's no telling what they'll do to me.*

That was yet another thing that Braim had worried about. He knew now that the main reason that the Void had successfully managed to enter Martir and almost kill everyone was because of his resurrection. He wanted to believe that he had nothing to do with it, but it was plainly obvious to him now that Diog was correct about Braim's resurrection having negative effects on Martir.

So far, none of the other gods had mentioned to Braim about doing something to him. It was possible, even, that they wouldn't harm him at all, seeing as he was a godling who was supposed to enter the Tournament of the Gods. As far as he knew, he and the other godlings were safe from the gods right now. Alira, at least, would keep Braim safe until he either won or lost the Skimif Bracket. He remembered how angry she had looked when he had told her about Diog kidnapping him. She seemed to take Diog's attempts to sabotage the Tournament as a personal offense.

Can't see them leaving me alone for much longer, though, Braim thought as he lay back down on his bed. *They're still angry at Diog for almost killing me, but once the anger fades and they can all think more clearly, then they'll probably listen to him and do something about me.*

Braim closed his eyes and tried to sleep, but he found it impossible under the current circumstances. He had thought that getting rid of Ragao and the Void would take his mind off things, but now that he had to worry about the gods listening to Diog and doing something about him, he found it hard to relax.

And there's still that darkness in the back of my mind that is still annoying me, Braim thought. *Almost forgot about that.*

Deciding that he wasn't going to be getting any sleep tonight, Braim sat up again, threw off his covers, and stood up. He thought about where he could go tonight, but even the idea of going anywhere was enough to tire him out, though not enough to make him go back to bed.

Indecision, Braim thought. *Nice. Like the gods.*

Braim shook his head. The gods weren't indecisive. Well, he supposed they could be sometimes. It was mostly that they were divided on most subjects that it made it impossible for them to do much of anything. He saw why the Powers went ahead and sent Alira to organize the Tournament, rather than relying on one of the gods to do it. As an impartial third party, she was the only one who could do this without getting mired in the petty politics of the gods.

And I am going to rule them, if I win the Tournament, Braim thought. *Still have a hard time wrapping my head around that one.*

Perhaps that was another reason why Braim felt so uneasy. Deep down inside, he wasn't sure he was ready for the position of God of Martir, or if he would ever be ready.

All this stress, but can't sleep it off, Braim thought. *Fantastic.*

Shaking his head, Braim began pulling on his clothes, getting ready to go and walk around the city tonight. He had no idea what the morning would bring, no idea at all. And he decided that he did not need to know, at least for now.

Continued in:

Tournament of the Gods Book #2:
Betrayal of the Chosen

Powerless and in the clutches of a mad god who seeks the secrets of his resurrection, Braim must escape the god's island in order to return to the Tournament of the Gods. But when the god's experiments leave him unable to trust his senses, escaping the deity's clutches may be harder than it seems.

Raya Mana wants a dress, which a famed katabans tailor has agreed to trade her for in exchange for one of her own dresses. Yet there is more to this famous tailor than meets the eye and Raya must do all that she can to uncover his secrets, because that is the only way she will save the gods and the world.

Carmaz believes that the secret to resurrecting his deceased friend lies in Braim Kotogs and so he helps a mad god kidnap Braim so he can experiment on him. Now Carmaz must ensure that no one knows that Braim is missing or that he is behind Braim's disappearance, otherwise he will be disqualified from the Tournament, which will make it impossible for him to ascend to godhood and help his poeple.

Now available in ebook and trade paperback wherever books are sold!

Glossary:

Aorja Kitano. A former student at North Academy who specialized in musical magic. Though she is good at pretending to be kind and intelligent, in truth she is insane and violent and is currently on the run from the authorities for her crimes against Martir. She has a 'pet' half-god called Zeeree who she managed to tame. She is also a mage known as a 'Limitless,' which means that she has access to unlimited magical energy (although that does not make her invincible).

Aquarians. A species of fish-like humanoids that live in the Undersea, which is the name for the part of Martir underneath the Crystal Sea. Like humans, aquarians worship the northern gods and can use magic, although they have different names for the gods and also do magic differently from their human counterparts. They have a variety of different appearances and races, much like humans, although their differences tend to be even more dramatic than the ones between humans.

Automatons. Mechanical beings created by the Mechanical Goddess to carry out her will, although the Carnagian Royal Family has been experimenting with making automatons of their own in recent years.

Darek Takren. The adopted son of Jenur Takren and a graduate of North Academy. He specializes in pagomancy, or ice magic, and is currently the leader of the Xocionian Monks. He was the protagonist in the Mages of Martir novels and is a good friend of Braim Kotogs.

Diog. The God of the Grave. Aquarian name: Hamafa.

Godling. Name for human beings who are destined to become gods.

Half-gods. The prototypes of the gods that the Powers abandoned in the Void after finishing Martir. Half-gods, while stronger than mortals, are not quite as strong as gods, although they can give the gods a good fight. They also tend to be more animalistic and lack some of the higher reasoning functions of the gods themselves due to their incompleteness, which makes it possible for beings who are weaker than them to control or manipulate them. The most well-known half-god is Zeeree, the Half-God of Poison, who serves Aorja Kitano.

Harnum. The world that existed before Martir. It was destroyed by Uron, one of its inhabitants, and everyone who lived there was killed off. The Powers arrived many years later and used Harnum's remains as the foundation for Martir, although some Harnumian buildings and objects can still be found deep beneath Martir's surface.

Jenur Takren. A native of Ruwa and current Magical Superior of North Academy and adoptive mother of Darek Takren. Like Malock, she was a major character in the Prince Malock World novels. In her youth, she was a member of the Dark Tigers Guild, an assassin's guild based in Ruwa, but eventually left it when she became disgusted with the Guild's mission. She adopted Darek Takren when he was only five years old after his birth mother was murdered by an enemy of hers.

Katabans. A species of intelligent beings who exist to serve the gods. 'Katabans' means 'minor spirit,' as katabans are spirits who often take on physical forms in order to follow the gods' commands. Their appearances range from human to beast, depending on their preferences, personality, and what they need to complete whatever mission given to them by the gods.

King Tojas Malock. The son of Queen Markinia and King Halock of Carnag. Current King of Carnag. He was the protagonist of the Prince Malock World novels and is married to Queen Hanarova. He is a fair and just ruler, although he spoils his daughter too much.

-Mancy. A suffix usually attached to Latin prefixes that denotes the name of a magical discipline. For example, hydromancy means 'water magic,' pyromancy means 'fire magic,' panamancy means 'healing magic,' and so on.

North Academy. The most prestigious and most difficult to get into magical school in the world. It is located in the northernmost reaches of the Great Berg and can only be reached with great difficulty. It is run by Jenur Takren, who is the current Magical Superior of the school.

Northern Isles. A region of the world located on the northern half of the Dividing Line that consists of thousands of island nations of various sizes. It is where almost all of Martir's human population is located, as well as many aquarians.

Northern Pantheon. The gods who rule the northern half of Martir. In contrast to their southern siblings, the northern gods are kinder and more respectful to mortals. They also tend to take mortal names (for example, Grinf), rather than titles translated from Godly Divina (for example, the Loner God).

Ooka. The God of Knives and Shadow. Aquarian name: Ooka.

Queen Hanarova. The katabans wife of King Malock and mother of Princess Raya Mana. Like Malock, she was a major character in the Prince Malock World novels. While not a bad person, she has a fierce rivalry with Jenur Takren that started in their youth and continues to this day.

Rock Isle. The most secure prison in the Northern Isles. Home to many of the most dangerous criminals in the Northern Isles.

Silver spoon. A slang term, common in the Northern Isles, usually applied to princesses, especially spoiled or bratty ones. The male equivalent is gold blood and the terms come from the folk song *Princess Silver Spoon and Prince Gold Blood.*

Skimif. The previous God of Martir. He was once an aquarian farmer who was chosen by the Powers to announce their return to Martir back in the Prince Malock World series. The Powers eventually made him into the God of Martir, but he was killed by Uron thirty years after his ascension.

Southern Pantheon. The gods who rule the southern half of Martir. In contrast to their northern siblings, they hate mortals and see them as no different than any other kind of animal. They tend to be more vicious and animalistic and don't understand humans as well as their northern siblings do.

The Almighty Ones. A group of four beings who live in the Spirit Lands and are responsible for judging and guiding the spirits of the dead. Originally consisted of the Dark Lady, the Arbiter, the Great Snake, and the Mysterious One before the Arbiter and the Great Snake were killed. They are far more powerful than the gods, but typically do not directly interfere with the physical realm, preferring to focus instead on the Spirit Lands where they rule.

The Dividing Line. The exact line that divides the northern and southern sides of Martir. This line can be crossed by any god or mortal, but if a southern god crosses it, then this god cannot kill any mortals on the northern side.

The gods of Martir. Super-powerful and immortal beings who each control a particular domain of Martir, such as the elements or even abstract concepts. The gods used to be one united force, but after the Godly War, they were separated into the Northern Pantheon and the Southern Pantheon and have remained that way ever since.

The Godly War. An ancient conflict that took place shortly after the creation of Martir eons ago. The War started over a disagreement between the gods over how to treat mortals. Half of them wished to use mortals for sport and food, while the other half wanted to have them as worshipers and followers. The two sides waged a war that killed many gods and countless mortals before the Powers stepped in, ended the conflict, and wrote up the Treaty to govern relations between the two sides.

The Ghostly God. The God of Ghosts and Mist. A southern god. Highly intelligent, but cruel and antisocial. Has an intense fascination with studying the dead and where ghosts go after their bodies die.

The Mechanical Goddess. The Goddess of Machines. A southern goddess. She is the creator of the automatons. Queen Hanarova served her in her youth.

The Mysterious One. One of the Almighty Ones. Originally pretended to be the mythical God of Mystery and Magic before revealing his true identity at the end of the Mages of Martir series. Strange and enigmatic, he nonetheless cares about Martir and does what he can to help protect it.

The Powers. A group of six powerful and ancient entities who created Martir, the gods, humanity, and everything else within Martir. Their exact nature is a mystery, but it is known that they are currently creating other worlds beyond the Void. They have only visited Martir once since creating the world but otherwise are not actively involved in the world's day-to-day functions, which are instead regulated by the gods themselves.

The Spirit Lands. A land where all spirits go when they die and where they are judged by the Mysterious One for their deeds in life. Those who are judged as righteous go beyond the Gates to rest eternally, while the ones judged wicked are banished to the Unknown to be tortured forever.

The Thief's Way. A magical discipline generally practiced by followers of the late Hollech, the former God of Deception, Thieves, and Horses. Practitioners of the Thief's Way can travel through shadow and also detach body parts and have them emerge from the shadows to attack someone or steal from them. Most practitioners of the Thief's Way are scorned by their fellow mages and generally treated as criminals even if they do not actually commit any crimes.

The Treaty. A document that governs relations between the Northern and Southern Pantheons, written by the Powers themselves.

The Void. A powerful and evil force that exists beyond the edge of Martir. Its sole purpose is to destroy and devour everything that exists. While the Void does not technically have a gender, it is usually referred to with female pronouns.

Tinkar. The God of Fate and Time. One of the oldest gods and a northern god. Aquarian name: Seyar.

Uron. A powerful being who existed in the world before Martir, where he was a bitter scientist who was hated by everyone. He allowed the Almighty One known as the Great Snake to possess him so he could get back at his people, but due to a series of unforeseen events, Uron and the Great Snake ended up banished to the physical realm without a body for centuries. After Uron got a body, he then attempted to destroy Martir, but was ultimately destroyed by Braim Kotogs and now no longer exists as a spiritual or physical being.

World's End. Also known as the Throne of the Gods. The final island in the southern seas and home to most of the katabans on Martir.

About the Author

Timothy L. Cerepaka writes fantasy as an indie author. He is the author of the Prince Malock World fantasy novels, the Mages of Martir fantasy novels, and the Two Worlds science-fantasy series. He lives in Texas.

Find out more at his website at www.timothylcerepaka.com.

Other books by Timothy L. Cerepaka

Prince Malock World:

The Mad Voyage of Prince Malock

The Return of Prince Malock

The New Era of Prince Malock

The Coronation of Prince Malock

Mages of Martir:

The Mage's Grave

The Mage's Limits

The Mage's Sea

The Mage's Ghost

Two Worlds:

Reunification

Alliance

Allegiance

Retaliation

Desinence

Tournament of the Gods:

Gathering of the Chosen

Betrayal of the Chosen

Standalones:

The Last Legend: Glitch Apocalypse

All of the above books are available in ebook and trade
paperback wherever books are sold!

www.ingramcontent.com/pod-product-compliance
Lightning Source LLC
Chambersburg PA
CBHW050552260626
47157CB00002B/529